T0326732

MAP
OF
OREGON TERRITORY.
BY
Samuel Parker
1838.
Copy right reserved.

Lamentations

A NOVEL OF WOMEN WALKING WEST

Carol Kammen

University of Nebraska Press
LINCOLN

Names: Kammen, Carol, 1937– author.
Title: Lamentations: a novel of women
walking west / Carol Kammen.
Description: Lincoln: University
of Nebraska Press, [2021]
Identifiers: LCCN 2021012557
ISBN 9781496227812 (paperback; alk. paper)
ISBN 9781496229953 (epub)
ISBN 9781496229960 (pdf)
Subjects: LCSH: Overland journeys to the
Pacific—Fiction. | Oregon National Historic
Trail—Fiction. | Women—Fiction. | GSAFD:
Historical fiction. | Western stories.
Classification: LCC PS3561.A435 L36 2021 |
DDC 813/.54—dc23
LC record available at https://lccn.loc.gov/2021012557

Set in Garamond Premier by Laura Buis.
Designed by N. Putens.

To the quick,
whom I love and who love me
And to the lately dead, who are missed
Michael and
AVD

The great Pacific, which had now become the
topic of conversation in every circle, and in
reference to which, speculations both rational
and irrational were everywhere in vogue.

—Lansford Hastings,
The Emigrants' Guide to Oregon and California

Women came in obedience to man's judgment,
whether or not in accord with her own.

—Mrs. Robert A. Miller,
"Women in Pioneer Times," *Transactions of the*
23rd meeting of the Oregon Pioneer Association

Contents

Preface

I began with women's voices in my head, but that led me to think about shoes. They might be the shoes women had in their previous lives—dainty for parties and sometimes of silk with bows, and walking shoes with neat buttons on the side, sturdy farmwoman shoes, broken in and comfortable for mucking the hogs or sneaking up on nests to collect eggs. There might also have been slippers, soft and supple to allow the foot to glide over the floor making but a whisper. And there were baby shoes, soft and loving on the feet of those who could not yet walk.

But then I began thinking of the shoes they needed to walk across the country: shoes that were up to the trip across the prairie, fording rivers, walking over the mountains. And then there were those shoes not suited—the ones they had come with; shoes that came apart with the sole flapping at each step and finally tied together or tossed aside; shoes that fell off. There were boots at first deemed ugly and then proving difficult to walk in because of the stiffness of the leather that caused blisters that swelled up and burst, leaving raw skin inside the boot to fester until it hardened over. Boots were needed to manage steep inclines and descents, to maneuver around stones and boulders, and boots with heels to dig into the side of the mountain to prevent falling forward or spindling down or even over a cliff.

Then I think too of the shoes of the Native women—soft antelope-skin boots decorated with quill stitching or soft moccasins that cradle the foot as if a babe.

We walk in our own shoes, in our own histories, but also in each other's shoes, we who write about the Overland Trail. There is a great simplicity to the story of the Oregon Trail and all stories are the same: people gather somewhere west of the Mississippi River, outfit themselves, and set out. They lose a wheel, encounter a rattlesnake, go along the Platte River, see buffalo, fight Indians, see Chimney Rock, endure cholera or thirst or long difficult walks; they pull wagons up the trail and then prevent them from going down too fast. In between there can be a murder, an act of cowardice, an evil trail boss, a guide, a love story, and items left behind—even bodies buried in shallow graves piled with rocks and marked with a wooden cross that quickly falls apart. These voyagers cross rivers, go over South Pass through the Rockies, and find they still have the Blue Mountains on their way into Oregon. At the end of the story, there is the relief of having made it across, of "seeing the elephant": of making their goal. Often the story stops there, as if that is an end rather than a beginning. For it is just that, the start of the real story. The trail taken is the hyphen between the old life and the new, between what once was and what might to be.

Excepting for the Civil War, which has its own set of legends, the Oregon Trail was the great American story until we discovered the Underground Railroad, which has in the last thirty years supplanted the romance of trails west. Yet, the trails remain.

For me, the Oregon Trail began in Roosevelt Elementary School on North Avenue, in Cranford, New Jersey. I sat on the floor, hiding my brown oxford tie-up shoes as I read through the books on the shelf marked "Trails." I moved on to the Cranford Public Library and read Francis Parkman, A. B. Guthrie, Bernard DeVoto, and Wallace Stegner. And yes, I also read Ezra Meeker, who re-created the trail, but backward, from west to east, and wrote a romance about it as well.

Then for a time, for me, the trail went cold.

Moving to Ithaca, New York, however, I found a state roadside plaque that marked the place where Dr. Elijah White had lived. Missionary to Oregon, it noted. And the trail west was again clear as I followed this very complicated man and his wife, Serepta, to Oregon and back. If Odysseus was *polytropos*, or a man of many twists and turns—a complicated man—Elijah White might be labeled *kako tropos*, or *mal tropos*, a man of bad or devious ways—a complicated man. In Oregon, White served as a physician at the Methodist Episcopal mission, where the couple's young child drowned in the Willamette River.

Jason Lee, head of the mission, dismissed the doctor on complaint for "pressing his female patients." Within this story, there was another complicated man, a *psychopomp* named Lansford Hastings, who contested with White to be captain of the 1842 company heading west. It was Hastings's book touting a trail into California that led the Donner Party to its death. *Psychopomp* is the Greek word for one who leads others to Hades.

But back to Elijah White: although dismissed from the Methodist mission, he was not through with Oregon. After returning home to Ithaca, he published his memoir, *Ten Years in Oregon*. This followed the 1838 publication of a book called *An Exploring Tour*, written by Dr. Samuel Parker, also of Ithaca, who had taken Marcus Whitman west in 1835 to site missions for the American Board of Commissioners for Foreign Missions, the ABCFM. Parker sent Whitman back to New York to marry Narcissa Prentiss, and the newlyweds went west the next year to establish a mission site at Waiilatpu, near present-day Walla Walla, Washington. They and William Gray, their guide, departed from the Ithaca Presbyterian church on DeWitt Park in Ithaca. Circles within circles: I came up again and again with an Oregon connection to follow.

In the winter of 1842 Secretary of War John Spencer heard of—and possibly read—Dr. White's book and called him to Washington to learn more about the Pacific Northwest, as its ownership was contested by both the United States and Great Britain. By the time Dr. White left the capital, he had a commission from Spencer to become the "sub Indian agent" and, as White believed, governor of the territory when the United States formally claimed it—and then possibly governor of the state of Oregon. None of that was to be.

When Secretary Spencer asked White if more Americans might make the overland trip to Oregon, to settle the area before a war with England broke, White answered that of course families could make the trip and he would lead them. But White had never crossed to Oregon by land, having gone earlier by sea, with a crossing at Panama, and also returning that way.

In the winter of 1842 Dr. White returned to central New York to say goodbye to his parents and friends. While visiting at the Crawford home in Havana, New

York, young Medorem Crawford decided to go west with White to serve as his clerk. The two set off, got to St. Louis, and made it known that they were ready to take a group of families to Oregon. Wandering Americans of all sorts responded.

By the time White and Crawford moved onto the trail west in May 1842, they had a company of more than one hundred people. Crawford kept an account of the trip, and several people later wrote memoirs of the crossing. This was a momentous undertaking—the beginning of a great migration of people and a moment in history when the story of the mountain men and the plunder of the West comes to an end and the story of the upending of western Native peoples begins as Americans made claim to the land.

This story has been told as a dynamic part of America's manifest destiny—to conquer and use the land, from sea to sea; to dominate the landscape; and to tell a new story of expansion, individualism, and enterprise. For many the overland migrant was a rugged individualist who faced vicissitudes and persevered. That story is not actually the truth, for the trip west required cooperation, community, and compassion.

This story contains a problem that needs to be faced. The people we call pioneers were determined to make a new future for themselves and to claim the land for the country. But the land was already claimed by any number of peoples who saw it as their own; the Indians, the Native Americans, lived on the land differently than the settlers planned to with their maps and deeds and governments. Native Americans were on the land first, but the newcomers could not or would not see them as owners or even as members of civilized cultures. While today we are conscious of this wrong, the people heading west believed in their own destiny despite evidence to the contrary, overlooking Native rights and customs and having no regard for the Native presence. To write the story to please our current understanding of the great wrongs inflicted upon Native Americans would be to erase what those traveling into the west thought and believed. I have tried to hew to the truth of the 1840s and not to revise history to make us feel better about the past.

In Cranford when I was nine years old I wanted desperately to have gone west on the trail. I saw myself as a happy girl, skipping westward, my yellow dress billowing in the breeze, while I was smiling and laughing with the people around me, avoiding the snakes, and ending up with an Indian friend.

All that of course was bosh, and knowing myself now better than I did at age nine, I understand that I would have been a dreadful addition to any wagon train. I would have hated the dust, complained about all the walking, reacted badly to the mosquitoes and the food. I would have gotten underfoot and been a general annoyance, if not a danger, to others. I would have been a cowardly Indian captive, a pain in the butt to those moving cattle along, and a general crybaby.

The Oregon Trail has become a popular subject for children's literature, with a child as the central figure. Some of the titles I found include Jean Van Leeuwen's *Bound for Oregon* (1994), Stacey Lee's *Under a Painted Sky* (2015), and Kristiana Gregory's *Across the Wide and Lonesome Prairie: The Oregon Trail Diary of Hattie Campbell* (1997). Even "Hitty," a doll, has her story of going west. Dennis G. Miller's *Mollie Sees the Elephant: A Novel of the Oregon Trail* (2020) is one of the latest; according to publicity about the book, it features an "optimistic child" and life-changing experiences and is "loaded with trivia," which is what many of these stories feature: wagons, food, cooking, gear, trail markers, and so on. There are Oregon Trail games with challenges for children to address as they "travel" the trail: work together to overcome calamities, get at least one member of a party to Oregon, stop to rest, decide which of their company will die of dysentery. Children are also invited to write their own name on a tombstone—to see how it fits, I assume—all according to "The Oregon Trail: Card Game," which contains fifty-eight trail cards, thirty-two calamity cards, twenty-six supply cards, and a laminated wagon party roster.

The romance of the trail has also been well documented, beginning with Ezra Meeker's *Kate Mulhall: A Romance of the Oregon Trail* (1929) and continuing through the years to *Impatient with Desire: The Lost Journal of Tamsen Donner*, by Gabrielle Burton (2019), and *Brides in the Sky*, a 2019 collection of short stories about the Oregon Trail by Cary C. Holladay. There is also *Backwards to Oregon*, an LGBT take on the Oregon Trail, moving from brothel to Oregon. There are also mail order brides on the trail, one example being Carré White's *Crystabelle: A Mail Order Bride on the Oregon Trail*, number six in a series called Brides of the Rockies. There are stories of the trail told as if in a diary kept by a participant, and there is Jane Kirkpatrick's book about women taking charge, *All Together in One Place* (2002), which is part of the Kinship and Courage series.

Even at age nine I wondered about the women. What did they think? What did they want? Women were nonparticipants at trail company meetings and were often ignored. They were wives, daughters, burdens, or sirens. Once the company embarked across the prairie from the Little Blue River and then traveled along the Platte River, women had to endure. Those who crossed the country in 1842 have left us no word of their thoughts, their troubles, or their delights, for all the documents concerning that first crossing of American families were written by men.

Over the years and at the Huntington Library, at the H. H. Bancroft Library in Berkeley, from documents at the Oregon Historical Society, the National Archives, and Yale University, and the resources of the Cornell University library, I have put together what I think the fifteen women on that 1842 journey might have thought about, worried over, considered, and lamented. I was especially interested in what they could not say, the errant thoughts that would have been dangerous or outrageous or even scandalous to voice aloud, to say to another. There are many diaries kept by women who did cross the country on later wagon trains, and they tell us of many things: of the beauty of the land, of flowers never before seen, of illness and death, of despair and fear. These are things that could be written and could be shared.

But there were other thoughts, dangerous ideas about the land through which they passed, about ownership, about the state of being married, about the Native men they saw who rode into the camp with their shocking demands, about their own religious beliefs that bordered on the pagan in a country of orthodoxy and fixed social mores. These were the things that women could and would not speak aloud to parent, to husband, even to trusted friends. These were thoughts that were unsayable, things that society would find unacceptable. It is around these thoughts that this book is written and that give the story its shape and tone. These are the things that were mulled over, thought about, worried on, contemplated, and that caused a lament in the soul that could not be shared.

This is a work of fiction based on years of research. The people mentioned, excepting a very few, were listed on the census that Elijah White took in October 1842 in Oregon, and the events are all real, recorded in memoirs and records—some on this journey west, some on others. The characters, however, are my own, and I feel a need to apologize to those whom I have portrayed as having been wanting in kindness, to have been cruel, to those I have used to let the women on the journey tell their own story. They might well in truth have been otherwise.

Lamentations is told with a number of voices, but if there is a central character, it is the land itself—the prairie, the rivers, the mountains, the rocks, and the trees that needed to be passed in order to get there. While now quite an old woman, I think back to myself sitting on the floor of Roosevelt Elementary School, seeing the journey. I think of the years of reading, of pulling documents from boxes and writing for more information.

I have crossed the country many times by airplane and three times by car, wearing sneakers for the most part. In 1976 my husband and I, accompanied by our sons, went west, traveling from state capitals and college campuses to national parks until we followed part of the Lewis and Clark route into Oregon. The second was in 1993, when my husband and I, our sons having gone off on their own travels, drove west from Ithaca by way of utopian communities: Kirtland and Zoar in Ohio, Bishop Hill and Nauvoo in Illinois, the Amana communities in Iowa, and on into California, before traveling back again to the Shaker Village of Pleasant Hill and then Berea in Kentucky. My last trip across the country, after being widowed, was with a dear friend, and we went joyously the entire way, across New York, south in Ohio to complete the journey via Route 50. As we left our first lunch on the road, at a Seneca Indian restaurant near Jamestown, New York, all the patrons turned and wished us a "blessed journey."

I think of the years I have lived with this 1842 crossing. I have put in what the records show and then some of what I imagined. I found voices for the women on the trip, and then they gave me voice. I trust I have not got it wrong, because then I too would lament.

The 1842 Company of Travelers

GABRIEL BROWN, with family and hired hands (two wagons)

LEVI GIRTMAN, with his wife and daughter

COLUMBIA LANCASTER, with his wife and daughter

McKAY BROTHERS, with horse and pack mules

JOHN SMITH, with his family (his wife and children plus his parents) and hired men (two wagons)

W. T. PERRY, with his wife, as well as her widowed sister and her baby

SIDNEY MOSS

L. COUCH, with his wife

JOHN FORCE

GERMAN MEN (five of them)

NATHANIEL CROCKER

D. TOMPKINS, with his wife and four children

SHADDEN, with his wife and children

VARDEMON BENNETT, with his wife, sons, and one daughter

HUNTERS and hired men working for the company to pay their way

DR. ELIJAH WHITE, company leader

MEDOREM CRAWFORD, company clerk

LAMENTATIONS

Part 1

STARTING OUT, LOOKING BACK

May 16, 1842: In our company were 16 waggons & 105 persons including women and children & 51 men over 18 years of age.
—Medorem Crawford, *Oregon Trail Journal of Medorem Crawford*

CAROLINE TOMPKINS

Behind her the wind picked up. Caroline could feel her skirt push against the backs of her legs. She walked and then turned to look back for a final time. She was at the end of civilization, of her country, of all she knew. She saw the small collection of buildings recede in the dust that obscured the edges of the barn and the house where she and several other women had spent the night. The mule in the yard continued braying as it had since morning. She felt sad leaving behind the two women who had been so glad to have someone to talk to, someone from outside—to talk about things from the East, where they had never been but that were of such great interest.

They had eagerly filled her cup over and over again as she described the journey west, leaving her home, the boat ride down the Ohio River, what St. Louis had been like with the bustle of people going places, carrying packages here and there, of the noise, the clang of the church bells on Sunday, the scraping of boots as men and women entered buildings trying not to bring mud inside. The two women living at the edge of the country wanted to know everything, and even when Caroline told them a second time about the goods in the shops, they didn't mind at all, they having no shops but needing to await the peddler who might come their way. They wanted it all, and Caroline felt drained by their need. How could she tell them everything when their need was so great? It was the whole world they were missing.

Caroline had liked those frontier women and admired their bravery living so alone, of bearing children so far from help, of having only themselves and their lives to talk over, even as their husbands and sons went off to hunt or explore or busied themselves with making things, tending the animals, watching the crops, or seeing Indians: the Otoes, she thought. Even the men's lives, to those two women standing in the dust, waving good-bye, seemed to be full of excitement as they worked or joked and rode off, leaving them behind watching. The thought of Caroline going even farther west than Elm Grove thrilled them while at the same time it filled them with fright about what was beyond, out there, in the land where even they, at the edge of the world, had never been.

Caroline turned away from the settlement, from the three houses, the barn, the squat blacksmith shed and faced in the direction of the company ahead. She faced into the West. The last wagon was a ways before her, and here she faltered: how could she describe distance out here? At home the last wagon would have been five, even six streets farther on, but here there were no streets; there was nothing on the land to help demark space. The wagon, slowly going away from her, was how far? She was not used to judging distance; in the countryside at home, distance was talked of as acres, or in time; about a half hour away, her grandparents would say about the next house, or as a horse trots—a good trot, a short ride, a spell ahead.

Here on the prairie she didn't know how far the space was, but she could see the wagons recede even as she watched, the pail at the back swinging gently, the canvas in full billow, the people getting smaller. The company was a good distance ahead. She could see the bunches of cattle, the clean line of wagons with their canvas tops moving, and people slowly walking to the sides, pushing into the land beyond.

Leaving those two women behind, holding each other in their loneliness, she walked steadily along the bent grass left by the heavy wheels, the horses, the gaggle of cattle at the rear. She leaned forward into the space, wanting to overtake the herd and to place herself between them and the wagons, where the dust would be less. She wanted to walk alone, at least for now, as the journey began, before she knew the other travelers. She appreciated having the confidence that her children were old enough to care for themselves—for the most part. There was Ellen of course, still coltish, prancing about; she bore watching. She thought of the women herding small children on the trail and was grateful she was beyond that; she didn't have to reach down for a small hand, or pull a child forward who was weary of walking, or carry one just too heavy to hold with ease.

She was now well beyond the small community they were leaving behind. She could walk with her own thoughts—at least for a while—with her doubts and hopes and her sense of guilt for having pushed for change and achieving it in a way she had never expected. Was this going west ultimately her fault?

The Women

The women had not expected the weariness of the trail, the walking, tripping over thick tufts of grasses, high even this early in the season. They had not counted on the snakes and the noises of the prairie and the wind—the endless wind that blew particles of dirt in their faces and into their ears, that carried into their nostrils specks that made their noses twitch, their mouths hang open. They had not thought about their dresses dragging on the ground or picking up burs and little insects that crawled up the front skirt panel, onto the apron, and sometimes even into a pocket to surprise and disturb them.

They hadn't known about the dryness in their mouths and the longing for fresh well water or for the weight in the hand of a newly laid egg found behind a lilac bush in the backyard, or for the sound of women in the general store evaluating the newest fabrics from Boston or New York or Baltimore. They didn't know that the touch of a china cup would be something to long for, or tea, carefully brewed in Grandmother Fitch's old English pot, was only something to remember. They didn't know that their shoes would wear thin and that the ugly, sturdy boots brought home by a husband or father would be welcome on feet used to town shoes made from their own shoe last. And then, they didn't know that to wear a pair of boots for a long walk could leave them hobbled; they needed to be broken in slowly, like a frisky colt.

There were some delights, such as the sage hens that ran ahead of the horses and seemed almost tame, and the marsh quails, the flights of wild geese, and the droves of snipe running about looking for ground snails. They appreciated the quiet after dinner when some sang and a Frenchman plucked a guitar-like instrument; these felt almost like chapel meetings, everyone tired from the day, boots pulled off, quiet conversations with neighbors, the softness of the evening as it fell and the sounds of nighttime. The rains interrupted of course, as did the wind. The lack of trees was disconcerting to some, or the infrequency of them rather than the forests they had known at home, where the trees were too many to count. Here trees seemed to spring up individually, as if only that one tree was able to draw enough moisture from the land to sustain it.

CAROLINE

Caroline walked by the clutch of cows that had stopped momentarily to lick at wet leaves, to mouth the grass, which might be in short supply farther along. She tapped one brown cow on the rump as she passed, getting a blurping sound in return. She came to the space between and moved off from the trail of the last wagon, to the side where there was little dust. She stepped around a dead snake that someone had decapitated, its tail still twitching. None of them liked the snakes, just now emerging from their winter dens, slithering across the land, or rising upward from a coil to challenge their forward motion. Caroline saw the revulsion in the faces of the women, the fascination of the children, and the savagery as the men dispatched them, removing one danger from the journey, alert for others. No one, she observed, reacted kindly toward the snakes. Snake in the grass, she thought. Was that the same snake in the Garden of Eden, she wondered, and was this the Garden of Eden they were entering?

Ahead the land was empty. There were no streets for judging distance, no church tower to know when she had arrived—or a bell; no store or courthouse lay ahead. Just land: undulating, rising, dipping, rising again with a sure downward tilt beyond. They were crossing unknown space.

By the time she came to their wagon, Caroline was happy to see the welcome smile on Dan's face. "I worried," he said.

"About me?"

"Yes. Please don't wander away, out of sight." She touched his hand and felt roughness where once it was smooth, a clerk's hand once, now a working hand. She rubbed softly at a callus growing on his index finger. "From the lead on the horse," he said gently and with some pleasure.

She smiled, saying, "You keep track of us, don't you," and he grinned.

"Yeah. I do. I count all the time."

"One to five," she countered. "Well, six, including yourself. Do you count yourself?" she asked.

He nodded.

"You do that in church too, as we sit and wait for Reverend Wisner to start. I have seen you tote up the heads of us along the pew; good thing we only have four children, Danby Tompkins, you would be the whole time counting rather than praying."

He grinned. "More would have been all right, too."

"Four is quite enough, Mr. Tompkins," she said with a smile in return. "Do you count the horses too?" she asked suddenly.

He laughed. "You know I do. I worked for years as a store clerk. I counted everything!" Then he rode off, and Caroline continued to walk, a slight flush on her face.

A good man, she thought to herself, even if he is leading us on this wild journey. It would help me if I knew more about where we were heading and how we will get there, but Dan seems confident about this move—about our going west, being first, well, early, out there, of making a new start. And I agree with that, for sure, I do agree with that.

She thought about Dan and how he was changing even while they were getting started, all concerned with harness and water tins, the cow, and other things he had never bothered about—or needed to. Dan was a literary man, at home with books and papers and pen and ink, at his desk, working away, thinking. All this was quite different for him, and he seemed as pleased and perhaps as surprised by it as she.

*

May 16. Started at 9 o'c. detained ½ hour by losing the trail. Left the Santa Fee trail at 2 o'c and camped at ½ past 3 evening, weather very warm. Traviled about 12 miles. 1 more wagon and 3 men came on.
—Medorem Crawford

CAROLINE

Caroline stood rooted as the company shifted its course to cut across the prairie toward the trail to the north. They had gone two miles before someone noticed they were headed wrong. There had been sharp words among the men, and one had thrown down a hat in fury at having been led off-trail so early on. That one had picked up his hat, slapped it against his thigh, and walked off. Others kicked their feet into the dry earth covered with wisps of grass, then shrugged their shoulders as if there had been little harm in it, as if two miles was minor cause for worry. She couldn't hear them, but their bodies held rigid, shoulders pushing toward each other, their hands to their sides told the story. Danby rode up to her and leaned over to touch her shoulder. He explained that they had followed the wrong trail, the road to Santa Fe, while they needed to veer to the north along the traders' route to the Platte River, the trail that no one had noticed or been alert to see.

"Rather a bad beginning," she had murmured to him before he rode off. She worried about it. Others around her picked up their sticks or grabbed the hands of children and set off, but she stood, watching the party shift, watching the set of resignation in the posture, the haughty righteousness shown by the leader, a self-regarding man, small of stature, with a thin, bony face. She had distrusted him at first meeting because of the importance he ascribed to his own experience, and she feared he would keep proving her right. Then Ned moved next to her, trailing a horse. He asked if she wanted to ride. She shook her head, saying, "Not yet. We have only gone a few miles and we have a long way ahead of us." Ned nodded and moved on; his father would have insisted she accept his gesture for her comfort, insisted she move along rather than giving her time to think. She looked with approval at Ned, a good son, but she feared they were expecting a lot of him.

They were expecting a lot of everyone. Little children were expected to keep up, women to keep families fed and healthy. Men were assumed to know where they were going, where there was game and water, and yet here at the start they had already gone wrong. She wondered briefly about Jane and Martha, worried about Ellen. She shrugged her shoulders slightly, felt the stiffness that had set in from the walking, and shrugged again, pushing her shoulders up and down, back to front, front to back, to loosen her muscles. She had never expected it to be this way, she had never expected this at all, and yet it had been she who had urged their leaving. It would be because of her insistence if things turned out badly, and she worried about that responsibility. She looked down at her dress and decided to cut inches from the hem to get the cloth out of her way for the next day's walk. She had already tired of kicking at the fabric, catching her boot in the hem as she strode forward, feeling the cloth pull back against her thighs. She wondered how high she could cut without causing comment.

Caroline walked on, keeping up with the last wagon, staying ahead of the cattle that kicked up billows of dust and dirt, avoiding the barking dogs that ran alongside the wagons or accompanied their masters. She would walk alone for a time and watch. Her eyes narrowed slightly as she tried to see into the distance, but all there was in front of her were wagons and men on horses. There didn't seem to be a horizon for her to navigate by.

At four they halted and created a circle with the wagons, a circle that bulged on one side, the wagons making odd angles at they came up to the next. Circle was too neat a name for the enclosure they created. The animals were tied with long ropes and staked on the prairie to graze.

*

May 18. A violent rain this morning much excitement in camp about Dogs: 22 dogs shot, stop[p]ed raining 9 o'c. Started at 1 o'clock without a track endeavoring to find the right trail. Camped on the right trail at 7 o'c. Traviled 10 miles.
—Medorem Crawford

CAROLINE

Caroline Tompkins knew immediately that it was Martha bellowing "Mother!" Martha was not a bellowing sort of daughter, more a whiner until she got her way, but this was a distinct howl. Caroline turned to the sound and saw Martha and Ellen running to her, their eyes red, their faces full of fury. Jane, they explained, was in the wagon hiding Wooley, with whom she would not be parted. Wooley, rather aged and even shaggy, had endured the trip from Ithaca, on the boat along the Ohio, and then up the Missouri. Here on the open prairie he could run about in his doggy fashion. Wooley was a great comfort to Jane, and to him and only to him she was able to talk, just as she could sing, without stuttering. He tolerated being dragged about by Jane and favored her in all things.

"The dogs!" wailed Ellen. Caroline felt women's eyes from all directions turn to them. "The dogs," said Martha, and now that she had collected herself into a major news source she announced coldly and distinctly, "The dogs are to be killed."

"The men decided, Mother," said Ellen. "They want to shoot Wooley. Whatever will Jane do without him?" she asked. "What would we all do?"

Steely voiced, Caroline replied, "They cannot do that to our dog."

"But they voted, Mother," said Martha. "The men decided that the dogs would go mad and turn on us. Dr. White told the men who were making the laws that while crossing the mountains the dogs will become rabid and be a danger to us all, especially when water is scarce. There was a case, recently, he said, of a mad wolf that had bitten eleven people . . ." She stopped. A wounded dog came suddenly between two of the wagons, seeking safety with his mistress; blood dripped from his ear as he came forward and then with a jerk of his head he dropped down and lay dead near a wagon wheel.

Caroline looked about and saw the alarm in the faces of the women. In the distance they heard woofing and scrambling, and above the screams of the women and children there were gunshots and howls from dogs as they were put down.

Farm dogs, hunting dogs, family dogs—the dogs people kept with them for comfort, to alert them to the presence of Indians, to keep their families safe. Companions, they were.

"They are not yet rabid," said Caroline in a determined voice as she turned in the direction of her wagon. When first on the trail, the dogs had made a commotion, getting used to each other and to the routine of walking and staying near; they had barked all the first night, keeping everyone awake. But they were settling, as were the emigrants, into a pattern.

"They annoyed Dr. White, however, who wanted to exterminate the entire canine race, old and young, male and female, wherever they might be found— within our jurisdiction, of course," said Reuben Lewis, who came striding into the camp area. Lewis had been at the meeting along with Gabriel Brown, with whom he was traveling as a hunter. He reported that Dr. White said dogs could not be taken through—that the dogs would die before they had traveled half the distance and that their incessant barking and howling would notify the Indians where the wagon train was.

"Well," said another man standing by, "the Indians probably know where we are without the dogs telling them—and the dogs might even alert us to Indian presence."

"Wouldn't the advantages of having the dogs be counterbalanced by the disadvantage?" asked Lansford Hastings, rather portentously. He was among those who had newly joined the company and strode about assessing everything, commenting, offering small, cutting criticisms. But Elijah White had insisted, and finally enough men agreed about danger from the dogs, until there was a vote at the council meeting and two-thirds of the men reluctantly voted yes. So the shooting began.

A Bennett boy, no one could tell them apart, came near the women and choked out, "They just shot Benny. He was mine." The boy's eyes were red, his face twisted in pain, the word *mine* stretched like a scarf into the air behind him. Mr. Carter exclaimed loudly that if any man should kill his dogs, he would kill him, regardless of consequences, and so the shooters backed away. A man Caroline didn't know came over toward his wagon and threw his gun inside, looking fiercely at the women, as if it had been their idea to destroy the dogs. "Well, I'll have no part in it," he said as he turned and stomped off, the Bennett boy following.

"There had been a story of a rabid wolf that had menaced men coming back on the trail," said Reuben Lewis to no one in particular, although Caroline heard him. He had walked away from the slaughter. "Can you imagine?" Caroline said to herself as she headed to their wagon to stand with Jane and Wooley as the camp erupted in the screams of women and children and of the victims who had not been clean-shot.

Then it was over. Twenty-two dogs were killed, men's tempers were fired up, and disgust showed on their faces. A few dogs remained, some hidden like Wooley, some moving to their owners' wagons to safety, for none of the men was willing to enter the circle of wagons to kill the dogs in front of the women and children.

The ordeal was over.

"It will leave a very bitter taste in many mouths," said Dan to Caroline that night, putting his arm gently on her shoulder and pulling her head close to his. "Jane was smart to hide Wooley. He should be safe now, but we will have to watch. We are in no position to deal with rabies." He paused. "We might have to put him down if he poses a danger . . ." He let the sentence die in the silence, his shoulder leaning heavily against Caroline as he spoke.

"I know he is old and he might not make it to Oregon," said Caroline, more fiercely than she intended, "but it won't be because we shot him." She pushed back slightly to settle their shoulders together, closing out the presence of others.

*

*May 19: Severe rain this morning; laid out and got very wet. Started at ½
past 9. detained by crossing 2 creeks stoped at 2. Traviled 5 miles.*
—Medorem Crawford

The Women

When the wagons had come to a stop and the animals attended to, the women
watched the men move away from the camp to hold an owners' meeting.
The older boys, uncertain they would be welcome, for they were not voting
members of the company, hung around the edges, where they could nod at the
proceedings, hear the discussions, and appear to agree with decisions made by
the others. They were reluctant to remain in the camp with the women and
children. The surviving dogs followed their masters, several sitting attentively
as if participants, while others slept in the waning sunlight. The dog decree
had been rescinded, leaving no one happy but the remaining dogs, safe for
the time being.

They agreed on regulations: that every male over the age of eighteen would
have one mule or horse, plus one gun, three pounds of powder, twelve pounds
of lead, and one thousand caps or suitable flints. Each would have flour or
meal and bacon, with a suitable portion for the women and children traveling
with them.

Dr. White showed the men at the meeting the document from the War
Department, which he read aloud, explaining his appointment to any office in
the Oregon Territory. White was elected captain for one month. They agreed
that Columbia Lancaster, Captain Hastings, and A. L. Lovejoy would be a
scientific corps to keep a record of the conditions of the road, a document to
be sent to the government for the aid of future emigrants. They knew they
were the first. James Coates was appointed pilot and Nathaniel Crocker,
secretary. They appointed an official blacksmith, a wagon maker, a road and
bridge builder—all with the power to direct others to work as needed.

They also resolved that a code of laws be drafted and submitted to the
company, rules to be enforced by reprimand, fines, and finally by banishment.
They resolved there would be no swearing or obscene conversation or immoral

conduct on pain of expulsion. Then they wrote out a roster of all those on the trip to be registered with the secretary and called the meeting adjourned, to be reconvened at Fort Vancouver on the Columbia River on the first day of October next, "the power of Heaven willing."

They were ready to move forward.

The women spread wet blankets on the ground to dry and busied themselves at the small fires, pushing coals from one side to the other, a pot hanging from a wooden tripod. Cooking out of doors was new to most of them, and they felt awkward squatting before the fires. Most of them were used to different equipment, kitchens with forks hanging nearby, a knife next to the grinding stone, salt sitting in a crock with a wooden lid. While the women cooked, children played simple games, but they were quiet, exhausted from the exertions of the day.

CAROLINE AND MRS. LANCASTER

Caroline Tompkins made her way across the camp. Earlier she had decided Mrs. Lancaster was her sort, an educated woman, knowing instinctively that many of the others in the company were most likely not. Certainly not Mrs. Bennett, the giantess who could no more speak softly than a rock could read, nor that dreary, child-worn Mrs. Shadden, her skin as translucent as parchment, her hair hanging in gray streaks alongside her thin face. Nor was Mrs. Girtman her type, she thought; she seemed vague, but there might be some sharpness behind her guarded eyes. Mrs. Smith might possibly be, could possibly be a companion, but she was older and bound to be conventional. Caroline had had enough of that sort of bossing from her mother-in-law.

"Mrs. Lancaster," Caroline said in greeting, leaning in to the young woman, "I have come to call," she said, as if she were entering a Seneca Street drawing room with a tea service on the little table, the Irish maid hurrying in from the kitchen with warm cakes. "Do sit down," Mrs. Lancaster said to her guest, indicating a wooden ledge cleverly set against the side of the family wagon. Then with some edge to her voice, she asked, "You have not come to pray with me, have you?"

"No," said Caroline, who lowered herself carefully onto the plank and then sat back, grateful for the support for her spine. She eased against the wagon. "So nice," she murmured about the plank seat, "so very nice to have something to rest against. I feel I have been holding myself upright for days."

"Take your ease," the young woman responded with some enthusiasm, and the two women sat a moment in silence.

"Your child?" asked Caroline after a time.

"She is sleeping just now, but she suffered gravely all this day. It is the flux, says the doctor."

"Have you a good tea?" asked Caroline. "At home, we used a worm tea made by an old woman who steeped it for several days. She sold it in the market each spring."

"Susannah, that young woman from Virginia, the one with the large bonnet? She offered me some herbs she said would help. I didn't know what to say, for I don't know her, do I? Yet, she was very kind and spoke soothingly, so I took what she offered—some dark leaves, all crumpled and sour smelling. I didn't give them to Clarissa, though. I couldn't. Besides, Dr. White came by and gave the baby an elixir he trusts," said the young woman, "and that seemed to stop it . . . for the moment. But I fear . . ." and she paused, unable to finish her sentence.

"The worst?" provided Caroline gently, for no mother would doom her own child with premature words.

"Yes," she said simply. Tears slipped quietly down her face. "She has not eaten for days, can keep nothing down, and she has the diarrhea."

"It is in God's hands," Caroline offered, spooning the words toward the other woman as if words were sugar. But she was uncertain about God's hands and how safe any of them were in such a place. Caroline was rather uncertain about God himself. She did not think herself a disbeliever, just one not yet convinced. She liked the society of religion if not the tenets.

"Yes," said the young mother, nodding in agreement. Then, rather angrily she added, "Well, no. It was not God who propelled us on this mad journey. It was Mr. Lancaster. It was his ambition to get early to the new country, to be a pioneer in Oregon. Missouri, where he could have been a senator, wasn't big enough for him, he said. He needed to be first: first out there. And I, I acquiesced."

"You had no choice," soothed Caroline. "What woman in this company, excepting possibly the one called Mother Bennett, desires to be here? What woman willingly gives up her home and family?"

"Is that true?"

After a pause, Caroline said. "We do what we have to do." She thought how it was not women's choice to leave homes where their lives fit, where the linens were folded in the cupboard, the preserves on the shelf. But perhaps it wasn't a husband's choice either. "It is the times that propel us with all this talk of Oregon and the West."

"Columbia would go."

"As would Mr. Tompkins. And the others. Each has his own reason that I am sure he thinks good enough to act on. Each is fleeing something, chasing something. My husband is going to start life in Oregon as a newspaper editor. He has sent ahead a printing press from San Francisco."

"Have we no way to prevent this madness?"

"My dear, many women surely have said 'no' but find they live with a husband caged in his own rage. We have allowed our husbands to hurtle forward into the abyss, which is a different sort of rage, I think. We hope to be able to hold things together as best we can."

"But some who are innocent will die."

"Yes." Caroline paused, wondering how much she might say to this woman who was already grieving. "But innocents die at home, too."

"I suppose. We all die."

Mrs. Lancaster looked calmer now. She had said the awful word she dreaded, faced what the future would surely bring. The two women sat quietly looking out at the others going about their work. At the Girtman girl with her mother; the widow Abel, talking with Mrs. Perry, her sister, who was in the family way, but not due just yet; at the large Brown clan milling about; at others whose names they didn't yet know—the group of Germans, the two Indian boys who had passed the winter in the East and were returning home to Oregon, and the passel of children who disappeared into wagons pulled together for the night into a square that held their cooking fires.

"Did you know anyone in the company before?" Roxanna Lancaster asked.

"No. No, we didn't, but Dr. White, he is from near us, and we heard that he was heading west. And Nathaniel Crocker is from our county. I believe I knew his sister at school. There are a few others from our area, but I didn't know them." Caroline paused. "We know old Dr. Parker, who went west in 1835 to establish mission sites and then returned to our village, where he published a book about his travels."

"Dr. White has been to the West before?"

"Oh yes. He was with the Methodist mission at the Willamette Valley for several years. Dr. Parker told me about him. Now he travels with a letter from the government appointing him Indian sub-agent," added Caroline. "He seems less convincing in person than his credentials suggest." She paused, wondering how much she could say of her worry.

Caroline had already discussed Dr. White with her husband, who had come to her shortly after they had gotten to Elm Grove and there whispered to her, "Perhaps we made a great mistake in our leader." She asked what he meant, and Dan had explained that he had been with William Sublette in Elm Grove, who had come up from Independence. Sublette knew more about the West than anyone, Dan explained, as he was a great fur trader and importer. Sublette had come out to see the company as it prepared to go west. Sublette and Dr. White had then had a confrontation.

"Sublette," Dan explained, "thought White was headed for trouble of a sort the doctor could not imagine."

"What was said?" she asked. Dan explained that Sublette, who knew the West well, the land beyond Missouri, had advised Dr. White not to go forward. White protested that everyone knew that the Oregon Country was held between two governments, that of the United States and that of Great Britain, but that there was no doubt that it would ultimately become a part of the United States: it was slated to be. White insisted that he was needed there.

"Yes," Sublette had said, "no doubt, but Doctor, you do not know what is before you. I have many times crossed those terrible mountains through all those Indian tribes—and you, you have a fearful undertaking before you." And, he added cautiously but with great doubt in his voice, "you are taking women and children." Sublette insisted that White could not preserve order, discipline, and good feeling among the travelers while traversing difficult terrain. The consequences, Sublette feared, would be that everyone would be destroyed or cut off by the Indians.

"White was not to be deterred," said Dan. "He insisted that as Moses had brought the people of Israel out of the land of the Egyptians to lead them to the Promised Land, so too he, Elijah White, was on just such a mission." Dan looked carefully at Caroline as he repeated the words he had heard: "he thinks, the doctor that is, that he is Moses directed by God."

"He also said," continued Dan, "that according to Frémont, who had made the trip across the mountains and into California, the distance was twenty-seven hundred miles."

"You people have no map or guide," Sublette had said, but Dr. White insisted that he carried with him the book and map created by Samuel Parker, who had made the trip west some years earlier. And documents from the government in Washington.

"But through hordes of strange savages," Sublette had cautioned White. "You do not know what is out there."

Dr. White then said the idea of an emigration had originated with the secretary of war, John Spencer, in Washington and that it struck him, the doctor, as eminently becoming that he be in charge. When Spencer gave him his federal appointment, he talked about how impressed he was with Dr. White's description of the Oregon Country. When Spencer wanted to know if an emigrant party might make it to the coast, White assured him that emigrants could make the trip and that he would lead them. "But Caroline," said Dan, "White knows as little about the crossing as anyone. When he was last in Oregon, he went and returned by ship. He might know Oregon, but he knows nothing about the land between."

"You mean that we are being led into the wilderness as were the Hebrews by Moses, by a man who doesn't know the way?" Caroline asked.

"Well, Sublette said to White that the doctor was a man with little experience in border life and perhaps was, ah, a bit too amiable to attempt to control a party, especially one without a charter. And of course White said he would happily write a charter, just as he agreed that he would lead an emigrant train west, but knowing nothing." Dan said that Sublette's impression of White was that he was a man who would rather tell a lie than the truth, even when the truth would serve him better.

"He seems a good doctor," said Mrs. Lancaster, bringing Caroline out of her reverie, her internal dialogue.

"Yes. Well, I didn't mean as a physician, Mrs. Lancaster," replied Caroline a bit quickly. She paused. "He does not inspire followers, I think."

They sat in silence for a minute, exploring the odd man who was leading them forth.

"What are the men doing over there?"

"Voting laws for our company," answered Caroline. "Men like the business of making resolutions and amending them, of voting and creating procedures. They are drawing up a constitution for our little band, now that we are beyond the jurisdiction of the United States. The traders and trappers who set out always insisted on constitutions before they would venture into the West. Our men will have elected officers and a committee to hear disputes, and they will affirm regulations so that we don't become lawless."

"You don't think that wise, Mrs. Tompkins?"

"It is not that rules aren't important," said Caroline, trying to put her ideas into words, never having voiced them before, "but we aren't likely to become any more lawless here than we were at home. It is the importance that the men attach to the making of the regulations that concerns me." Both women looked up as a huzzah came from the assembled men.

"We will all be guided by these laws, yet we, and the young men, and the hired men, have no hand in making them. They legislate for us as if we were children, to be led by the wiser parent." She paused, trying to find a way to justify her attitude. "They know little more than we do about this journey."

"Mr. Lancaster is surely wiser than I about things of the law, as he is a lawyer," stated the young woman rather strongly. "If not wiser about things that are practical," she added quietly.

"Yes. Well, I am glad to see Dan so involved with this. In his lifetime, he has been too often regulated by others. I think it might make him feel good to be the one to enact the regulations for once." Another cheer went up from the men gathered to the side of the camp.

"I should go back inside in case the baby wakes."

The two women shook hands. Caroline saw Mrs. Lancaster into her wagon and heard the young mother talking softly to her infant. It was bad enough, she thought, to face the illness of a child at home, with family around and the familiar to give strength. There, she thought, we know where to reach for blankets or for a pan to fill with water, where the stick is kept that can brace open the window for a bit of air, where the heat remains longest so that towels could be warmed on the stove before being placed at a baby's back. They were not yet friends, and might never become well acquainted, yet they talked easily, bonded by their motherhood, though one of them could barely remember her children as infants while the other feared, knew really, that her child would never live past this day or perhaps the next.

Here, nothing is familiar; everything serves to put us off balance, for we are strangers, thought Caroline somewhat bitterly. We are not intended to be on this foreign land. It doesn't belong to us nor we to it, she mused as she walked slowly back to her own family's spot. And what of the people already here—the Indians—she wondered. She skirted the fires, where supper was cooking in pots; around the camp site where the German men kept to themselves, locked away in their own language, understood by few; past the animals tethered to wagons or stakes. Across the way the men in council seemed to come apart as water spilled on a kitchen floor goes in various directions.

This was their fifth day on the trail after moving off from Elm Grove. It had taken the company several weeks to gather, and even now there were people who were said to be coming along behind them for whom they had waited until they could delay no longer. They headed into Indian Territory, where the marks on the land were few, their meaning ambiguous. They had traveled through hot dry weather, the air clogged with dust, and then they had experienced rain, at first in a fine shower, then torrents, and some hail. The wagon covers soaked through and then the oilcloths sagged, some of them ripping from the weight of the water. Even goods locked into trunks had gotten damp. They had crossed two difficult creeks, swollen from the rains, and they were now moving slowly, like a caterpillar, across the rolling prairie.

This day they had camped early because everyone knew that the Lancaster child was gravely ill. The men used the time to hold their organizational meeting, to set rules that would get them through. That is what they said, "to get us through," meaning across Indian Territory, along the River Platte, over the Rocky Mountains and on, through to Oregon. That is the way they envisioned the journey, in stages, each to be conquered before the next goal was contemplated or even spoken of.

Caroline couldn't help but think how very odd it was that she and Danby were actually here, in the middle of the prairie, outside their own country, heading into the unknown. They were an unlikely couple to be pioneers, yet Dan would go.

Caroline walked past the wagon that belonged to those two young people from Virginia. She was called Susannah, Caroline thought, but she didn't know the husband's name. He was dark-skinned, furtive in manner, as if he were hiding. Caroline thought them odd, a rather skittish pair. And young, she thought, very young. Then it came to her that perhaps they were running from something at home, that possibly they were newlyweds or, more probably, eloping. That would explain their reticence with others in the company, their preference for being alone, for not joining in. She shook her head, wondering just what their story was.

Caroline had the habit at times of speaking aloud to herself, though she took care to do so quietly so others wouldn't notice or hear. She mouthed the words that raced through her brain, saying them and hearing them at the same time—and sometimes forgetting them just as quickly as the thoughts and words came to her. Her children, now intent on lives of their own, didn't pay attention. As she walked back to her own wagon, she was in deep conversation with herself, commenting about what she observed:

> That's a poor-looking horse over there, and we are less than a week out on the trail. I wonder if it will make the trip, and since some won't get to Oregon I would think this a candidate. . . . Look at that smart wagon with all those pockets at the back with loops for tools to keep them handy when needed. I like that . . . I like the kind of mind who would think where to keep things. . . . I wonder whose wagon that is . . . ah, yes, Gabriel Brown's, I think. A tidy-looking man, too, now that I think about it, for when they arrived, not now of course, but at the beginning his beard was trimmed close to his face, his jaw square as if his beard were the dressing

round a window. I haven't met Mrs. Brown yet. He seems to have several hired men traveling with him, possibly relatives. One gave us a hand the other day, a steady sort and older, than most of the young men working their way west. Reuben, I think I heard someone call him. A well-spoken man. I noticed right off that he carries something small that he moves back and forth, from hand to hand, like a talisman. He has a book in his pocket, too. I don't think it's a Bible, though it could be a small edition, but it seems to be more like a novel or book of poetry, perhaps. It would be nice if it were poetry, although one wouldn't expect that on the trail.

THE WOMEN

The creeks proved to be a problem, each different from the last. Some were shallow and filled with rocks, some approached from steep banks, some with water racing by, enough to swamp the wagon beds; there was quicksand in others. The men placed planks across wagon boxes on which baggage was placed to keep goods and women dry. Then they moved the wagons forward, one by one, and brought them across the water.

This trip west was not what most of the women had thought it would be. For some, to be sure, it was a continuation of a life on the move, from one farm to another, from one hoped-for opportunity to another, moving, roving, seeking the better place, the next place; never owning, never planting anything but babies left behind in graveyards that other people would tend—or leave uncared for; never having more goods than would fit in a wagon and never having money for more anyway. For those women, married life had been a continuing series of new places, people to shy from, people who looked down upon them knowing trash when they thought they saw it. It was a life of rumors to chase down, then rumors to live down. Mrs. Shadden knew this life, and Mrs. Bennett, too. They had come to Elm Grove, and from there Dr. White was to lead them west. They had come without plan and were here only because Missouri was the next place in their meandering journey through life, a journey of no destination but one that spun endlessly forward. It was a life of shy hello and hasty farewell, sometimes said silently when already out of town and owing: at least for the Shaddens, it was often that way. It was sometimes a departure just ahead of the sheriff. No real crime about them but poverty, which generated more poverty.

Several of them didn't have the money to buy into the company, but Dr. White had offered to take them along, seeking to increase the number in his party. It wouldn't take money so much as grit to get them through, and who knew in the long run who would have the grit needed and who would fade or fail to meet the challenges ahead. Fording rivers and crossing mountains would not depend on money; White simply wanted to arrive in Oregon with a great entourage. So the Shaddens and the Bennetts had been allowed to come along. Each man with a vote, and each with a chip on his shoulder about the hand the world had dealt him.

The Bennetts had come from Georgia and carried that place in their speech. They had willingly left, for there was talk about them at home, and people would point and remember she was the wife that little Bennett had gotten off of her daddy to pay a debt.

For the other women, though, the journey with its trials was a surprise. Most of those other women, Mrs. Abel the widow; her sister, Mrs. Perry; as well as Mrs. Brown, Mrs. Tompkins, and Mrs. Smith, were not really prepared for what it was actually like. How could they have been? One day there was heat, another day a torrent of rain and even hail; they watched a waterspout that had come racing down the river, striking the water and creating a great foam and then passing along as if it were a tornado. One day they were alone on the land and the next they saw a flat-bottomed boat piled with furs floating neatly past them. One day there was plenty of wood and water, the next the land was arid.

*

May 20: Verry heavy rain last night & cloudy this morning. Moved camp about one mile.
—Medorem Crawford

The Tompkins Family Boots

Only Ellen, of the females in the Tompkins family, was happy the day her father, wearing a new leather large-brimmed hat, had come striding into the house with four pairs of boots for Caroline and the girls and announced that they were to wear them on the trip west. Only Ellen had put hers on and broken them in. And her boots already showed where her right ankle tipped slightly out on the one side, the heel of the other boot scuffed, listing slightly inward as she walked.

To her sisters, Martha and Jane, the boots had been an affront. Their father had returned home one day, along with Ned, who was wearing a new pair of boots himself, breaking them in, and had said, "And you should too." They scoffed as their father had placed the sturdy brown leather boots on the drawing room floor. He had said, "These are from George Frost, made from the family lasts. The hat's from George, too, to keep the sun out of my eyes." Martha and Jane had looked at him in disbelief.

Caroline had said, "And what are these ugly boots for, Danby Tompkins? Surely not for us to walk about town?"

That is when the family learned it was about to leave. To leave home and school and church and the dear streets lined with linden and chestnut trees, and houses painted white, or stately in black, in which their friends lived. To leave all that they knew about in life—the sewing circle at the church, the music lessons with old Mrs. Elmer, who was always grumpy and who smelled, to leave the long, interminable sermons of the Reverend Wisner, to abandon the rhythm of their lives, which included Sunday dinners at Grandmother's house, where everyone was quiet all day and time hung languidly on the children's hands while the adults sat at table and drank tea to make the hours pass. They would leave the very stores on Owego Street that never carried the true blue cambric that Jane sought, or the sheet music that Martha longed to learn to play, or the right dishes for the dollhouse that the girls shared—those very stores that were always inadequate suddenly became dear to them, homey, familiar. They knew the ways of the shopkeepers, which one would give the children a candy and who would not, who had a heavy thumb on the scale, and who saved the newspapers for Mr. Tompkins and made sure they were not touched by anyone else so that they would be tight and make crinkling sounds as he opened them each day.

All that they had taken for granted, all that they knew and loved, or knew and belittled, or knew and had always found wanting was suddenly to be left behind. The boots became the symbol of that change they neither wanted nor looked forward to. They were comfortable at home; they had a place, and a good one, each thought, in the order of life in the small town. They were from a respected family with enough money so that a child who wanted, really wanted, a new doll or a piano could actually expect to get it.

To all but Ellen, that is, who embraced the idea of the adventure, the new sights and new times, and the things to be seen and learned. She thought of the new land they would help create. Just as she embraced the boots that her father brought home and placed on the drawing room floor, she embraced the idea of the journey west.

So Ellen, throwing off the pair of shoes she wore to school, pulled on the new boots ever so carefully, first over the toes, then the foot, her heel, and then her leg disappearing down the long shaft of leather. Making a quiet thud, her heel slipped into place, the sour smell of the leather coming to her nose as she tugged at the sides. She pulled on those boots with as much ritual and care as her mother and sisters would have employed when they initiated a pair of long kid gloves, but of course the leather in each case was quite different.

Martha and Jane walked around the collection of boots as if by doing so they would go away, just as they hoped that this new situation would disappear. Caroline hefted the boots and carried them to her sewing room, where she sat and wept. Danby had finally made a break with his family, just as she had encouraged him to do all these years, just as she had hoped he would do, and yet he had done it ever so differently than she had envisioned. How could he? How could he simply come home and announce that they were about to depart, that the house was as good as sold to Mr. Timmons, who had just moved into town to open a singing school, and that what they could not take with them could be stored in his mother's house. After all these years of not making a move, not speaking up, not rebelling against his family's wishes and plans, how could he make such a break that would disrupt them all? She hadn't expected this, not this. Other possibilities she would have greeted avidly, for she was as anxious as he to change their circumstances. She had thought they might move to Schenectady, where Danby had had the offer of a teaching position, or to Rochester, where he could start the literary magazine he had talked about, or to Brooklyn to write for one of those national journals. But this? How could he do it—and not even tell her beforehand?

In other homes the decision to leave, the decision to go, the decision to try elsewhere, to get in on the early phase when the good land would be there for the taking, when the territory needed families to claim it for the nation, in other homes the decisions had come in various ways. In some it was mutually made: the Perrys had decided they didn't want to remain in Indiana and that Oregon sounded possible. "A young man's country," Mr. Perry had said. He assisted at a sawmill, but in Oregon he would open his own. The Perrys, young people looking forward to a new land and a new challenge, made the decision together. Widow Abel had no choice but to go along. She didn't complain much; she didn't say much at all—not since Frederick's death. The Perrys were sure that the change of scenery would be good for her. "Besides," Susan Perry had said, "there will be plenty of men out there looking for a good woman and she can marry again and forget the past."

Mr. Perry had surprised her when he commented that perhaps Widow Abel would not forget but learn to live with the past. Susan looked sharply at him and then smiled that he understood.

The Browns had left willingly too, because they had lost three children in the lowlands near the Missouri River where they lived. Ague, they said, and each time they made the trip to the cemetery they vowed they would leave for a better place. The problem was, where would they go? They were already on the frontier, as far as the country went. Then they read about Dr. White and his commission from the president of the United States to take emigrant families to Oregon, and, having heard of Oregon for years and years, they were willing to try it—to keep their living children in this world, to give children yet unborn a chance.

In other families, there were reasons to go, situations to draw away from. In places they were leaving, the land was worn, or the deed wasn't solid, or the family disapproved, the neighbors had divided on the issue of slavery, or the times weren't good. And there were attractions, in Oregon. This was the right time, said the men, and opportunity beckoned. Think of climate so mild the cattle could feed themselves through the winter; of fish in the rivers so plentiful they flew onto the shore; the grass so lush, the trees so tall, the land so empty. It called loudly to some.

The Women

The trail was not what anyone had expected. Their feet hurt, unaccustomed as they were to walking all day. Their dresses tore. Even this early in the spring they needed bonnets to keep the sun from burning their skin. Who would have thought that singeing the end of an axe would create an oily residue that could be wiped on the lips to keep them from cracking? Whoever thought that up? They needed to keep the bugs from their eyes and out of the food. They had new worries about the children, and they watched their men change from city ways, or migrant ways, or agricultural ways, to men of new purpose.

Most of the women had expected to ride west. Excepting Mrs. Shadden and Mrs. Bennett, the women had envisioned traveling in carriages with prancing horses moving proudly across the countryside. Some of them had been led to believe that crossing the country would require little effort on their part. The *Indian Advocate* even printed a series of articles about how effortless women travelers would find the journey. That magazine promoted the idea of the trip as a time to see the landscape, pick new wildflowers, to see the sights. Women, the articles had promised, would find less work on the trail than in their own homes; they would be fascinated by the wildlife; they would revel in sights of native peoples; they would carry with them American civilization. Which of course was the point.

But it wasn't like that. The trip was proving to be hard work. They discovered that the first week. It was hard work to get food ready; wood needed to be hauled or found; fires made; ingredients, a paltry few, cooked; dishes passed out and gathered together again; dishes washed with sand when no water was near. It was work managing the lumbering wagons that were the only vehicles that could make the trip; loading the goods, making sure they didn't shift and fall on a body while under way, storing things needed close at hand and safely at the bottom of the wagon. Those goods simply making the trip across the country to be there when they got to Oregon tucked safely at the back or hung from the top. It turned out to be hard work to pull the canvas forward when it rained, to yank it back when it was so hot you could cook pancakes inside the wagon at midday—and this was only late May. It was hard work to get in and out, hauling one's self up the sides and into the back of the wagon, especially when the wagons were in motion, for then you had to be careful not to get thrown forward, into the dark interior of the canvas house, or even off the moving wagon, only to be pinned under the slow-moving but heavy wheels.

It was hard, too, to walk. It was tiring to walk all day, up and down, over and about for women who had walked little, for girls who walked only to school and back and to music lessons. They learned to avoid the holes in the ground, to walk around the horse droppings, to look out for snakes, to watch the children running about and ensure they did not fall under a wagon wheel or get run over by a horse whose rider rushed into the camp heedless of the youngsters.

The younger women—the Girtman girl, Mrs. Perry and her widowed sister, sometimes that Virginia woman, Susannah—found plenty to interest them, and they chatted while walking forward. Susannah noted the plants beneath their feet and collected twigs and leaves, pulling off bark to use as medicine. Mrs. Perry watched the hawks and buzzards swooping overhead, the birds graceful as they caught an air current, when they seemed to float forward, or swoop rapidly to the ground if there was something of interest. They talked of here and of before; they did so mostly without regret, though in a guarded way revealing little of consequence. They were in the process of knowing each other but were not yet known and comfortable. Some of them, like Martha and Jane, were decidedly not happy about this move away from the lives they once knew.

The women of middle age, with more pounds on them than when they were newlywed, found the going difficult at first. They felt stiff in their joints, tired in the calves of their legs, discomfort in their women's parts. There was this place in the middle of the back where a sharp pain appeared and stayed. They felt awkward at the lack of privacy. Even while lying in the wagon bed ready for sleep they could hear others talking, laughing in the night. There was no outhouse or even chamber pot, and bodily functions were performed alone or behind the skirts of other women. At the back of the wagons there were wooden pails with water for the monthly cloths, the motion of the wagon agitating the blood they had just left on them.

The trip was not what they expected. And while they slowly met, warmed to each other, and began conversations about the bewildering character of men and the danger children got themselves into, they began to feel their bodies ease, their boots take the form of their feet. They lengthened their stride until they were walking with their heads bent slightly forward, their backs straight, their pace not what one would expect of a city woman with shops to look into and neighbors to greet. But this easing into a physical comfort was not quick or smooth; it took time to work first the legs, then the back, then the shoulders, finally the boots. It took time for them to see that dresses that swept the ground only made their walking harder. At night, at the campfires, they ripped strips from the bottom of their skirts so that their dresses hung to the ankle but no farther. Absolutely no farther down. Petticoats were put away, used later for shrouds for the dead, for bandages for the injured, the lace pulled off to make pretty things for dolls that the few younger girls carried with them.

All these things took time for the women to learn and know.

Excepting for Ellen, who abandoned her old self in a flash, with no regret as she quickly found the person she knew herself to be. She was an excited, interested, probing girl of twelve who climbed trees, pulled apart insects to see how they were made, looked under rocks, and carried stones away with her. She traveled about with a small pail into which she put things. When she met up on the trail with the McKay boys traveling back home after a year in the East, she remembered having previously seen Alexander McKay, who had spent the year in Ithaca living with Reverend and Mrs. Parker, but she had never talked to him. Now, however, there were three of them: wild young people on the wondrous earth, a caution to the mothers, something scandalous to the older sisters.

*

May 20: All gone ahead except 3 wagons who are detained with a sick child.
—Medorem Crawford

Martha Tompkins Writes a Letter Home

My dear Letty,

I promised to write to you when I left home and thought to send
a letter from St. Louis but as there was much to do and see in that
city, I never got to it. I was so lonely for you and all my friends at the
Academy that I didn't feel much like writing anyway, nor did I have
anything to say but how I missed you and even Miss Thayer, and my
piano, and even silly Tad Hoskins.

Now we have gone on the trail, everything has changed. There are
no more cities, no more boat travel, no more interesting people to
meet for we are alone out here, absolutely. And we have had a death! I
can almost not believe it. People died at home. I even knew some who
died like that fat Harriet Besom and old Mr. Ayers, but this was so
shocking to us all. It was so sudden.

I should explain that there are a lot of people in this company,
probably more than one hundred. Some are families, most are men
working their way west. There are two Indians with us too. Remember
that Indian boy McKay who lived with Mrs. Parker, old Reverend
Parker's wife on Seneca Street last winter? Well, he is here along with
his brother, who had been at school in Connecticut. They came east,
well, went east last year, and are going home now, traveling along with
us. And there are some others, an odd Frenchman from Canada and
a group of German men who have very thick accents so no one can
understand them. How they came to be going west, having just arrived
in this country—or the United States for we are beyond your country
now—I do not know. But they are. We have a great number of wagons,
some well fixed and others rather loosely put together even at the start.
I don't know how some will get through.

The Germans are traveling in a democrat wagon with an open top. They replaced the fine wheels with heavy wooden ones and have braced the wagon with extra planking. Each evening they take out a tent that they erect instead of sleeping under their wagon bed, which is full of tools and things. There are five of them, I think.

Well, yesterday, one of those German men was taking a musket out of the wagon bed and in pulling it away from the shovel and tent poles, it went off! Can you imagine!

And instead of the bullet just flying into the air, it shot into a young man named Bailey, who was standing on a wagon nearby, hitting him in the abdomen. There was a great shout from Bailey and there was a great deal of blood. I did not see it, but Ned told me as he was not far off when the accident happened, and he ran to find Dr. White for help.

There was little the doctor could do as the wound was too dreadful so he gave young Bailey some laudanum to ease his pain, since alcohol is not permitted in this company, and Bailey seeing that death was near called his friends to him and told them to put their trust in God for no one ever knows when death will take them away, and after a time, Bailey, whose first name I do not know, expired.

It is all so dreadful, and Bailey was a very lovely young man though I had not yet had the opportunity to meet and speak with him. Yet, I miss him already. He was traveling with another young man working for a family named Carter. Mrs. Carter has a little boy.

Now the horrible part is that he had to be buried right here on the prairie. Some men went off the trail and began digging a grave and someone else built a coffin from boards from the side of a wagon. Mother brought a small blanket to cushion the box and Bailey was put inside. Then we all walked to the open grave and Dr. White said some words of comfort for Bailey's friends and warnings for the rest of us. He called this death a caution to which we should pay especial attention for the journey on which we were going was untested by emigrant families and we are the first company of families and wagons to make this crossing. We will be at great risk.

Then, surprisingly, Jane stood up holding the hymnal Mother had brought along and sang a sad song about dying young and there was hardly a dry eye to be seen. Then we sang "Jesus, Lover of My Soul," with the awful line "Let me to Thy bosom fly," which was what Bailey requested while Dr. White was tending to him.

Then the men put the coffin in the ground and covered the hole with dirt and the whole company walked over it back and forth. Some men put stones on the grave so the wolves would not dig it up. Ned made a small cross and put Bailey's name on it but no one knows who his parents or family are so there is no one we can notify when we get a chance to send a letter back. It is all very pathetic and I felt faint for much of the rest of the afternoon. But once the service was over, we walked back to our wagons and set off—never to see this spot again and no one will ever know that Bailey is dead or that he is buried there. Isn't that just too dreadful?

The German man who sent off the shot was named Horn. He was prostrate with grief and could not attend the service.

Not everything is so dreadful. The prairie is quite beautiful.

The prairie rolls, rather like the way I imagine the ocean would, with one short rise following after another short rise, and so we go up and up and down, and up and up and down, all during the day. We are heading now for a river called the Blue, and we will travel along it for a time until we get to the Platte River, which is the river we will follow west all the way to Fort Laramie.

There could be Indians nearby, Osages or Pawnees. I think it is the Osages to whom Miss Palmer went off to be a missionary several years ago. Do you remember? It is she for whom we take the missionary collection at church each quarter; for her, and for Mr. Allis, to whom she was afterwards married. They are our church's special missionary concern. Your church, that is. Not mine any longer.

As you may suspect, Ellen is loving every minute of the trip except for the death of Bailey to whom she said she had talked the previous day on her quest for information for her account, which she calls her Observation. Mother has set her to keeping a history of this trip and for it she goes all over the camp talking to anyone. I think she will end up a heathen and not a proper young lady at all but Mother says we should encourage her to keep a good record of this journey because she is missing her education at the Academy.

I will put this letter away and when we get to the Fort Laramie, which will be in about a month, or if we meet a trapping party heading back to the States, I will send it on its way to you, my very dear friend.

Yours in friendship and love. Please don't let all my friends at home forget me.

Martha Elinore Tompkins
On the Oregon Trail
In Indian Territory
Don't forget to write to me.

What the Widow Abel Noted in Her Diary

There was a burial yesterday of a young boy accidentally shot. Dr. White gave a short sermon and a girl sang. It was dreadful that this young man Bailey was cut down in his prime, and I should be full of sympathy for him, but I can think only of Frederick, who was also cut down in the prime of his life, and I hope so that the Lord will "receive his soul at last," as the girl sang. After the service we walked over the grave to tamp down the earth and then we started up again and drove through beautiful country and camped. The night was rainy & cloudy cold & uncomfortable. Baby slept peacefully while I lay and listened to the raindrops on the canvas above me. I am glad to be here with Brother Perry and my dear sister, but I feel disloyal at the same time leaving Frederick lying in a grave in Indiana with no one to tend it.

*

May 21: Another rainy night & cloudy cold & uncomfortable morning. Mrs. Lancaster's only child, a daughter 16 months old, died 10 o'clock. the Doctor called the disease symptomatick fever accompanied with worms. Continues to rain moderately.
—Medorem Crawford

Mrs. Shadden Speaks Her Mind

They stopped the wagons after the Lancaster baby died. The doctor said it was fever accompanied with worms. Now, isn't that interesting. Worms: even the high and mighty get pulled down like us ordinary folks. We made a camp circle, and some men went off to dig a grave. The area was rocky, and so they went about a three-quarters of a mile off the trail. In the camp, one of the men built a tiny coffin and some of the ladies donated pieces of linen for a lining. The older Mrs. Smith, traveling with her son's family, but in her own wagon with old Mr. Smith, went off to wash and dress the child. Then when everything was ready we all trooped off to the gravesite, and that Tompkins girl sang again and people said prayers.

I could have gone and washed the baby. I have done it many a time, for my own and for others too, but it seemed that the Lancasters and the Tompkinses and the Smiths had it all decided between them. The likes of Flora Shadden was not needed. A bunch of swells they think they are, if you ask me.

This second death has put everyone in a downcast mood, especially following the day they killed the dogs about which people are still real resentful and the death of that Bailey boy. Even the children seem to be playing more quietly than before. A boy, perhaps it was a Bennett child, brought a snake into camp, but it was quickly beheaded and he was scolded by that mother of his. A big loud woman; she doesn't act much like a woman neither, with her shouting at her family, telling 'em what to do and where to put things and when to move and the like. Her mister seems to take orders from her just like the children do. It makes one wonder.

Anyway, after the burial, which was nice enough with plenty of tears shed for the little baby and the family grieving and all, we came back to the camp and some of the men began to make preparations to move off. Mrs. Lancaster wailed and screeched that she couldn't just drive off and leave her baby in the wilderness where it would never be mourned and she would never again see its grave. The Lancasters stayed back when we left the gravesite, sitting on the ground, clasped in each other's arms crying. They looked as though they would never leave that spot, but what can they do. They can't stay here and we cannot stay here either. We have far to go.

By the time she had got all that steam up, Mrs. Lancaster was ill herself, lying prostrate on the ground in front of their wagon getting her nice clothes dirty and all.

That Mr. Lancaster, a nice looking man with a large fine head, you know, watched her and shook his head with dismay. He and the doctor seemed to think there was nothing to be done but to put Mrs. Lancaster in the wagon, so the two of them, and Mrs. Tompkins too, sticking in her head where it ain't any of her business, I would think, helped and they dragged the poor woman to the wagon and put her to bed. The doctor gave her something to make her sleep. After a time her yelling got less and then it stopped altogether. So the company hitched up the wagons and we moved on for the rest of the day.

I must say that I do understand the grief of leaving that little grave all alone where no one will ever see it again. It wasn't easy for any of us to go on, and it wasn't even our baby. We are all feeling folk and we have had our share of tears over dead children. For myself I can say I have three babies buried in Kentucky from where we come, and it was no small feat leaving those little children behind. But at least they were in a graveyard where others will come and pay some attention; out here in the prairie, as soon as the marker weathers or is blown away, that little grave will be totally unmarked and unknown. Even Mrs. Bennett mentioned how hard it would be to simply pull away. She said she had left babies in graves in Mississippi and in Louisiana, and the Mississippi one was her first born, too.

We traveled farther that day of the burying, and we all thought about death, let me tell you. I had to do a heap of explaining to little Joey about why we couldn't bring the dead baby along with us. Camped, but there was no singing after the dinner chores were done as nobody felt much like picking up a tune. The next day we traveled on. It was said around camp that Mrs.

Lancaster was not quite right in the head and that the doctor thought we should stop so she could recover or go slowly so the bumping of the wagon didn't disturb her more. He feared for her, he said. That's what Shadden said to me he heard the doctor say, anyway.

But the company didn't want to wait because we have a great long way in front of us and every day counts. We need to move along when the weather is good and we are able, and today the weather is fine. All this talk of delay makes me wonder, if it was Flora Shadden who was ill, would Dr. White want to delay the company? No, I think not, for Flora Shadden is little more than a poor Kentucky woman with a lot of children and Thomas Shadden is not a lawyer who was suggested as a candidate from Missouri to the U.S. Congress, as it is said that Mr. Columbia Lancaster was. But if he was so mighty important in Missouri, why would he be taking his family to Oregon? That is the question I asked Shadden at supper, but he had no answer and thought wanting to be first in a place could attract any man, rich or poor, shiftless or a lawyer. That's what Shadden had to say about it.

Well past the Kansas River we drove over a beautiful country. We traveled some twenty-five miles, they say. Then we stopped while the men fixed the wagons.

The next day there was a crisis, and isn't it the high-born educated ladies who always seem to have a fuss that gets everyone involved. It seems that Mrs. Lancaster is despaired of, her grief is so great. But the men in the company, especially that Lansford Hastings, who joined the company late and who struts about acting as if he is the captain even when the men voted Dr. White the captain, urged all the men to say they wanted to keep going while the going was good. So there was a meeting of the company, that is, of the men who are voters, and Shadden said that at that meeting Dr. White was outvoted and Mr. Hastings—he likes to be called Captain Hastings—urged the body of the company to move forward and leave Mr. Lancaster to decide what to do for his own family by himself. Then Shadden said that Dr. White said he would remain with the Lancasters as the missus would be needing a doctor, and that boy traveling with Dr. White, the Crawford lad, who seems like a good sort, said he would remain behind with the doctor too.

It was decided that Captain Hastings would lead most of us forward along the trappers' trail, which is pretty well marked, and the doctor and some others would remain with the Lancaster wagon. We parted, which seemed very strange since everyone had pledged to keep together because there could be Indians about, as this is Indian Territory, and lone people on the trail could be attacked. Or they could run into other trouble.

I watched the wagons as we pulled off and wondered what would happen since this company is Dr. White's. He is the one with the government certificate, which he allowed everyone to see, giving him the duty to raise a company of emigrants to take to Oregon. We went on forward, some six miles, I would estimate, by the time we traveled, and then we camped for the night.

Next day we moved on, north and west, heading to the Platte River. We moved on right smartly as the tracks in the prairie were pretty visible, made as they were by the traders who came in from the mountains earlier in the spring with their pelts. We found some old objects like a pail and the remains of campfires along the way, and Natty Shadden found a bottle that one of the traders had tossed off and it only had a chip from the lip; it wasn't even broken all the way across.

Our party was divided until Dr. White and the Crawford boy came back into camp. But they didn't come alone, for some other men who had been trailing us caught up with them, and so while the Lancasters headed east, back to Missouri, we have three new men along, which should make us even safer if there is trouble. One of them is Stephen Meek, said to be a mountain man wanting to go back west again after time in St. Louis. They had to ride two days to catch up to us, one of those days for twenty-five miles, which is a long time to sit on a horse. At dusk the doctor called a meeting and said he was in charge again, which made Captain Hastings look dark, said Shadden, who thinks there will be trouble between those two before the journey is done. Neither one is a following sort, and each is too big for his britches already, liking to stand up before the men and tell 'em where to next.

Shadden reported that the doctor said that Lawyer Lancaster had decided to return to Missouri rather than risk the health of his wife, for he feared losing her too. According to the doctor, Lancaster said he would get to Oregon yet, and get there in time to help turn it into a state, but this was not the time for him to push on. So the doctor and Crawford and the others rode back a ways with them to the Kansas River, where they should be safe enough from the Indians, and bid them good luck.

＊

May 23: Some rain last night & cloudy cool morning. Started at 9 o'clock. . . .
Distance 10 miles.
—Medorem Crawford

CAROLINE TOMPKINS

Caroline noticed a small bird, something smaller than a wren, she thought, light brown and tan below. It flew close to the ground and then landed gently on one of the longer grasses. It hung there, swaying back and forth on the stalk. Then it flew off.

She mused about the bird, so free, almost weightless. Nearby Martha was fussing with the dried peaches they had brought along, and she could hear Jane singing over near the horses. The girl sang all the time, thought Caroline, remembering with satisfaction the sure tones of Jane's voice when she sang in the service for the young man who was shot, and then again for the baby. She had done very well, and Caroline was pleased, for Jane had such difficulty expressing herself, her speech most often erupting in stutters. She was unable to get through an entire sentence. Yet, she could sing. Caroline wondered, and not for the first time, how that could be. How could she sing and not stutter?

"Where is Ellen?" she asked.

"I haven't seen her, Mother," Martha replied. "Perhaps she went off with Ned or with Father."

"Your Father and Ned are with the animals, staking them for the night."

"She has made friends with those Indian boys, Mother," Martha said in a complaining way. "The McKays. She might be with them, though they are hardly good company for a nice girl. Whatever would Miss Sherman at the Academy think?"

"Probably not much, Martha, but it gives Ellen pleasure to have interesting company for her exploring, and I would rather she is with those boys than wandering alone. Otherwise she might go off away from the rest of us . . ." She let the thought drift off.

About Ellen

Ellen was not with the McKay brothers. Their father was a trader in Oregon, a rather well-known man, Dr. White had said. Their mother was the daughter of a French trader and his Canadian Indian wife. At the moment the McKays were off with Ned and some of the other young men, spinning tales about the Indian maidens they were to meet. The McKay brothers had traveled east with Dr. Whitman when he was sent back to New York by Dr. Parker to wed Miss Prentiss, and their knowledge of the West, and of the crossing, gave them something like equal footing with the young men in the party. For not only were they considered half-bloods—though by true reckoning, they were quite a bit less than half Indian—they were younger than the working boys and found themselves chronologically between groups in the company, and so aligned with no one.

Most of the families with children had little ones, beneath the McKay boys' interest, except for lively Ellen, who knew a great deal about animals and wasn't afraid to pick up bugs and things. The older youths were all assigned jobs, either by employers or by parents who were depending on them to work their passage just as if they had been hired. At fourteen and sixteen, and traveling on their own, the McKays found themselves much alone. They traded their knowledge of the West, of the trail, of the people to be encountered, for acceptance by the older boys. Some of the lore they offered was rather unlikely to be true, but their stories kept the young men interested and guaranteed admittance to their circle.

Ellen Tompkins also found herself an outsider. She had little tolerance for the interests of her older sisters, as she was impatient with talk of dresses and schools, music and books. She thought Martha and Jane insufferably dull and their clothing inappropriate for this crossing on which the family was embarked. There was one other girl on the trip who looked to be about fourteen or so, but she stuck close to her mother and their wagon and seemed an unlikely candidate for adventures.

The other children were younger, babies and toddlers, and were of no interest.

By temperament and by inclination, Ellen was perfectly suited for this journey. She adored being out of doors, she liked hiking and walking, she reveled in the insects and other wriggling things she found, many of which she collected and stored in a tin bucket or brought back to the wagon to observe. There were of course many things that Ellen did not like: Ellen Tompkins did not like neat penmanship, stitching, embroidery, sitting in the parlor listening to singing, church, teachers, school, being quiet, being ladylike, or Sundays. She did not like lace or fine shoes, lining up embroidery threads or anything at all about sewing, eating slowly, or giggling. This journey to the West provided her with an opportunity to avoid most of these things.

Upon leaving the Younger Girls Division of the Academy, her teacher, Miss Sherman, had a long talk with her mother, and the two had agreed that it was sad indeed that Ellen would have to be withdrawn from such a fine school, especially since she had not finished her education. Both women acknowledged that Ellen knew a great deal about the natural world; the girl could name all the trees, she knew about insects, and she observed closely the world around her. These things, they could count on Ellen continuing. But there were other subjects that both women deemed necessary for Ellen to know, and so stowed in the wagon were three novels and a spelling book written by Lyman Cobb, who happened to live in their community, the book containing a great many words to learn. That left the problem of composition, at which Ellen did not excel.

"She must be kept at it," Miss Sherman had said energetically, and Caroline Tompkins agreed, adding that when Ellen finds that which she really wants to write about, she will do well. They hatched the idea that Ellen would be appointed the historian of the Tompkins Family Crossing, and to that end she was given three lovely new pencils and a tablet in which she was expected to keep a daily log of what the family saw and did on the journey west.

"Oh, Mother," Ellen had complained when she saw the size of the book she was expected to fill. She lessened her antagonism a bit when Caroline also provided her with a small drawing tablet so that she could make anatomical and botanical illustrations and map the journey.

"But," cautioned Caroline sternly, "you may not substitute the illustrations for writing daily in the journal. They are in addition to your observations, which you will write out for us."

Ellen groaned, but there seemed to be no way to avoid the task, and the joy of going west—and of not going to church and school as a regular thing and ending once and for all the hated piano lessons with Mrs. Elmer, who smelled of stale clothing—outweighed the onerous task she had been assigned. But the composition book remained unopened all during the trip from New York State to St. Louis, and then it was placed at the bottom of a trunk and was therefore unavailable on the trip up the Missouri River.

It was when the family camped at Elm Grove that Caroline stepped in and demanded that Ellen get busy. It was a requirement that each day Ellen would find time to write or she would get no supper. This seemed to Caroline, who was a mild woman and sympathetic to Ellen's restlessness with the tidier aspects of life, a bit extreme, but she was also concerned that she would be derelict as a mother if she allowed her unorthodox daughter to abandon all learning in favor of running freely about.

It was because of the Tompkins Family Observation that Ellen had made the acquaintance of Medorem Crawford, and it was Mr. Crawford she was with when her mother asked about her.

Ellen had resented the chore of keeping the Observation, as she called it, until she realized that as historian she could write what she wished. So while Martha or Jane or even her mother might have made notations about who came to visit the campfire or about the condition of the ladies' dresses, which is all that Ellen could think they might find of interest, she turned the chore to her own concerns, and that freed her to go about the camp site looking for things she considered worth mentioning. This had led Ellen to Medorem Crawford, a young man who also came from central New York. He had joined the journey west when Dr. White had gone to say good-bye to the elderly Crawfords at their home in the town of Havana. That very afternoon, listening to the doctor talk about the new country on the Pacific shore and of White's government commission, young Crawford had decided to go along. At least that was the story people told about him.

Dr. White appointed Crawford his clerk, to keep track of company meetings, because he wrote a clear hand, and lacking a wagon and an outfit of his own, the young man could not be a voting member. Crawford kept a small diary account of the distances traveled each day and something of the day's events. He was a good-natured fellow and was interested in the land through which they were passing. Each evening when the company stopped, he allowed Ellen to look into his diary and copy out whatever interested her.

The Tompkins Family Observation

The first time she did so, Ellen's entry in her Observation was a mirror image of Crawford's, and indeed she was guilty of merely copying his words rather than writing anything of her own. She entered, as he had, "May 23: Some rain last night & cloudy cool morning. Started at 9 o'clock. drove to the Kansas river and crossed with safty, Distance 10 miles."

When Caroline asked Ellen for her Observation that evening, she handed over the book. Caroline noted the misspelling of "safty" and the lack of punctuation. Ellen looked carefully at her feet as the lecture began.

"This is note taking, Ellen," Caroline started. "This can hardly be considered writing, and that is writing we have set you to. Gathering information from others is all well and good, my dear, but it is up to you to write about it, not to copy from someone else's book." She spoke about essays and paragraphs, and of beginnings, middles, and ends. About copying others' work.

"Ellen, dear," she said, and the girl's eyes glazed over ever so slightly but not enough to notice. "Ellen, you must consider the precision of our language. You might comment on someone's shoes, for example, but are they shoes? Well, possibly not. For some wear shoes, but others wear boots, and some boots are tall and black and others stubby in the front and brown, and some are worked with a burning tool and decorated, while most are plain. Do you see what I mean?" she asked earnestly in her most educated, schoolteacherly voice. Ellen noted the wear marks on her own boots and the long scrape in the leather near the heel where she had gotten too close to a wagon wheel and it had grazed her boot.

At the end of Caroline's lecture Ellen said, "Yes, Mother," and she vowed she would do enough to avoid another talking to. Caroline, for her part, thought she had gotten through to the girl the importance of the task she had been set, and Caroline recalled her days, though they had been short, when she had taught at the Girls' Academy at home.

The following day Ellen wrote more, and she found that there was more indeed to write about. It had been a rainy night and the wagons were crowded, the blankets damp. But there were other things to tell as well.

*

May 31: Started at 5 oc. Stopped for dinner, camped on Blue River at 4 o'clock. traveled 15 miles; most splendid spring water there
—Medorem Crawford

ELLEN TOMPKINS

What interested Ellen this day was the fact that at noon, by standing on the wagon to look where they were headed, she could see clouds of dust far in the distance. Since it was a windless day, there was no natural reason for the dust to rise. Ellen decided it must be Indians. She had seen a few Indians in Elm Grove while they had waited for the wagon company to gather, and she had noted how they spoke quickly to each other, not seeming to use more than a few words, and precise ones, she was sure, though she could not understand their language.

They seemed to her very quiet. Very still. A white man sucked in the air and expelled it; he occupied space and let everyone know it, warning off other men from his spot, moving head or arms, or even tapping a foot or slapping gently on his thigh with a whip handle or a pocketbook. Or he might jingle coins in his pocket. His stillness wasn't at all like that of the Indians she observed in Elm Grove or even Independence.

Their stillness was complete: she could see no movement. Their bodies remained motionless; the air around them remained unruffled. They emanated silence. They pulled their clothing close and stood quietly, their chests barely moving in and out as they breathed. She could not read their faces; their eyes were as if hooded so while they might look out, she could not look in; their hands lay silent as if in waiting. She thought them beautiful and mysterious.

Because Ellen was a small girl and curious, she stared at the Indians and at the Mexicans, who came to the trading center at the end of the Santa Fe

Trail. The Mexicans were easy to pick out, for their clothing was not of animal skins, but woven and colorful. They carried striped blankets pulled about their shoulders, their heads topped by large black hats, some shiny, others of fur. Their faces danced, their mouths spoke so quickly that even had she known Spanish there is no way she could have understood what they said. And they spoke, many of them, from under a lip topped by a curled mustache astride it, like a man on a horse. Their skin looked like cakes warmed in an oven, glistening with sugar coating. Some had musical instruments slung across their backs, and they made music of a kind that Ellen had never heard before, nothing like the songs played in the parlor at home or at church. Their music stirred her in ways that made her feel unsure. They too wore boots, black ones, and higher than the boots her father had bought for Ned and himself and taller too than the boots of the other American men, with heels. Ellen was very conscious of these foreigners who were at the edge of the United States. She knew that soon she too would move beyond the country of her birth into a foreign land where she would be the stranger.

The Indians came from that other world. It was Indians ahead moving toward them, Ellen thought, agitating the earth, sending up the cloud of dust. All during the afternoon, Ellen walked off to the side of the wagon train, to get away from the company, to get a view of those who were approaching. She wondered if the Indians would trade, if there would be children with them or if dust heralded a war party of young men in paint. She wondered what sort of Indians these would be, knowing from the McKay boys that there were many different nations, each with a particular language, clothing that marked their identity, and habits that distinguished them one from another.

The missionary literature had called all the people of the West "Indians." But the McKays talked about differences, of the prairie Indians who lit the grasses each spring in order to clear the land to make it ready for planting and easier to cross, of the horse-proud people who dragged their skin houses and poles behind them, of the coastal tribes who lived in Oregon Territory and who fished and paddled canoes down the giant river called the Columbia.

The McKay boys dressed as everyone did, except that they had told her they would trade for deerskin trousers at Fort Laramie to wear when the thorny growth began to tear at their cloth pants. They were ruddy looking, not at all like the Negroes she had seen in St. Louis and along the Missouri River. Nor did they look like the Indians at Elm Grove. The McKay boys were short, and the older one, John, was stocky.

At the Blue River the company stopped and camped. They found a spring of delicious water, and containers were filled for the next day's trip, though there would be no shortage of water for a while. That would come later. They started fires for supper, and the odors of cooking hung in the air, speaking to the empty stomachs of the assembled company.

Ellen found Medorem Crawford and asked how many miles they had gone that day. He answered fifteen. Then she pointed to the dust cloud still moving toward them, and he went off from the camp to look.

"Indians, Mr. Crawford," Ellen announced.

"Possibly. We haven't seen any yet, and we are well into Indian Territory now."

So the two sat quietly together as the cloud approached, and then after a time Ellen pointed out that she could see riders emerging from beneath the haze and Medorem Crawford nodded yes, he could see them too. After a time the cloud was close enough for everyone in the camp to see that it was made by men on horses and four heavy wagons.

"Must be traders in from Fort Laramie," said one man. "We were told to watch for them and to follow their trail out."

"Wagons moving mighty slowly," said another.

"Heavy load of skins, I imagine," observed a man with a bandage on his hand.

"Look at those oxen they have pulling," commented a third. "My ox never got that big, for sure, but at the same time those animals look spent."

Among the men there was a great deal of discussion about the value of the pelts the men were bringing in for trade, of the free life of the trappers, the long winters spent in the mountains. There was something of a sneer when they talked about what the trappers must know of the Indians.

The women looked at the men and wagons approaching with a different anticipation. Those men had been where the company was going. They knew the trail, had seen the Indians, had drunk from the safe springs, forded swift rivers. These men knew the way west; they had been there and were returning. Their presence encouraged the women but sobered them, too.

The two parties came together, the traders keeping outside the circle of wagons. There was a good deal of how-doing and exchanges of information. Dr. White introduced himself and stated his mission, even pulling out his papers and showing them again. The traders said their goal was St. Louis, as quick as can be.

"You should come with us," called out one man, but the traders shook their heads. They were owed money by the company. They looked forward to having a spree until it was time, once again, to return to the mountains.

This passing was significant: one way of life was supplanting the other. Families heading west to claim land were passing by men bringing out the treasure of the land and living free while there. But the pelts were running out and the market was changing. While there was always more to explore, it was the families who would settle and stay.

"Have supper with us," invited someone from the company, but the traders said no, they had good light yet and miles to go. They would, they offered, take letters to the States, and here and there people like Martha, who had thought to have letters ready, laughed joyfully as they ran to get them, to have them carried on.

"And so soon," said Martha. "I didn't think I could send a letter back until we got to Fort Laramie." Others complained that they had not written and would like an hour to do so, but the traders said no, they needed to push on.

"Have your guards look snappy at night," they said to Dr. White while Martha was handing over her letter. "The Pawnees are near, and they will steal your cows if they can."

"And your horses," added another, "if they can get them."

"They want the things that they see white people bringing in," offered the leader of the group. "Keep everything tidy and tell the guard to stay alert. That way they won't give you any trouble, I shouldn't think."

"Unless you trouble them," added one of the guards riding at the rear of the caravan and giving Martha a grin.

And suddenly, more suddenly than they had come into view, the traders with their four lumbering wagons full of fur were gone from the landscape, hidden behind the rise of a bluff, dimmed by the waning light of the day. It began to rain.

*

*June 2: Tremendous rain & wind last night. Commenced standing guard
last night. Cold wind & disagreeable morning. Started at 1 o'clock Camped
at 7. traveled 8 miles*
—Medorem Crawford

What Mrs. Shadden Had to Say

Now the company is whole again, with Dr. White back, and if Mr. Moss
will stop arguing with everyone about guard duty we can have some peace.
Shadden must stand guard tomorrow night, so I will save up some dinner
things for him to take while he waits in the dark. Little Natty said he wanted
to go on guard with his pa, but Shadden said it wouldn't be allowed, that the
rules of the company seemed to take in every situation, and that guards had
to stand alone and they had to be standing at all times so that they don't fall
asleep. Most of the men think this is a good idea. After hearing the trappers,
the idea of Indians is making folks edgy.

It seems to me, however, the men like the idea of exposing themselves to a
danger that probably isn't there because it makes them feel important. I just
hope they will be as brave when the danger is real. I suppose we'll have to wait
and see. Right now they seem to be enjoying all the fussing about with guns
and duties and guarding and dividing up into teams, each to take charge of
one night, each man to have a particular two-hour shift.

Seems that Virginia woman, Susannah, a girl really, isn't too keen about
her man being out there at night. She said something to the Girtman girl,
who reported it to her mother. Mrs. Girtman told me. "Lorenzo is such a
deep sleeper," that Susannah had said. "If he falls asleep a whole posse could
get past and him never knowing."

Wants to have her Lorenzo home with her in their little wagon, I suspect,
but every man has to do his duty, and that Lorenzo, an odd man he is, dark
like a Negro. Scowly, too, she thought, a boy really—that Lorenzo has a wagon
and a full vote, so it is his responsibility to stand guard even if she doesn't
want to be alone. Probably she's frightened, that Susannah, maybe more for
him than for herself.

*

*June 3: The company started at 5 oclock & left myself with 3 others to wait
for Mr. Burns and others who were detained by Mr. Lancaster.*
—Medorem Crawford

TOMPKINS FAMILY OBSERVATION

We are traveling with a number of different animals. Some wagons are pulled
by oxen, some by mules, one by small horses. There are also the riding horses,
and almost every family has a cow tied to the back of the wagon. This makes
a lot of animals at night, and they are usually set out in strings with one of
the hired men to watch them. Now, of course, we have guards on the lookout
for Indians. A number of horses got away last night, however, and stampeded
a short distance. This morning we had to wait while they were rounded up.
One is still missing.

We still have dogs in the camp, but people don't complain about their
barking. Dr. White doesn't like them and I have seen him kicking at them
when he passes, but some of the men think the dogs will warn us when the
Indians come near. I know that the Girtman girl, I think her name is Cynthia,
has a small cat in their wagon. She hasn't told anyone, but I saw it one day
when I was looking around.

Mr. Crawford told me that we traveled twenty miles yesterday and fifteen
today. That is good time, he said, and even so, it will take us more than four
months to get to Oregon.

I asked him why he had decided to go to Oregon, and he said for the trip,
for the journey. When I asked what that meant, he told me that his father has
a small farm in a place called Havana in New York State and that he has three
brothers. They all can't inherit the farm, and it barely supports his father and
mother as it is. He had never been farther away than to the Glen at Seneca
Lake and had to do something: going to Oregon was what came up. Oregon
has land and needs people, he said.

I asked him if he really left the day he heard about Dr. White's going. He
said yes. The doctor went to his parents' home to tea, and by the time he was
packing up his letter from the government after reading to it to his parents

and as Dr. White was ready to leave, Mr. Crawford decided to go with him. I looked at his feet and asked if he already had boots and a gun; he said that he and the doctor got outfitted in St. Louis when they were there. They got to St. Louis the same way we did, by going down the Ohio River on a riverboat. Their boat rammed another along the way and one of the horses Dr. White was bringing along got injured, so in Cincinnati they traded it for that mule he has.

Our boat didn't ram anything so our trip was pretty tame. Our boat, the *Cambria* it was called, didn't even go very fast, and just about every other boat on the river passed us. I am never where there is any excitement.

Mr. Crawford said that other people had different reasons for going to Oregon. I told him I thought that was a good thing because his reason seemed weak to me. This was a rather sassy answer, but Mr. Crawford is only twenty-two years old, just a year older than Ned, so he isn't a real adult yet.

He said that the Shaddens were going for land and a new place to try. The Bennetts were going for land and because with all those sons they thought the boys would be welcomed, especially if there was to be war with England over the Oregon Territory. It's a good thing those Bennett boys will be on our side because they are big and cruel. I saw one shooting at a hawk that was eating a rabbit the other day. That seemed mean to me.

Why is Dr. White going? I asked him. Mr. Crawford said because the government was sending him and he expected to be the governor of the Oregon Territory one of these days. For now he will be the Indian agent and the only federal official out there. He has the responsibility to send messages back to Washington.

Mr. Crawford said that Reuben Lewis, along with some of the others working their way across, were going to Oregon because they were opposed to slavery and didn't want to live with all the arguing about it. Some of them think it will lead to war, and they want no part of fighting over colored people. He said the Oregon Territory will be off limits to slavery, just like the Northwest Territory was, and he thought that no Negroes will be allowed in the Oregon Territory. So slavery won't be an issue, which will be a relief to many people because of all the arguments that adults get into over it.

Of course, I am against slavery as there isn't any in our state, that is, in New York, and because I don't like the idea of owning other people. My parents are against slavery too. They know Governor William Henry Seward of Auburn, who speaks out against slavery. I know that my mother and father both signed a petition against slavery one Sunday after church service and that the petition was sent to Congress. Mother said that the women knew that their signatures wouldn't count because they are not voters, so the women signed all along one side of the document, the men using the middle of the page. Nothing ever happened about it that I ever heard.

Mr. Crawford said he is a pretty good farmer but that he might be interested in doing something else in Oregon. He will see what is available once he is there, or what is needed. I told him my father is going to set up a newspaper in the territory, which will be the first one. He has shipped a small press by boat around to California, where it will wait for us until he tells them to send it on to Oregon. Father is very happy about becoming a newspaper publisher after all those years working as a clerk in Grandfather's store. He has promised to show me how to set type. He says that women's and children's fingers are very nimble for typesetting but that I will have to be careful about spelling, which might be a problem. Perhaps Jane could set type and I could run the machine through which the paper goes to get printed on.

Mother is going to write an article for women for the paper. I suppose she will write about hats and dresses and sending children to school and the like. She might also write about things she calls "social ills." When I asked her what, she said "suffrage," but she didn't explain. She is a very educated woman, having gone to the Academy, where she stayed an extra year so that she is qualified as a schoolteacher, too. Father says she is most accomplished, and all her friends think she is amazingly widely read. She learned Greek from her grandfather, who had many books in Greek in his library.

I talk with Mr. Crawford about all sorts of things, and he seems glad to see me. I invited him to eat supper with us tomorrow night, and he said he would be glad to join us. I think he is tired of eating his own cooking. Mother said this was agreeable with her as I am taking up a great deal of Mr. Crawford's time. Ned will have to leave for guard duty as soon as supper is done, as tomorrow is his night to stand the early shift. Father goes after that. Though the traders said to keep watch for the Indians, we have seen none yet, Indians that is. People think they must be elsewhere.

Part 2

OBSERVING, MARVELING

June 8: Cloudy morning started at ½ past 7 o'clock. Stoped for dinner at ½ p. 11: started at ½ past 2. Camped at 7 o'clock on the head waters of the Blue R. which we have been following up for the last 3 days, good water & wood, traveled 16 miles.
—Medorem Crawford

THE COMPANY

They spent these early weeks learning to work together. They got better at maintaining a safe distance so one wagon would not ride up against the wagon in front. They learned the advantages of being in the lead, where the wagon driver didn't have to contend with the dust that clogged the air, but they learned too that the lead wagon had to keep a keen eye out for the trail, which they had actually missed once or twice when the lead wagon master fell into a reverie and failed to watch ahead. And they decided at one of Dr. White's meetings to switch about each day with a different wagon in the front to give every driver a chance at clear air. Dr. White insisted that any man who misled the company would forfeit his right to be lead wagon.

The trail itself was a series of grooves or depressions in the ground. These were well worked into the land from years past—from fur wagons of other years that brought beaver pelts and buffalo hides back to Independence and St. Louis, from explorers' trails, and from the Pawnees and other Indians who traveled along the riverbanks. There were camp sites, too, clearly marked by charred circles where fires had burned. Sometimes there were unburned logs left at the firesides, to be used by the next people who came along; sometimes a bit of harness was left lying on the trail or in a camp, sometimes a broken bit of a bottle or piece of clothing remained, and usually there were bones from the rabbits or deer that the hunters shot for dinner.

Caroline, looking at the trail, thought of their progress as moving from one refuse heap to another. They did not usually camp where the trappers had made their fires because often there was a foulness there of human and animal leavings, which attracted ants and fleas and other insects. They usually headed farther on to find a fresh place of their own.

They also learned how to camp quickly at night and to get under way in the morning without loss of time. They established a routine of eating breakfast early, just when the sun was coming up, and traveling until the heat of the day. Then they would stop to have dinner. The men would make repairs or see to ailing animals or rest themselves. The children would sleep; the women washed, or they prepared food for the evening meal so that it would be ready when they stopped again. That way the little company moved along at twelve and fifteen and even eighteen miles a day.

They became used to each other, too. The children knew which of the hired men would help them mount an extra horse with shortened stirrups so they could ride a while. They also learned to stay away from that Lorenzo Couch, the man from Virginia, as he didn't seem to get along with anyone.

The women discovered which of their group they could talk peaceably to, which women were prickly. There had already been some trouble between the Girtmans and the Carters when the Girtman wagon had narrowly missed running over one of Carter's dogs. It was generally known that Mrs. Bennett was formidable, and behind her back she was called The Giantess. To her face she was Mother Bennett. The children learned to be wary of her children, who came in a variety of ages, from the eldest boy, Vardemon, and his wife, to the little girl everyone called the Bennett girl as if she had no given name of her own. One of the middle boys offered that the family hadn't gotten around to naming her yet. They, too, called her the Bennett girl.

When Mrs. Bennett thought one of her sons was missing, she ran about the camp with immense strides—screaming and hallooing equal to any wild

Indian, Dr. White insisted, wringing and clapping her hands and tearing her hair.

"Where is my Philly?" or "My Philly is dead!" she hollered as she called for the men to fall out and look for him. Many took her shouts and actions comically, but her agony was terrible. As the men picked up their guns and prepared to set off, Philly suddenly appeared, carrying on his shoulder a large piece of buffalo meat, quite unconscious that he had been the subject of an alarm. That's when they learned he had a name.

The buffalo meat, however, was greeted with enthusiasm, for the travelers had not yet seen buffalo even though they were expecting herds of them. "One," said Philly to a group of hunters. "There was one lone buffalo," insisted the young man, who indicated where he had come upon the bull.

The hunters, still expecting a giant herd of animals, went out immediately, found the carcass of the bull Philly had shot, as well as one other animal. They drove the cow into the river and killed it, crowding about to get a view of the slaughtered animal.

"Three times the size of a common ox," said one with amazement. They all anticipated facing a herd of such giants.

The children also learned the behavior of the trail. They stayed close to their parents' wagon, walked nearby, and didn't cause problems by straying, at least not after one of the Shadden boys had wandered off and caused the company to stop so the men could go looking for him. They found him, too, and just in time, confronting a rather large rattlesnake that had just come from its den. The men dispatched the snake but tied the rattles to the child to remind him to stay close to home.

They all learned, too, to avoid certain bushes that pulled at their clothing, tearing at the cloth, for there was little replacement to be had, not if they wanted to have anything to wear as they rode into Oregon. That is what the mothers said.

Some grew tired of Dr. White's fussiness but more worried about the growing hostility between the doctor and Captain Hastings. The rules that the men had voted on at their first meeting were honored not at all, so one could hear cussing around the animals, and it was generally known that Mr.

Moss probably drank a little, judging from the bottles the children found now and again on the trail.

They felt glad, however, that they traveled with a doctor and relied upon his plasters and tonics when this one tore a thumb or that one had the runs for more than three days. He doctored and nursed and was gentle with one and all. But he liked to call meetings of the company, annoying some of the men who regarded him as a soft, inexperienced easterner without much practical knowledge. In fact, you could hear some of the men saying that those two half-blood boys were better at watching the trail than that Dr. White.

The McKay brothers traveled happily. They were anxious to return home. Some thought their presence might even be helpful if the Indians ahead proved to be hostile, while others scoffed and pointed out that they were only boys, after all. Some pointed out that they were barely Indians anyway, or at least not enough to make a difference. This was the opposite of what they said when they insisted that the McKays were Indians and not quite trustworthy.

There was a good deal of general talk in the camp at night about the Indians. And there was talk and anticipation concerning the buffalo. As yet, neither the Indians nor great herds had been seen. Still, the guards were set in the evening and each man was required to take his turn. Lorenzo Couch did, despite his wife's concern, as did Ned Tompkins and his father, Dan, and the other wagon owners and hired men.

Some days began in cold rain that flooded the camp; other days the sun burned hot in the sky. There were insects everywhere. Whatever the weather, whatever the challenge of the day, the company moved slowly ahead.

They left the Blue River behind at six one morning and headed north following the marks on the land that led off into the distance. The day was fine, and they traveled happily. That night they camped within sight of the Platte River or, rather, at the edge of the forest skirting it. The children raced about picking up sticks and small branches to stow in the wagons for later. Water, too, would be scarce farther on, for Platte water was not to be drunk and the nearby springs were suspect. Their route lay along the southern side of the river to South Fork, where they would cross over to the North Fork and to the Black Hills. Farther on, the Rocky Mountains loomed.

*

June 9: Crossed the Pawnee Trail at 8 o'clock. Stoped at ½ p. 12 for dinner without wood or water except what we carried with us. Started at 2 oclock & traviled through a ridge of country destitute of wood & water. Camped at 7 o'clock on the Platte R. traviled 25 miles.
—Medorem Crawford

A Conversation in the Couch Wagon

"I collected some early cress this morning just before we left the river," said Susannah.

"It was odd when we turned north, wasn't it? Now that we have come to the Platte River we will have that to follow, giving us some direction, with a definite way to go—like a road would, but along the water."

"I know. We won't have so many little hills to go over. Probably better for the oxen, Lorenzo." Her voice was soothing.

"Virginia was never like this."

"No. No it wasn't. Virginia was green with colorful flowers and fine houses. This is all pale green tinged with yellow, and everything here billows." She thought of the grasses, and the emerging field flowers, the way the birds seemed to hover and then fly up as if over a bubble of air, then light on the earth again. She had watched a great blue heron that day, sailing over them toward the water ahead, its neck crooked, its head jutting forward. It seemed to pump itself, unlike the hawks that soared and floated above the earth before dropping abruptly to scoop up a meal of field mouse or rabbit.

"Sometimes it seems that I can see the air move in front of us," he commented as he got ready for bed.

"When it is very hot. Yes, I have seen that too." Her voice seemed to hold smiles in it, rising softly at the ends of words, dipping low as she ended a sentence. The lilt of Virginia was in her tones.

"It is the distance here that unnerves me," he said quietly.

"I know," she agreed. She thought a minute about the differences between this prairie and home. "At home we looked from one boundary to another; the boundary between the house and the fields; the boundary fence between the land and the road; the boundary between one plantation and another; the boundary between the land and the sky. There were boundaries between people, too." She paused a minute to think how to phrase the next part. "Here it seems there are no boundaries. The land flows over the ridges, up and down and up again with no fences, no lines or marks, no indications of it belonging to anything. The land and the sky even seem to flow into each other. It is free feeling out here," she said slowly. "I rather like it."

"You make it sound beautiful, Susannah." He pulled off his britches and pointed to a tear at the seam; without words she nodded, acknowledging it, giving a silent pledge to mend it in the morning.

"It is, Lorenzo. It is beautiful but in a different way than what we have known."

"We have come a long way from home." He worried the idea of being so far away, wrestled with the consequences of leaving.

"We had to leave." She put the cool palm of her hand against his face, pulled her fingers along his cheek, touched his ear.

"I know." He nodded assent, pushing his face into the curve of her hand.

"It will be different again from here, where we are going," she added wisely, as if preparing him for the next surprise. She moved her hand against his neck and rubbed softly, pushing his hair up.

"I know. We have mountains to cross." He considered the problems; she looked at the beauty. They were so different in their outlook. "Would you have ever thought you would be camped at the Platte River?"

"We will have to be careful for the animals," she said, "for the river isn't good for drinking." Then she asked, "When is your next night to stand guard?"

"In two nights. With one of the Bennett boys. The older one, I think."

"He looks handy with a gun."

"He says he is." Lorenzo pulled the linen sheet over them.

"But you can handle a gun too," she said encouragingly.

"We aren't out there to shoot," he replied. "Mostly we are there to look, to make sure no one sneaks up on us. Crossing the Pawnee Trail today made the idea of Indians very real for the first time. Until now they were something out there, an unseen worry. Now, crossing the trail, seeing that it was recently used, made the idea of guarding more than just an activity the doctor thought up to show who was in charge."

"Those traders we met a week back said to set guards." She felt him run his hands along her arms, cupping her elbows in his large hands.

"I know. But the men are gonna pay more attention now that we actually saw Indian sign."

"Less like boys at play?" she teased.

"It wasn't play before. Just not . . . urgent. You know?"

"Sometimes, when I collect an herb, it doesn't seem urgent. Then, when there is a fever to bring down, the herb is there waiting to be used. When it is needed, then the fact that it is there makes it . . . crucial."

"Yeah. I guess." He was quiet for a time. Then he asked, "What did that Mrs. Tompkins want today when she came over poking about?"

"She saw me picking cress and wanted to know what I was finding. Then she asked where we were from. She is from the North, New York, I think. I didn't say anything to her, but she seemed to want to suggest she understood about . . ."

"Us? As if she could," he said scornfully.

"Oh, no, Lorenzo. She was nice. She said she remembered when she was first married and how special their world was, as if there was no other besides the two of them. As if, as if, no one else could understand how they felt."

He said nothing.

"She is ever so much older than I am, but we talked easily. She likes to talk about her children. . . . She is worried about the youngest girl because she won't get to finish school."

"I'll bet that boy of hers is older than us."

"He could be. She is pretty old."

"Be careful, Susannah."

"Lorenzo! I am careful and you know it. You are the one to take care." They talked on for some time until he touched the front of her bodice and pulled the little ties apart to allow his hand to slip under the soft fabric to find her rounded breasts, which he held in his hands as if holding water for drink.

"We went twenty-five miles today," he said as he pushed himself between her legs and buried his head into her neck. She ran her hands over the orb of his head, gently fingering the scar near his ear. She smiled as they moved together.

＊

*June 10: Started at 8 o'clock & followed up the Platte R. Stoped for dinner
at ½ past 12, started at 2. Camped at 5 o'clock traviled 12 miles.*
—Medorem Crawford

ALL ABOUT MR. MOSS

"There's been some trouble, Caroline."

"What is it, Dan?" she asked, coming quickly from her sleep, blinking at
the darkness.

He reached out to touch her arm and said quietly, "We are going to have
to have a meeting."

"Now?"

"No. At the noon stop, I would think. Dr. White is furious."

"What happened?"

"It was Moss. Do you know him?"

"I don't think so."

"The man traveling alone in the small wagon."

"With the mules that give him so much trouble?"

"Yes. He's the one."

"What happened, Danby?"

"Well, Moss has complained a lot about having to stand guard. Didn't
want to, didn't want the company telling him what to do. He said he was his
own man and all that."

"He's a member of the company, isn't he, Dan?"

"Well, the fool Moss heard something and went out and shot it. It turned
out to be the Shaddens' cow!"

"Oh, my goodness," she exclaimed, reaching out for him. "It's about the
only thing in the world those poor people have that isn't tied onto that ram-
shackle wagon. Whatever will they do?"

"Shadden wants to have a trial."

"A trial? Here?"

"Well, the company set up a judicial committee, of White and Hastings and one or two others. Maybe old Mr. Smith. Shadden wants them to fine or punish Moss."

"This could be dangerous."

"Yes. Well, anything that hurts the company is dangerous. We have a long way to go, and none of us could make it alone. We need each other. That was the point of forming a company in the first place. To make sure we could make it through."

"So what can the committee do to Mr. Moss?"

"I don't know. He doesn't have a cow to replace the Shaddens'. I don't know if he has any money to pay for their loss, but even so, that wouldn't replace the milk for all those children. And he might not be willing to pay up, either."

"What's happening now?"

"Well, Shadden is out there yelling at everyone about his valuable cow, but he's butchering it, too, at the same time. He seems to be afraid that if the cow isn't in his cooking pot, Moss will claim it for himself, especially if they make him pay a fine. Shadden wants to make sure his family, and not Moss, get to eat it."

"What do the others say?"

"Well, Gabriel Brown, a sensible man, thinks the judicial committee should take the case, and perhaps they will decide something fair. But with both White and Hastings on the committee, they could spend their time arguing between themselves."

"I am glad you are out of it, Danby."

"I am too. Moss is an angry man and claims no one has any jurisdiction over him. That's why he left the States, he says. To be his own man."

"Mr. Moss sounds unrealistic, if you ask me. We need each other out here. Too bad his wife isn't along. She might be able to talk some reason into him."

"He has a wife?"

"Yes. At home. That is what Mrs. Lancaster said about him. He was also from Jefferson City, in Missouri. She knew of his family."

"Better get up and get breakfast going. We are going to leave early so we have time at noon to have a meeting."

"I didn't hear the horn sound."

"You will. Get up, sleepyhead."

Later, when Caroline spoke with Mrs. Smith about the events of the night, Mary Smith shook her head and said, "You don't see the women making such claims and causing trouble, do you?"

Caroline said, no, she thought not.

"Women can make trouble," insisted Mrs. Smith, "but not the sort of trouble that can jeopardize a company, that would put children at risk. They wouldn't do that."

"Everyone seems ill at ease," said Caroline. "All of a sudden people are edgy."

"It's the buffalo, I suspect," said Mrs. Smith. "We are getting nearer and the men are anxious about them."

"Anxious?"

"Yes. One of the trappers we met in Missouri, long before we joined up with the company, told us to watch for the jitters to hit when we get to buffalo country."

"I would have thought it was the Indians that would cause anxiety," remarked Caroline.

"They do. But of a different kind, I suspect. The buffalo are a challenge to our men . . . their first real challenge, I suspect, since we got going. Now they are going to have to face 'em, and shoot straight. Those buffalo might look big, but to bring them down the aim has to be true, just below the hump, said the trapper. Higher and they keep going; lower, they keep going and die of blood loss elsewhere."

Caroline looked rather astonished. "Buffalo jitters," she said. "I wouldn't have known."

"Wait and see, my dear. Wait and see."

*

June 11: Difficulty between Doct. White & John Force. Started at 8 o'clock, stop[p]ed for dinner 2 hours, camped at 5 ½ o'clock. traveled 10 miles.
—Medorem Crawford

WIDOW ABEL'S DIARY

Some fool has shot a cow and now the company is in an uproar. First we have an accidental shooting, then a baby dies, and now this. The men are going to have a trial of the man who shot the cow, to find a way to recompense the family for its loss. Well, what can the committee do? They can't force Mr. Moss to replace the cow, he doesn't have one himself, and there is no place to buy one. And they can't really force Moss to pay for the cow. How could they compel him, anyway, to hand over cash? He might not have much money, anyway. They have no authority; no one does. But the men will have a go at it, I suppose.

That Walter Pomeroy keeps hanging around, complimenting me on Baby, how pretty she is, "just like her mama."

The man must be near fifty years old.

MARY SMITH TO CAROLINE TOMPKINS

"They act like little boys at play," said Mrs. Smith.

"Well, yes, I suppose they do. So earnest." Caroline found that walking along with Mrs. Smith was most agreeable. Although Mrs. Smith was years older and had a husband, a son, and his family for company, she seemed to spend a lot of time on her own.

"They will have a trial, I suppose." Mrs. Smith looked concerned.

"Dan said that the judicial committee could render a judgment on its own." Caroline looked at the other woman, her face hidden in a hat, her skirts short by the fashions of the East, boots on her feet. She didn't look like an educated woman or someone Caroline might have known back home.

"Mrs. Shadden is moaning everywhere about that dead cow." Mrs. Smith looked off to the side, noting a small plant pushing its way up between some rocks. A cactus, she decided.

"Oh my, yes."

"But that cow gave barely a pint of milk a day, so poorly has it been fed all its life," observed Mrs. Smith, pulling at the wool she carried in her pocket, clicking her needles. "The children will probably get as much milk now as they did when the cow was alive."

"I didn't know that," said Caroline, watching the stitches pass automatically from one needle to the other, one loop pulled along by the others already on the needle. "How do you do that," she asked, "knit and not look at it?"

"Experience, my dear. I've been knitting for my family since I was six. My grandmother set me to it, making socks, and I have been at it since."

"But it's summer," observed Caroline.

"Yes, dear, I know. But after a time, wool socks will feel good on feet that have been walking over this hard earth, especially when we have to ford a river and get wet." She pulled more wool with an automatic jerk and dug the needles together. "Like today," she added. "Besides, I think best when my hands are working at something. I like the feel of the wool passing through my fingers."

"What do you think should be done, Mrs. Smith?"

"About the cow?" she asked. "Well, I would think Mr. Moss owes the Shaddens the price of the cow. Morally, he certainly does. But who is going to make him do anything out here?"

"I have been thinking just that. There is really little one can do."

"The committee could require Mr. Moss to work extra for the company, I suppose."

"The men could see to it. But will any man act against Mr. Moss when his own time of conflict might arise? He might need Moss's aid or something Moss has; he might even worry that he'll fall afoul of the judicial committee and will be wanting an ally."

"No one needs an enemy out here," said Mary Smith. They walked together in silence for a bit. Then the older woman pulled at her wool, then spoke again. "This scenery along the river is delightful. Look over there, the bluffs seem to be all in a chain, each one large enough to be a mountain by itself, but each totally disconnected from its neighbors. And between them there is the sweetest little vale. No scenery I have ever seen bears any comparison to it."

"It is certainly nothing like home," added Caroline.

"Where was that, Mrs. Tompkins?"

"On Cayuga Lake, in New York State," said Caroline, thinking of the green hills and the rocky ledges along the long blue lake, and of the small town on the flats at the foot of the hills.

"I was born in New York. Outside of Troy," said the older woman. "I went west to Lake Erie when I married and have lived there since. Then our son John wanted to leave, to try something else before he was too old to do so, or to want to try."

"And so here you are," finished Caroline.

"Yes." There was a pause. "I really don't mind. Perhaps I was the only one in the family who understood why John wanted to go to Oregon, why he wanted to see what else life held besides his Cattaraugus farm. I always wondered, myself, what else there was to life. Would it be more interesting to live in a city? Or in Illinois? To join the Mormons? To visit England? The world seemed so wide to me that I felt confined on the farm, as if I was missing something that I would only get one chance to see. I think I would have gone anywhere but never had the opportunity to. So when John wanted to go, needed to go . . ."

"You encouraged him?"

"Oh, yes. And you know, at my age I might not even make it all the way across. I am a grandmother, after all, and my grandchildren are well grown. But even that I don't think I'll mind."

"And Mr. Smith?"

"Oh, he minds. He feels railroaded into this. He gave up his own farm some years ago. I think he expected we would live out our days with John and his family. On the farm. Not so far from town that he couldn't get there for the farmers' meetings and for the Sunday service. He is a great one for Sunday service. But John wanted to go, and his family was willing. And I wanted John to have this dream . . ."

"It sounds as if you wanted to go too," teased Caroline.

"Yes. It seemed the chance to do something one last time. So Mr. Smith found that his entire family was about to depart. He had little choice but to join in. But it's not really his cuppa tea, and he'll do a hoot of complaining along the way once the going gets rough. He fears he will die on the road and not have a proper cemetery in which to lie."

"You are admirable," said Caroline, as she looked at this very unusual woman. "I guess I am really more like your husband, liking church services, and stores, and women coming to call, and the talk of books."

"They told me you are a well-read woman. Your girl Ellen did."

"Did she?" said Caroline, thoroughly amused. "Ellen boasting about a well-read mother? That is interesting, especially since it is a punishment for that girl to sit and read herself."

"Well, she wasn't boasting now," said Mrs. Smith.

"More like complaining?"

"More like a statement of fact, like the fact that your eyes are . . . ," and she looked around Caroline's bonnet to see, "blue."

"Look there," pointed Mrs. Smith at something growing nearby. "That is a plant I have never before seen."

At this Caroline smiled. "Well, I see what you and Ellen have in common, Mrs. Smith. She is very interested in each and every new thing. I just hope she will be careful."

"She has sense, that girl," said Mrs. Smith approvingly. "But she'll bear watching, too."

Mrs. Smith seemed a most sharp-eyed woman, knitting and walking and noticing plants and animals. But also seeing, too, what happened around the camp. "That's Dr. White coming from Mr. Moss's wagon. We'll know soon what the outcome will be of his shooting that cow." Following the doctor from behind the wagon was Mr. Moss, a most aptly named man, thought Caroline, for he was rather small and green tinged. While most of the men had switched to leather pants and vests to keep the plants from tearing their clothes, Moss had retained his woolen clothing and seemed soft and even fuzzy, where others looked hard and angular. Moss was scowling; *that* Caroline could see.

"Dr. White isn't looking pleased," said Mrs. Smith. "I'd better be off to see what the judiciary committee decided to do about the Shaddens' cow. Mr. Smith is on the panel, you know."

"Walking with you is very pleasant," replied Caroline. "Thank you for coming over."

"My pleasure, my dear. And don't you worry about that Ellen. She has a good head, a good head." And with that Mrs. Smith darted away to her own wagon.

*

June 12: Sunday, Started at 7 o'clock. Stop[p]ed at 12, found a band of Buffalo near the camp nearly 100 killed 3 very good Bulls. Started at 3, saw many Buffalo. Camped at 6 o'clock. traveled 14 miles. Buffalo came close around the camp killed 6.
—Medorem Crawford

CAROLINE CONSIDERS HER COMPANIONS

Caroline watched Mrs. Bennett stride across the way, her legs moving quickly, her arms swinging one way and the other. They called her a giantess because of her size. Her children called her Mother Bennett, even when speaking directly to her.

An odd woman, said Caroline to herself. She seems uncomfortable with her own body, as if it is so large she doesn't quite know where to put it, lest she or someone else should trip on it. But her hair! So unexpected it is to see it glisten red and gold in the sunlight. It is so beautiful. She seems an odd contradiction, both bold and timid, yet how can a woman that tall, who has such a voice on her, be timid? Yet, somehow the word is right for her, I think.

Any number of people in this camp appear to be contradictions, she mused. That Mrs. Smith now, a grandmother and older even than I, yet she is sturdy and walks on all day without seeming to mind. A practical soul, yet, a dreamer too. There's Mrs. Girtman, a vague sort of woman, but a reader. Traveling with books in her wagon. She has *Gulliver*! I shouldn't have believed that when I first met her.

And the men aren't without contradictions, either, she thought, pushing away a large beetle with her boot.

Another Sunday, she said quietly to herself, thinking of sitting in the church at home and shushing Ellen, who liked to kick ever so lightly at the pew in front, listening to Dr. Wisner or one of the guest ministers who frequently came to speak to the congregation. Gathering together like that was important to Caroline, who liked feeling part of a group and of being with her own family within that group. She liked sitting with Danby, their shoulders gently touching, their children strung out, like a knot on a blanket of knots, hers tight and together. That unity sustained her.

There had been discussions about Sunday when the company first started off. What to do? How would they observe the Sabbath? Would they travel on that day? Caroline had been surprised to hear there were so many nonbelievers in their midst, people who had never paid much mind to churchgoing, like the Bennetts and the Shaddens. They had said they hadn't been to church themselves. If others wanted services, that was their business, but being on the trail every day counted. They seemed to exercise more authority about moving forward than Caroline could have imagined them exercising in their previous lives—given the evidence, that is, of shiftlessness and nomadism.

That thought lacks any Christian charity, she said quietly to herself. Because there was no proper minister in their company, it was somehow easy to put aside ideas of holding church services and regard Sunday as another travel day—especially since they had had the two deaths and had held services at those times. So on Sunday they traveled, as they knew they had to. Church services would have to wait until Oregon, where there were already missionaries aplenty and regular services.

Until then, Caroline mused, I hope we can have peace. Mr. Moss seems the least of our troubles with Dr. White and John Force, that man who came out with him, feuding about something. Probably horses; they all talk about horses a lot—what they will be worth in Oregon, how much they cost at home. Force, I think, worked at the Inlet at home. He probably heard about this trip as we did, when Dr. Parker began talking about Elijah White going west again and how wonderful Oregon is, how beautiful the way across is.

She wondered, Are we all really here because of nice old Dr. Parker? She thought about the preacher at home and about his obsession with the idea of missionaries getting to the Pacific Northwest. It had been his passion to go there, to site missions, to see for himself the worthy natives waiting for the word of the Calvinist God. So it had all come to pass. Samuel Parker had journeyed to the Oregon Territory, he had crossed the continent, and he had come home and published a book about his experiences. So here are we, more than one hundred people following along in Reverend Parker's dream. But is it ours?

68

It is curious, she thought, that even though there is much to do to keep the family going, there is still time to watch our fellow travelers and wonder about them. This company on the trail is really barely a company at all, more a packet of individuals or individual families, like a bag of buttons, each with its own interests at heart. Making Mr. Moss pay eight dollars for that cow and then charging it to the time he owes the company doesn't help the Shadden family much, and now they are angry at the committee and Mr. Moss both. They have all yielded, I believe, to circumstances but not to leadership.

There's the Girtman girl; Cynthia, I think her name is. Sad little thing, so thin-looking. She keeps to her mother and spoils her as a mother might favor a child. She and Ellen are about the same age, but so very different from each other.

I have watched Martha question Ellen each time she goes to see Mr. Crawford. Ever since he was here for supper that night, Martha has been watching out for him to come over to talk. Though he is very friendly with Ellen, he hasn't been back. Could be he is shy, or even spoken for at home; there's no knowing. But Martha keeps watching out for him, I am pretty sure, and what Martha wants, Jane wants too. What Martha decides is good enough for her, Jane usually agrees, but Jane needs to learn that Martha generally gets her way. Dear Jane is going to have to find what she wants and stop copying Martha. Dear Jane needs to find a way to stop stuttering; it makes people so uncomfortable. It makes her so uncomfortable with people.

Ned is steady. We couldn't be doing this trip without Ned. He has picked up this life on the trail as if born to it; happy to be doing this, he is. Dan should be pleased he has such an ally in Ned . . . and Ellen, too. He gets a lot of resistance from the girls, though possibly he doesn't even know that it is resistance to this trip that is behind their anxiety. He probably thought that once he had decided to go west, we all would consider the decision as agreed upon by all of us. That we would all want to go because he had decided. Well, Martha and Jane miss home, Martha more so, I suspect, as she had beaux there and was very popular with her schoolmates.

But Ellen. This is the answer to her prayers; it has saved her from church and school and going to piano lessons and sitting up straight and having tea. Such a daughter I have. She amazes me. I understand Martha and Jane; they are like me in so many ways that I can anticipate their reactions to things; I understand what they want. But Ellen! Where did she come from, with all her action and her many interests?

Muse away, old lady. It is time to get supper ready.

BISON

"Look at them go!" cried Mrs. Perry. "I have never seen William Perry move so fast, not in his entire life. He is no slow-moving sort, either."

"Well, something had to happen. We couldn't keep on with the men so jittery like they have been," said Mrs. Girtman. "Had to happen sometime."

"Mama," called out Cynthia Girtman, "here comes Father back for something," and there he was racing back into the camp grabbing up a sack, which he then slung over his shoulder before racing out again.

"Whoopee!" called out the Bennett girl. "My mama is a'going too, she is. Better shot than most men."

"She got eight acres of hell in her," said a man nearby, somewhat under his breath, but loud enough for some to hear.

"I imagine that's right," said Caroline to Mrs. Smith, standing next to her. Mrs. Smith looked sharply at Caroline and said, "But she is not to be discounted for her looks and ways." Caroline felt stung, as if slapped. An odd tension hung between the two women.

They all stood, the women of the company and the children, watching the men race about gathering guns and bullets, sacks and ropes, getting their horses ready, hopping on and racing off.

Everything had been normal that day. They had gotten started at seven o'clock and then stopped at noon for dinner. The women had readied the food at the small fires they got underway. The men were watering the oxen when suddenly the earth rumbled. Many looked skyward to see if thunder was approaching the way it did over the prairie, moving toward them with dark swirling air, but the sun was out and there were no clouds in the sky.

Then there was a cry of "Buffalo!" and a herd moved slowly into view, veered a bit from the camped wagons, and moved past. Thousands of buffalo, their lumbering feet thudding the ground so that everything shook. Even the fires seemed to flicker; there was a smell of dust and heat. The men raced about for their equipment, food forgotten; the women stood and stared. Then the men on their horses were gone from the camp and amid the buffalo herd. Guns popped, there was the screech of wounded animals, the thundering of hooves, the cry of men and horses and dogs.

"They have gone off with such joy at the opportunity to kill those animals," observed Mrs. Smith.

"It shouldn't matter," Caroline replied. "There are so many of them."

"But what will they do with all that they shoot? They are mad with killing. It makes me glad Mr. Smith knows himself to be too old to join in, though I suspect that galls him, too."

"They are like boys in their joy of it all," Caroline commented above the noise.

"Well, we shall have meat tonight for dinner," said Mrs. Perry.

"And buffalo robes?" asked the widow Abel.

"If they bring back the hides, I suppose, though who knows how to cure them? And can we do that while on the trail?"

"One of the hunters who joined us late, after the Lancasters went back east, will know," replied her sister.

The women sat together, saying little as the slaughter went on. The small boys ran about, while the younger girls, trained to fear loud noises, recoiled from the repeated shooting and the screaming animals. The women stood in wonderment at the excitement of the men.

In the end the men killed nearly thirty animals. "Three good bulls," Ned came in to tell them. Most of the animals were left on the ground, their tongues cut out, and here and there some of the hump meat, but who could eat all that had been slaughtered?

Later Mrs. Bennett rode back into camp with a small buffalo calfskin slung over her saddle. "For the girl," she said, pointing to the skin. "We'll cure it. Vardemon is bringing in the meat." She rode away to her wagon, where she left her horse for Victor, one of her younger sons, to rub down and cool off.

The pandemonium had started with little anticipation and ended as abruptly. There was the noise of the animals and then of the hunting. Then suddenly there was quiet, and all over the plain to the south lay heaving carcasses. The men wiped bloody knives on trousers, and each thought himself a bit taller. They had met the buffalo. Their pleasure was palpable, and it made them expansive.

"So that's buffalo," one called to another.

"Easier to hit than a target tied to a tree, I say," commented another.

"Got about four, myself," one called.

"Somebody shot pretty close to me," complained another, but without rancor or real concern. The day had been theirs; they had culled their trophies from a herd of a million animals, and the survivors were now running on to the south. There were dead animals on the ground. The men who had shot them looked over their rifles with pleasure; they slapped their horses and each other. The women watching could see in their faces that it had been a fine day to have been a man, a fine day.

Someone, probably Dr. White, decided that they should linger in this spot and cook the meat, clean the hides that had been brought in, and rest for the remainder of the day. "Give the horses a chance to get their wind back," commented one man as he patted foaming sweat from his mount. There were discussions among these hunters about the merits of one horse over another, who had shot truest, which horse had been the steadiest in the face of the herd, which men had shot but hit nothing at all.

"That Bennett woman is good with a rifle," said Mr. Perry to his wife.

"She got a calf and took the skin," Mrs. Perry remarked.

"Now she gotta clean it and cure it or we'll all smell the darn thing," he said.

"She'll get one of those boys of hers to do it. Good she is at giving her menfolk orders."

"Hardly a woman herself, if you ask me," said Mr. Perry, but with some admiration for her skill with a gun. "There was some wild shooting out there, believe me. Shots were going every which way."

"Take care, please. You have two women dependent upon you, Mr. Perry," said his wife with a proud twinkle.

"I do. I do. And don't forget two babes."

"Well, Hannah's baby. Ours is yet to be born, Mister!" They smiled at each other and enjoyed the quiet moment. Then he was gone to fetch some water for the horse, to look over the meat he had brought back, to find out from the other men just how they would cure pieces of it to carry on their journey.

"Do you remember your school days?" Mrs. Smith asked Caroline. "When the teacher called recess, how fast those little boys were out the door."

"This was just the same," said Caroline amazed, "wasn't it?"

"Yes," said the older woman. "Just the same."

✳

June 13: Large herds of Buffalo in plain sight around the camp Started in good season. Saw thousands of Buffalo. Traveled 15 miles, little feed for horses.
—Medorem Crawford

ELLEN AND MRS. SMITH

I am not sure Mother noticed that I skipped a day, but having written every day up until then I felt sad to have missed one. I thought of going back and filling it in because Mr. Crawford said that he does that sometimes, but I decided this should be an honest account, so I won't. He doesn't have a mother sitting him down each day to write, so that might be the reason, but Mr. Crawford's diary is pretty skimpy, little more than the distance traveled and the weather, sometimes. Not much of what mother calls "Commentary." Mother likes "Commentary."

Mrs. Smith invited me to walk with her for a time. She is a really interesting person, for a lady, and for one so old. She knows the names of many of the plants, and of all the birds, I am sure. We saw some wild roses in bloom and yellow daisies. Mrs. Smith knew the names. She said she has a book that I might borrow.

Mrs. Smith said that one of the hunters had told her there was a deserted Indian village just off the trail. She and I walked over to it while the wagons rolled slowly on. She didn't seem concerned, the way some would be, to see the wagons move past us. "We'll catch back up," she said.

There were cultivated patches in some places, on the edges of the village, but it looked as if it was old and hadn't been used in years. There were some cedar trees, the first we have seen in a long time. The soil is very sandy, but the grass thick and lush. There weren't any houses, but we could see where fires had been lit and there were some bald places where people had walked and grass hadn't yet grown back in. While we were walking we saw some dust arise and then horses coming toward us.

"Pawnees," said Mrs. Smith in a pretty calm voice.

"Indians," I said, with more fright in my voice than I expected I would have.

"We will just walk swiftly back to the wagons, Ellen, but no need to run. We don't know that they are hostile, and they are probably curious about what we are doing here, looking about." So we walked back about three-quarters of a mile and the Pawnees never even came close to us, but we knew they were back there, watching.

When we caught up with the last wagon, we told people that we had seen Indians and everyone began looking out and around the wagon flaps to see if they could see them too. And some of the men reached for their rifles but then put them back because there was nothing to shoot at. Some of the women said, "Put up those guns before you scare the children."

We have had a hard south wind for several days, and even though this is June we all wore cloaks and overcoats and mittens in the early morning. Yet at noon it was warm when we stopped for dinner. This is the time when Mother sees to it that I write and read. She'd probably sit Mr. Crawford down too, if she thought about it.

The horseflies are very bad today. I never saw such large ones or so many before. The boys all lay asleep under the wagons at noon. They covered their faces with hats to keep off the flies.

The river here is full of sandbars, and up ahead we are soon going to have to cross to the South Fork of the Platte.

Talking out loud to yourself must be catching. We all know that Mother does it, but now Father seems to be doing it too. He is talking about editorials! Imagine!

*

June 14: Our animals alarmed last night by the Buffalo. . . .
—Medorem Crawford

CAROLINE TOMPKINS AND MRS. GIRTMAN

"Mrs. Girtman," called Caroline, as she was walking up to the Girtman wagon. "Have you a minute to talk?"

"Of course, Mrs. Tompkins."

"Please, I am Caroline."

"And I, Louisa."

"How lovely! I have come to talk about *Gulliver*! I never before read the second part, about the voyage to Brobdingnag, where everything gets topsy-turvy. In Lilliput, Gulliver is tall and the Lilliputians are tiny, but in Brobdingnag, Gulliver is tiny and the Brobdingnag people are huge."

"*Gulliver* is all full of contrasts," said Louisa. "I think that must have been fun to write, but I am not sure what the meaning of it is."

"What amused me the most," said Caroline, "is the fact that when the queen commissioned a house for him so that Gulliver could be carried around, he called it his 'travelling box.'"

"And we," said Louisa pointing around them, "are here in the West in our own 'travelling boxes,' aren't we?"

"Yes. Yes, but we have no eagle to come along to pick us up and deposit us on the other side of the mountains, have we?"

"No. No, we don't. But remember, Gulliver was alone and he doesn't fare all that well. In the end, Gulliver gets home and then retreats into his garden and sulks."

"And we," said Caroline, "we will have a better conclusion to this journey. We will have our families and we will make communities. At least, I hope we will."

"I think so," said Louisa. "I am going to teach at the Methodist mission, as is Mr. Girtman. They expect us, but most likely they think we will be coming by ship. When we heard of Dr. White's mission, and as we were already in St. Louis, it seemed sensible to join up."

"I do wonder about that," said Caroline a bit sharply.

"As do I," said Louisa, "especially as my eyesight is such a hindrance to walking. But I have Cynthia. She will see me across."

The two women parted, their faces adorned with knowing smiles about their small private joke about traveling boxes, each woman thinking of the folly of men, both fictional and real.

*

June 15: Started at 7 o'clock. Saw thousands of Buffalo near the trail stopped for dinner at ½ p 11, good wood and pasture, but poor water, very warm day.

The month for which Capt. White was elected being up the company elected Mr. Hastings by a majority of 12 over Mr. Meek. Concluded not to move camp today, traviled 9 miles.
—Medorem Crawford

Susannah the Healer

Sidney Moss traveled alone and kept his own counsel. But he had cut himself some days back, and Susannah Couch, seeing him bleeding, had gone over and brought him back to her wagon. Then she got out some slippery elm she had collected back along the Kansas River and some bandages. She cleaned off the wound, which was like a slice from Mr. Moss's arm, in the fleshy part. She put a salve on the cut, wound the slippery elm about, and tied bandages to hold it all together. Next she ripped another strip of cloth and tied Mr. Moss's arm to his chest so he couldn't move it about much. For about six days he worked with his animals with one hand, and got his water and his food and ate with one hand, until Susannah arrived to release his arm.

She brought water with her to wet the bandages in order to loosen them, she pulled the cloth off, and then removed the remains of the elm bark to expose the skin. Moss's arm looked pale white and rather limp, but he was healed enough that Susannah only put some salve on the scar. Then she covered it with clean cloth and declared him just about healed.

"How'd you learn this, girl?" he asked.

"Mama died when I was five, and Auntie Beechy raised me. She was a healer, and instead of leaving me home alone, she took me along with her. We nursed men with cuts and women in childbirth, children with rashes, and she could cure the sick headache and those who had had too much to drink. She doing all the work, of course, but always teaching, and I learned what I could. Fine woman, Auntie Beechy."

Susannah Couch was one of the few people Mr. Moss talked to. He confided to her that his second mule was getting lame. He asked if she could heal the mule, as she had fixed him up, and she tried to but noted that the mule favored one leg in an unhealthy way.

Lorenzo observed that Mr. Moss, a fat little man with a square head and no neck, looked like a jug with a cork in it. He peered at the sick animal and said that back home in Virginia they put horses down if they limped that way, that such weakness didn't heal and certainly wouldn't out here where the road was hard and there was alkali all about that would further weaken the animal.

Mr. Moss did not like that prediction, but he tried to be careful and kept his animals away from the little white circles that looked like salt but were alkali that formed from place to place. He held his mules back from the edge of the river, for everyone knew that no one should drink the Platte River water unless they really had to.

When Moss heard that the Tompkins girl and that old lady, Mrs. Smith, had actually seen Pawnees off to the south, he approached Lorenzo about going off to capture some Indian horses. Susannah had said most positively not—Lorenzo would not go.

Sidney Moss had crept off by himself.

That was all Susannah knew.

The judicial committee thanked Mrs. Couch for her account of what she knew about Sidney Moss and excused her. There were some comments about who wore the pants in that wagon and about men who didn't stand up to their women, but these were said after Susannah had left the area the men had set up as a "court." The constitution that Dr. White had drawn up for the company, and that the voting members had agreed upon, stipulated that any offense against the well-being of the company, or any dispute between members, be judged by a committee of three.

Everything else that the women learned about the episode of Mr. Moss and the Pawnee horses, they heard from their men.

Mr. Smith reported to Mrs. Smith that Moss was a damn fool who had set out alone to capture some Pawnee horses after hearing about the presence of Indians when she and Ellen Tompkins had returned to camp. Mr. Smith was disgusted with Moss for making the attempt. "Fool man could get us all killed," he said. He turned on Mary Smith, too, and yelled at her for going off "discovering," observing that she too could have brought the Indians down on them or gotten herself and that child killed.

Mr. Perry, also on the judicial committee, had told his wife and sister-in-law that Moss had actually gotten close to the Indian camp and had seen that the Pawnees were asleep, with the horses staked out nearby. He had crept up on the horses, but then they began to get restless, what with a stranger crawling about among them. Moss accidentally fired off his gun as he got up to flee. Mr. Perry had left out some of the details, because his wife was in her condition and he didn't want to upset her.

Danby Tompkins told his family at dinner that Moss had put the entire company in jeopardy by staging that stupid raid on the Pawnee horses. Who knew what the Indians would do? He forbade Ellen to go off from the camp, even if she was with Mrs. Smith. For the time being they both had better stay close. "No telling what the Indians will do," he said. He directed Ned to stay close to the cow and extra horses they were taking along. He himself would ride with the wagon for a day or two to make sure the Pawnees didn't attack, and he instructed Caroline to oil the small rifle that Mr. Frost back home had taught her to shoot.

"Well, I couldn't shoot at anyone," said Caroline, emphasizing the word *at*.

"You did well out behind Frost's barn. He told me you hit that target on the tree every time."

"Well, yes," she replied, "But there is a huge difference between a red circle and a real person."

"These are Indians, Caroline," Danby had said roughly, in a voice that matched the countryside. "You will shoot at them."

"Well, I doubt it," she had answered. "They were here first," but then she relented. "I will shoot at their horses' feet to see if that might turn them back. That is, if they come after us."

"What will happen to Mr. Moss?" asked Ellen, who had offered several times to learn to fire a rifle, which she would be sure to aim at anyone who approached the wagon. Her offers were declined as totally inappropriate, her father commenting that "it was bad enough that we have to ask your mother to shoot if necessary. I don't mean to have gun-toting daughters as well." Martha and Jane scoffed at the idea.

When Ned returned from looking after the animals, he said that Dr. White was showing everyone his commission from the government again because he was the appointed Indian agent, and any trespass against the Pawnees was a violation of his directions to maintain order. Such violations, he said, came under his jurisdiction, not that of the company and certainly should not be judged by some random committee. White warned that the Pawnees could come ask for goods in payment for the indignity of a white man creeping up on them at night with no obvious good intention and shooting off a gun, proving that he had not been peaceable. He said that Moss would have to pay what they wanted, and Moss had said he had nothing to pay them with and he wasn't going to give any damn Indian—"Excuse me, Mother"—anything anyway.

Sidney Moss had retreated into his wagon and refused to come out.

The judiciary committee called on him, but he remained inside.

Children gathered in the campground across from Moss's wagon to watch. Some of the women walked across the campground more often than necessary in order to see what might be happening.

Dr. White went to the wagon with the intention of dragging Moss out, but when he approached the entrance, a rifle appeared from within and Moss refused to budge.

"I'll shoot you," he had called out. "I'll shoot anybody who gets any closer than that," he threatened.

Then Mr. Smith called over to Moss to be reasonable, and there ensued a whole lot of yelling from outside the wagon to the man inside, first someone from the company telling Moss he had put everyone at risk and Moss not saying anything at all, and then another man telling Moss that he was in violation of the judiciary committee ruling and Moss spitting loudly so that everyone could hear. Dr. White hollered to Moss that his authority as Indian agent made him the person who should set the punishment, and, if the Pawnees appeared, he would probably rule in their favor as Moss was definitely in the wrong.

Things went on like this for the entire evening until Moss called from the back of his wagon, doing so quite softly but in the direction of the Couch wagon, to ask Lorenzo to feed his animals, which Lorenzo went off to do.

Except for this, all the shouting came from the men of the company, with some jeers from the children, who were on the verge of calling out "Coward!" They were immediately silenced by their elders, not wanting that word to encourage the fury that gripped them all. Moss went to sleep.

The next morning, when it was time to move on, Moss emerged from his wagon, hitched up his animals, and drove off. This completely surprised the remainder of the company, so everyone else hurried to hitch up too, and they set off without breakfast, following along in Moss's path. At noon Moss stopped, unhitched his mules, retired into his wagon, and refused to be seen. No one could engage him in conversation. Susannah said to Lorenzo that he better tend to Moss's animals, for she believed he had gone to sleep.

That evening the company came up to Moss's wagon and camped around him. The judiciary committee approached Moss's wagon, but when they got within fifteen feet, a rifle jutted forth from the canvas and Moss began shooting. His bullets hit the ground and the men fell back and to the sides to get out of range. No one knew if Moss was a good shot, but no one was willing to find out now.

That night was Sidney Moss's turn to stand guard. He showed total defiance, leaving the committee with few options.

"We could storm his wagon," said one.

"He'll shoot us, sure as rain," answered another. "No point in one of us getting killed."

"We could set his wagon on fire and drive him out," suggested another, but no one knew what to do if Sidney Moss refused to come out. Or, what to do if he came out shooting.

"You mean, you think he would just burn up in there?" asked old Mr. Smith.

"Who knows what that crazy man will do," Dr. White replied. "But if he burned up, I wouldn't be sorry."

"Well, we can't have that. It's not civilized."

"We could abandon him," said Gabriel Brown, an even-tempered man who was now riled at Moss's treatment of the company and its rules.

"What do you mean?"

"Well, we could simply tell him that he is on his own. That we refuse to allow him to travel with us anymore. That he is a party of one."

"That is like condemning a man to death out here."

"So is burning down his wagon or shooting him."

"It's not the same thing."

"Well, if you can't abandon him, you can't burn him out, and you can't shoot him, then he wins, 'cause we can't do anything at all about him."

"Then we are going to back down?"

"Let's wait and see," said Mr. Smith, who returned to his wagon to report to his wife.

That night, when the first shift ended, Gabriel Brown went out to stand guard. Around the camp people watched Sidney Moss's wagon to see what he would do. At exactly eleven the wagon cover opened and Sidney Moss appeared. He carried his rifle and the tin of water he always took when on guard, and he had the whistle around his neck to use as warning if there was cause to alert the camp. He walked quietly across the center of the campground, moved beyond the Shaddens' wagon, and joined Gabriel Brown on the watch.

Susannah Couch turned to Lorenzo and said quietly, "I bet no one ever mentions Pawnee horses or Sidney Moss's trial or the judicial committee again."

Lorenzo turned to her, replying, "But they almost killed him for putting us at such risk."

"I know," she said. "But they are decent men and they couldn't do it. They just couldn't do it. And he broke them; he defied their authority and won."

"He backed them down. So who is going to do what the judiciary committee says after this?"

"No one, Lorenzo," she said. "There won't be a judiciary committee from now on. The women will talk quietly about this for a time, but I wager that you men never mention it amongst yourselves again. Not once."

The Company

The company had agreed to abide by its rules for one month and at the end of that time there would be another meeting and another vote for captain. The men who owned full shares in the company gathered off from the wagons while the women and children remained in the camp. The hired men, who were not voting members, worked tending the animals or fixing things in need of repair. The McKay brothers took their horses and rode out to hunt for game, while Ellen and Mrs. Smith walked along the river to look at the birds; those left in the camp wrote letters or read. There was plenty of light, as the sun was high in the sky, and there was a soft breeze from the west that lightly stirred the few trees along the water and moved the grasses in a languid manner.

Caroline had finished the supper dishes and had taken up *Gulliver*, which she had borrowed from Mrs. Girtman, easing herself against the rim of the wagon wheel so that it supported her back. She had brought out a pillow and a mug of tea. She felt grateful that her children were old enough to care for themselves, that she needn't worry about youngsters at the end of the day. Caroline realized suddenly that she was not alone.

"Ma'am," said the hired man who was traveling with the Brown family. "Mr. Tompkins said he had a good awl in the wagon that I might borrow."

"Mr. Lewis?" she inquired, both saying the name she thought was his but asking too, in case she had it wrong, "I don't know where it might be. He is off now, at the meeting."

"I saw him on his way, Mrs. Tompkins. He said it was in the pouch, under the seat. May I look for it?"

"Of course," she replied, returning to her book.

Some minutes later he returned with the tool in his hand. "Thank you, ma'am," he said, and he started off.

"Mr. Lewis," she said, "do you know what is happening?"

"A bit, ma'am. I usually eat with Medorem Crawford, and he thinks that Dr. White is going to lose this election. He fears with all the disagreements the doctor has had, with Hastings, and then with John Force—and of course, about the dogs—that he might not be reelected. Some would like Stephen Meek to take over, as he knows the trail, but there is the issue of Captain Hastings, who likes to take charge. And Meek is only riding along; he don't have a stake in this company."

"But Dr. White has the government commission," she replied.

"That may be so. But he doesn't get along well with folks, and he has to contend with Lansford Hastings, a man with an opinion of himself as big as the mountains we are supposed to cross."

Caroline shivered. "What will happen?"

"Well, I don't know exactly. But Mr. Moss is pretty angry at everyone who was in power during his difficulties, so he isn't about to support Dr. White. Hastings and his crew of men will happily block White, so I guess that Hastings will become captain, in reality as well as in name, and that the doctor will just have to go along with it."

"Are there no others who might lead the company? Others who aren't as cantankerous as Dr. White and Mr. Hastings?"

"My money would be on Stephen Meek, ma'am. He is a good man, and he has been along the Platte River before—all the way to Fort Laramie, they say, and even into the mountains. He is one of those who came in when the Lancasters turned back, among the party rushing to overtake us. Problem is that Meek doesn't have a share, that is, he is traveling along with the company but doesn't have a vote, so maybe the men with votes won't trust him to be cautious enough, as they are the ones with the greatest to lose."

"What will happen if Hastings is made captain?"

"I dunno, Mrs. Tompkins. I try to keep out of the discussions, not being a voting member myself."

"Why are you going west, Mr. Lewis?"

"For the land. Like everyone else, for the land."

"But you are older than the others working their way across, Mr. Lewis. If I may say so."

"Yes. But I would still like a chance, and I couldn't put an outfit together. Besides, the work is pleasant and the politicking isn't. I'm content." As he talked he rubbed his fingers on a small lead object.

"I have this theory, that everyone here is running from or running to," said Caroline.

"I am definitely running to, Mrs. Tompkins. It is the future I am after, not the past." He tipped his hat just slightly to her and moved away.

About the same time, Ned, calling to her, approached the wagon.

"Here, Ned. By the far wheel." She greeted Ned with a smile, for his presence gave her enormous pleasure. Her firstborn child, Ned was a capable young man and he was making this trip possible. No one in the family could think of the trip without Ned. Dan was a splendid man but not exactly a practical one, or handy. Father and son were different, and their difference had become even more obvious as Ned grew older. But they were alike too, physically, and also in the precise way in which their minds worked.

"What do you hear about the meeting?" she asked.

"Father came over to tell me that they had voted Mr. Hastings captain by a majority of twelve votes over Mr. Meek. The doctor was not even in the running, and now he is full of dark looks. They changed some of the other rules, like how long we need to keep guard at night and the order of rotation. They also want to start earlier in the day and rest longer in the middle when the heat is worst. Father said that Captain Hastings was gathering himself up like a little Napoleon, all full of brisk orders."

"Will there be trouble, do you think?"

"Father thinks we will all just have to make do with the change. No one can go alone."

"Dr. White has a temper. That you have seen yourself, Ned."

"Yes. . . . Look, here comes Father."

Danby strode over to them and squatted down on his heels. "Elijah White is furious and Hastings hasn't the decency not to gloat about winning the vote. Stephen Meek seemed resigned to losing the election, but he still knows more about traveling along the Platte than the other two combined. And Moss—he is looking as if he has just prevailed."

"I talked to Ellen's Mr. Crawford," Dan continued, "and he thinks that the doctor will split off, not being able to stomach Hastings in the lead."

"Don't they realize that we all need each other?" asked Caroline. "This journey is dangerous enough without squabbling amongst ourselves. How can we get through if we fight each other?"

"Mother, at the moment, a split wouldn't be so awful. The path is marked by the river, first crossing the South Branch, then along the North Branch until we get to the fort. The way along the river is fairly flat, and it is unlikely that one company could get very far ahead of the other, so we would always be in sight of the entire company."

"Ned is right and it might give Hastings and White a chance to cool off. Remember, the mountain men who passed us last week were traveling with only four wagons and twelve men. Even if we split, each company would still have more than that. We should be able to make it safely to Fort Laramie."

*

*June 16: More difficulty and misunderstanding in the company. Doct. White
with a few others concluded to leave. Rain this morning. The majority of
the company started at 8 o'clock under Capt. Hastings. Two wagons and 13
men remained [with] Capt. Fallen. Started at 11 o'clock passed the other
party and camped at 6 o'clock.*
—Medorem Crawford

Tompkins Family Observation

Dr. White has left the train. Father decided to remain with the largest part of
the company for safety. We can see Dr. White and his party of two wagons
just behind us. They have Captain Fallon, who joined the company riding
in late with a few others, to guide them, and we are with Captain Hastings.
Mr. Crawford has gone with Dr. White, so I won't be able to get mileage
from him at night.

Halfway through the day, Dr. White and his party got going fast enough
that they overtook us where the way was wide. Some of them waved as they
passed, but people in our company thought they wasted their energy being
smug moving along so quickly. Captain Hastings picked up the speed somewhat, but there is no way such a long line of wagons as ours can keep up with
that small company.

The McKay brothers have been out hunting, and since I do not have a
horse of my own to ride and because Father has said I must remain close to
the wagon, I have been walking with Mrs. Smith. The horseflies have been
very bad, and I never saw such large ones or so many of them before.

The men killed a buffalo last night. It had gotten close to our animals and
so the guard shot it. I think it was a Bennett who did it. They shared the
buffalo meat with a number of wagons, but the hunters take only the good
parts, that is, the tongue and heart and liver and some of the hump meat.
There was not enough for everyone.

The way along the river is very pleasant in general, and it is level. The soil is
sandy, but the grass is good and the animals get a lot to eat. Mrs. Smith and I
watched two large blue herons fly low over the water and extend their necks,

and fly off. Because they look different in the sky with their necks pushed out, I didn't know what they were at first. There are some small herons here too, green and shiny looking, with large necks, probably so they can swallow fish whole. We camped about a mile behind Dr. White's company, and we could clearly see their campfire and could even hear their voices, which carried in the breeze.

*

June 17: They passed us again and camped 3 miles ahead, traviled 14 miles, quite cold.
—Medorem Crawford

Tompkins Family Observation

Very hard west wind today. We started early, calculating to stop and rest our teams as soon as we came to good grass. Mrs. Smith and I found some toads with horns and long tails. They are about three inches long and very slender, and their tails are as long as their bodies. They are spotted, white, yellow, and brown and they can run as fast as any man. They are very wild. Mosquitoes annoy us very much, and sometimes the air seems to be filled with large bugs. But it is the dust that is most troublesome, as it clogs our noses and makes our eyes sting. There is some white larkspur along the riverbank and also a very pretty dark red flower, a stranger to Mrs. Smith.

The road is good, however, though water is now scarce and there is no grass. No timber either. At noon we came upon a dead buffalo in the road, killed by the company ahead. We had heard the shots but didn't know the reason for them. Then a buffalo came near our camp and Mr. Williams went out to kill him, which he did some way off. Mrs. Bennett and Susannah Couch took a wagon to get the buffalo meat. Alexander McKay shot a badger right near our camp, and he and his brother chased some prairie dogs in their village. Someone killed one of them to see it closely, but we have been told they are not good to eat. Mrs. Smith warned me that prairie dogs live underground in burrows along with rattlesnakes and so I should never reach into a hole. That's worth knowing.

Mother mentioned that our teams are getting tired and that Mr. Moss's lame mule is no better. It has been decided that we should go slowly so we don't tire the animals. It is fortunate that the way along the Platte is safe and easy walking. The grass, however, comes and goes; at one place there is plenty while at another little, but now we seem to have moved past all the good grass and the animals have to chew on some of the harder weeds that grow near the water's edge.

We went about twenty miles today and can see Dr. White's company about a mile ahead. It seems that as fast as they go, they only go fast enough to keep ahead but not out of sight. There was a buffalo near the camp again today, but because we had meat no one fired at it—so I got a good look. We camped near a spring and everyone enjoyed the sweet water. Mother decided to wash and she recruited all of us to help. I carried water and spread out some clothes on bushes and the sides of the wagon after the others had pounded them.

Martha had the sick headache last night and today too, so she rode in the wagon. That meant that Jane walked with me for a time and we had a good talk. We ended up talking about Father: how happy he seems to be heading west and how much he talks about what he will put in his newspaper. He makes it sound important and rather exciting.

I like walking with Jane when Martha is elsewhere, but when the two are together Jane is as silly as Martha. Jane sang while we walked, and some of the people in the near wagon joined in the chorus.

*

June 18: Started at 7 o'clock. Cold wind & extremely uncomfortable. Commenced to rain at 10 o'clock stoped. Started at 2 camped at 7 on the South fork of Platte traveled 18 miles. For 2 days we have seen no Buffalo. Capt. Fallen brought us some meat.
—Medorem Crawford

Tompkins Family Observation

Cold and rainy today, which makes everyone disagreeable. Some remain in the wagons but then they are heavier for the animals to pull; some walk and get wet in the rain or walk in puddles and splash others. The animals have to walk through mud, and some of the wet spots actually have quicksand, which we try to avoid. One wagon wheel crossed the quicksand and got stuck, so all the men had to come heave it out. After that, everyone was careful about the dangerous spots and most everybody was in a bad mood.

After a time, the pathway that Dr. White and his party took moved away from the water into the bluffs, which are of a rocky formation, a mixture, said Father, of sand and lime. We followed along in their wagon tracks. In about three miles we came to Ash Hollow, so called from the ash and cedar trees that grow here. We took tree limbs for fuel, and some cut long ones for fishing poles. This glen is very picturesque, as rocks rise almost perpendicular two hundred feet high, or even more. We have not yet camped in a prettier place.

*

June 19: Sunday, Started at 7, stopped for dinner 2 ½ hours within 1 miles of Capt. Hastings. Camped on the Platte within ½ mile of the other company at 6, traveled 20 miles.
—Medorem Crawford

Tompkins Family Observation

Mr. Crawford rode back to see how we were doing and told me the distance. We got an early start today and our route was back to the Platte River. We crossed a very deep ravine that had steep banks but was entirely dry. We saw three antelopes and two wolves. We are moving now along the South Branch of the Platte River. Mr. Crawford said that tomorrow we will ford the South Branch and go onto the North Branch, which takes us to Fort Laramie.

We have seen no buffalo today. The McKay boys brought in several large rabbits, and they skinned one and gave it to Mother. There is little game in this vicinity. But there are wolves and they howl in the night and especially in the early morning. They grew so bold they came near our camp and enraged Mr. Moss, who took after a leader of the pack, his old gun spewing shot and missing all of the animals, but then the wolves turned on him and chased Mr. Moss back into camp. He was not well pleased.

*

June 20: Capt. Hastings & comp. crossed over the river & we followed immediately.
—Medorem Crawford

TOMPKINS FAMILY OBSERVATION

We have come to the South Fork and crossed the river where it is one-half a mile wide—some said three-quarters of a mile—but the water is only inches deep, not having banks to keep it contained, so it flows where it wants. The men met to decide how to make the crossing. They chained the wagons together and paired the horses so there were six or eight teams. Men on horseback rode by the side, women and children rode on the tops of boxes strapped to the wagon seats. There are some spots of quicksand, but the lead horse took a safe route and we crossed without trouble. Dr. White's company had crossed after we did but farther up from us, and his camp is now nearby so that we can shout to each other.

From here, we move in a northwest direction along the North Fork. We traveled fifteen miles today.

*

June 21: The other company went south of us. Camped on the North Fork. The other company 2 miles behind, traveled 20 miles.
—Medorem Crawford

WIDOW ABEL'S DIARY

We came in sight of Courthouse Rock today. We came near it, at noontime, or within about four miles of the nearest point where the road approaches it. It is a massive stone heap, some three hundred or four hundred feet high, jutting out of the level prairie. It can be seen from miles away, and as much as we walk we don't seem to get close. This scenery is most enchanting, entirely surprising in its loveliness and unlike anything I have ever seen, but I have lived in Indiana all my life. Up until now.

Mr. Pomeroy asked if I would like to walk or ride with him over to see the Courthouse bluff, but I declined, though others went near. The monument is so large, however, it is hard to get close to it, and viewing it from afar gives one a better idea of the whole. There were large birds flying about it near the top and some suggested they might be eagles with nests up on the cliffs.

Baby is now walking any chance she gets.

*

June 23: Started early, kept along the river, water good. Saw some boatmen from the Fort stopped 3 hours for dinner. Camped early traveled 10 miles.
—Medorem Crawford

MOTHER BENNETT

Mary Bennett squatted down, her legs spread apart, her skirt billowing in the wind. She felt the stream of urine flow beneath her and listened to it hit the dry ground. As she relieved herself she watched the activity among the wagons off to the right. She eased down closer to the earth to defecate, feeling the pull of her muscles as she strained. She thought to herself, one day I have the runs; the next day I am all bound up. She wondered about the water they had been drinking.

Most of the other women defecated amid a circle of women all facing outward, their skirts creating a semblance of privacy in this land of openness, in this camp where there was no place to hide. Mary preferred to be alone. She had watched the women's heads jerk forward when they had circled. She could imagine their noses scrunching to block the odor of her stool. She was sure she created more odor than any of them, and she felt shame, even in this natural act.

Squatting down near the ground sometimes made her shake too, in remembrance. Squatting, her feet flat on the prairie floor, legs spread apart, she experienced time and again her last day as a girl, her first as wife. It was a memory that came unbidden, unwelcomed; yet it arose every time she relieved herself along the trail. For so many years it had been hidden and lay almost forgotten in her mind, but the experience of squatting in the open, of feeling her legs, now older and heavier, but stretched wide; lowering her body near the earth was all it had taken to bring that early experience to mind, and, once there, it was impossible not to relive it each and every time.

She had been fourteen the day her father had called her out from their Georgia cabin and ordered her to follow him.

"Where we going to, Pa?" she had asked.

"Just you follow along, Sis," he had said. "Gonna pay off a debt to Varde-mon Bennett. Man threatening to take me to the sheriff if'n I don't settle."

"What's the debt for, Pa?"

"Things, girl. Don't be pesky. We gotta get along," and after that the two had walked in silence away from the small family cabin, past her mother's grave and those of the three babies who had never breathed long enough to even be named, past the little field and the bullfrog pond, past the crossing to the Redmonds', and the next to the Smiths', where her friend Patsy lived. They walked into the little hamlet where the family bought things when they had money or traded when one of the boys had luck with his traps. At the store Pa stopped off for a drink and Mary fingered the calicos. She liked the yellow ones dotted with flowers, but she herself had never had a dress of store-bought goods. Her clothes had mostly been handed down from her brothers and remade, with a skirt cut from her ma's old dresses. The stiff new calico felt almost brittle in her fingers, but she admired the bright color.

Then Pa nodded to Fitch Jamison to come along, and the three of them left the store and walked to the crossing heading south. They trudged along, Mary watching the birds and looking for berries along the way, but there were none, as it was too early in the season.

"I didn't know'd you got some money lately," said Mary brightly to her father, hoping he would explain their mission or at least talk to her. The silent ways of the family lay heavy upon her, with no one ever explaining anything because she was the youngest, because she was a girl, because no one really talked to anyone any more than necessary anyway. It was a family that mostly barked orders to one another, that snapped answers as if words cost just as much as goods at the store. It was a family of silences and had been since Ma had died. Before that there had been music, but when Ma died it was as if they had buried all the notes in her grave with her and there were no others to be had. Or, those that were out there cost too much for the likes of the Fenner family.

Her father didn't answer. He looked at her harshly and kept walking.

"For that debt, Pa," she said, hoping to have him speak, but he pushed his thin lips together as if he had eaten something very sour. His pale blue eyes looked lifeless and sad. He said nothing.

After half an hour the Bennett place came into view. The cabin was poorly made. It didn't look like anyone took any care of it at all. Then from the side of the building, where boards showed a long dark green stain of water that had run along them for a long time, stepped Mr. Bennett, a small, tight-looking man. He was holding in his hand a coon he had been skinning, his hand crimson with blood.

"Bennett," said Pa.

"Fenner," said Bennett in acknowledgment. "Got the thirty-six dollars you owe me for that horse your boy ruined?"

Her father stopped walking, set his feet into the dirt before the cabin, and looked down. Mr. Jamison stopped some paces back. Then her pa put his hand on Mary's shoulder, clasping her as if to support himself. He was often an unsteady man when he was drinking. Mary held still as expected.

"Don't have no money, Bennett," said Pa. "I gotta give you goods for the debt."

"You owed it a good long time. You promised to pay it by today," said the small man, tossing the animal aside and wiping his bloody hand on his trousers.

"Yeah."

"How you gonna pay?" asked Mr. Bennett.

Mary looked from one man to the other. She had never known her father to have thirty dollars in cash, but he didn't own trade worth that either. She was young, but she knew about Pa. And about how things were at home.

There was a pause and then Pa said, "You can have the girl for it." The words hit her ears like a hammer on the smith's anvil, ringing back and forth inside her head. *You can have the girl for it. You can have the girl for it.* What did he mean?

She tried to jerk away, but her father kept her near him, his fingers digging tight into her shoulder.

Bennett swung his eyes to her, seeing her for the first time.

"Your woman died, I heard," said Pa. "They say she was sickly from the start and the young 'uns you got on her were weak and died too. That's what they say. You need a woman, probably pretty bad by now. This one is young, but you can learn her."

"You passing off a daughter you done with?" asked Bennett nastily. "I know about your oldest girl. You used this one too?"

Her father's eyes blazed. "Keep your dirty mouth offa my children, Bennett." Then Pa, remembering why he was there added, "I never touched this one."

"Some young buck got her in the family way, then," suggested Mr. Bennett.

"Nobody touched this gal," insisted Pa, who then turned her head to face him and asked, "Anyone get between your legs, girl? Anyone?"

Mary stiffened. Her eyes blazed wide and filled with tears. Her mouth went dry and words were impossible. "What do you mean, Pa?" she choked out.

But her father cut her off and pushed her forward toward the other man. "See for yourself, Bennett," he said.

Mary felt herself spun from one man to the other. Bennett put his bloodied hand against her back and propelled her toward the door of the cabin.

"Only touch, Bennett, for the proof. Don't you fuck her and claim she is used. Just you see for yourself nobody been there." Pa spit the words out like spoiled milk. Fitch Jamison looked sick to his stomach. "Aw, Fenner, you ain't gonna do that to yer pup."

As Mr. Bennett moved her toward the door of the cabin, Mary heard her father say, "Shut up, Fitch. Mind your own business."

Mr. Bennett moved forward with Mary, but she was rooted to the ground. She knew about animals, having lived on a farm, but she didn't understand what had been said about her now, or what had been suggested. She didn't know what was expected of her, what her part in all this was to be, but nothing sounded good.

As Mr. Bennett opened the cabin door, her father called out, "Go in there, girl; let 'em see you is intact." Then angrily he ordered, "You do what Mr. Bennett says, girl."

The cabin was dark and messy. She felt Mr. Bennett behind her, pushing her forward, could hear the catch in his throat as he asked, "How old are you, girl?"

She turned to him. "Thirteen. Fourteen next month." She could feel her skin where his hand held her, saw on her arm some blood from the coon he had been skinning. She moved back away from him, but there was no room to go farther.

He moved behind her and said, "Squat down, girl."

She didn't move. He commanded her again, "Squat down, girl, when I tell you," and he pushed harshly on her shoulder. Mary bent her knees and lowered her body until she was near the dirt floor of the cabin. She could see some old bones lying under the table and a blanket on the floor. There was a broken plate, too, near the corner of the room, like someone had cracked it and then tossed it away in disgust.

Bennett reached his arm around her shoulder and slid it down her body. He pulled at her skirts with the other hand and slid his hand beneath her drawers and thrust his finger into her body. She arched up in shock, knocking them both back, Bennett hitting the floor with her face-up on top of him. She had called out "Pa!" when he touched her, but the sound died as soon as it was voiced, as Pa was unlikely to help her now. She gasped for air, weeping and afraid.

Bennett pulled his hand away and pushed her off him. He got up and put his hand to his nose, savoring it, slowly, like a man with a new bottle of liquor just opened, the aroma flowing from the bottle neck as potent as the liquid within. Then he started wiping his pudgy fingers on his trousers.

"Go tell yer Pa I only touched you." When she didn't move, he shouted at her, "You do as I tell you, girl. You go tell your pa you is intact."

But at the same time Pa and Mr. Jamison were in the doorway.

"Well?" asked Pa.

"Yeah," said Bennett. "She's all right, I guess. Unless you are putting a trick on me."

"No trick," said Pa. "She's a good girl. You sign the note and Fitch here will marry you two."

Mary, looking up from the floor where Mr. Bennett had left her, could see spittle coming from his mouth. At the word *marry* both she and Mr. Bennett looked up sharply.

"Marry? You didn't say nothing about marry," whined Vardemon Bennett, but he was a caught man, having touched and smelled and imagined all he needed to imagine. Besides, the girl was young and he could learn her, and she just might be fertile; he just might get sons from her.

"You got her smell on your fingers now," said Pa, "but you'll smell across the whole county if'n you just take her and don't marry. She's probably like her ma, real fertile. She's not all growed yet. She'll get you sons." He paused. "And I don't want her back after you get through."

He turned to the man standing behind him. "Fitch," he called, "get up here with your book. Bennett, you bring out that note, and if you have a bottle in that hole of a house, bring it too and we'll drink on it."

After the first time it got better. Mary got used to Vardemon Bennett, and she did prove to be fertile. Seven babies she had had. But at home, in Georgia, people had smiled at them knowingly, and they had made remarks about them, for the story had spread about the neighborhood.

Mary had grown, too. After a few years she towered over the small man she had married, and she had filled out, each pregnancy leaving her not fat, but bigger. As she became a physical presence, he seemed to shrink. And she learned to have her way.

After a time the Bennetts picked up and moved on. The place hadn't been much to leave behind anyway, and the snickers that often greeted them weren't missed. In time Mary had forgotten or had enough else to do that she didn't dwell on that day. But here, on the prairie, each time she needed to relieve herself, squatting down near the earth, feeling her legs pull apart and the hot urine flow from between them, the memory flashed before her and made her feel weak.

*

June 24: Started early drove very fast stopped for dinner nearly opposite the Chimney a very remarkable mound rising like a pyramid some 100 feet and then a perpendicular column standing on the top probably 200 feet high. Saw a Buffalo crossing the River.
—Medorem Crawford

WIDOW ABEL'S DIARY

No one should travel out this far from home without a box of medicines. Already people seem to be having the summer complaint. Castor oil is needed. We should also have brought along some peppermint essence. It is from drinking the Platte water, I think.

Cows got loose last night and the men have gone out hunting them. As it is, many of the cattle are lame. It is plain to my mind what makes their feet wear out. It is the alkaline nature of the ground.

I must now keep an even closer eye on Baby, as she wants to walk when she is free of restraint, and she picks up and puts in her mouth anything within hand. I am lucky to be with my sister, who helps out.

We can see the rock they call Chimney rising like a pyramid some one hundred feet and then a perpendicular column standing on the top, more than double the base. There are buffalo nearby too.

Walter Pomeroy has come by again to see if I might walk with him. He will not honor the fact that I am in mourning for my husband. He seems to think that being on the trail to Oregon excuses his boldness. I have certainly not encouraged his attentions. Little black hairs stick out from his ears in a most unpleasant way.

Part 3

CLIMBING, DESCENDING

June 26: Sunday, Started early without breakfast came to good wood and water at 8 o'clock. Camped on the side of a hill in a grove. Started at 1 o'clock saw the other company coming on
—Medorem Crawford

MARY SMITH'S SOLILOQUY

There is a great deal of writing going on among the people in this company, as if each of the participants knows this to be a historic crossing that must be recorded. Caroline Tompkins has her daughter, Ellen, writing an Observation, but that, I think, is more a school exercise than a desire to record the journey. People I wouldn't imagine keeping a diary or journal at home are now doing so. I doubt that these accounts will be all that reflective, as what seems important to the writers is the distance covered and the weather. I suspect that most of the diary keepers are doing so in order to know the date, to have a sense of the passage of time since every day on the trail is much like the next. It is as if every day is Tuesday, so we have Tuesday that is Wednesday, and Tuesday that is Thursday, and Tuesday-Friday, Tuesday-Saturday, all through the week. There is little distinction unless it is Cross-a-Creek Day, or Go-without-Water Day, or Watch-for-the-Quicksand Day.

The smart thing to do would be to record the musings of those of us who are walking. There, I suspect, are the real reactions to what we are doing, and they have little to do with the distance covered. It is when walking along, and alone, that I seem to churn up what I really think—those comments that cannot be uttered, words left unsaid, those flights of thought that are out of the usual or beyond the conventions by which we live, those words and ideas that would be thought crazy or scandalous or even stupid if told to others. It is almost as if the action of my legs, moving me forward step by step, lubricates my imagination so that I go free in my mind as my body plods forward. Thoughts are not fleeting and momentary but are worked over and developed by the process of walking. Perambulating, it is called.

I don't dwell much on those back home. I wonder about the people out there—the Indians about whom I have heard but know nothing. I think about them and wonder if they think about us. Do they wonder what we are doing out here as our canvas-topped wagons move across this vast space? Do they wonder what we want? What can they make of our thin line making its way across their landscape? Are they watching, even now? We don't know where they are or what they are doing; they don't speak our language and we don't know theirs. Yet, we—they and we—are strangely connected by all that disconnects us, and I assume that the real connection is the land—their land, or land that has always been theirs, without political designation made on maps, and of our moving across it as if it is our right to do so.

And it is our right. We, we Americans, we have always moved on to something better. My ancestors moved from England to the New World, not Mayflower people, but afterward, and they came to better themselves. Then my grandparents moved up the Hudson River to find a better space, and when I married, I moved to the western reaches of the state and lived facing Lake Erie and the West rather than looking east. From that move we are now making this one.

I made that initial journey in a carriage, nursing my firstborn. During that trip the land moved past me as I jostled up and down, the movement forward fueled by horses. Now walking, it is different, for movement depends upon each step I take, and each day I must keep going, stepping forward, into the West. So I am the moving object on the landscape, and the trees and rocks stand still as I pass. And I pass by because I walk. When I stop, the world around me stops too. I am the actor that puts this journey into motion, however slow that is; it is I who make the miles pass. There is something thrilling in this, something eternal. I think we humans have always walked, moved forward, sometimes not knowing what the end will be, what the goal is. Just moving onward. And some, not ever reaching it.

I wonder if it is different for me, moving west with my family, than it might be for those men with us who are alone or who hire out and are moving because it is a job or a requirement of where they are. There are some young men here who work for others, and some just traveling west, and some like Ned, a nice young man, working to get his family west. I travel with my tribe, though that is a funny word because my tribe is so small, yet it is what I have in this world: my son, John, his wife, their young children, and my husband, John, on whom this trip has been forced. He had no other option, I think. But he doesn't travel alone, either. He is part of our tribe, and so we go forth together.

My son John came to me before he told his wife and family that he wanted to try Oregon. He knew me to be his ally, always knew me to want for him what he wanted. That link, that mother-and-son link is so close that we are as one in our hopes that he will have in this world what he aspires to—at least, some of it. I gave him life and I would do anything to further his life; I would back him in anything and against any odds. He grew knowing of that support. What a privilege that is, to live knowing that someone, even if just a mother, would do anything to foster what you want, to aid you, support you, and would go against tradition and expectation for you. What is it to know that there is someone fierce on your behalf? That is powerful. That must be a most liberating feeling, knowing that whatever the world says, this one person approves and always has, always will.

It is such a different relationship than that of man and wife, where there are tugs and strains; where there are different interests and desires, where the wife must always know that the mother represents total approval, where the wife is the adjunct to the husband, where the wife's true loyalty is to the son. I wonder if this is true, for all or even really true for me.

Look where my walking has led me. The endless walking takes my thoughts to places they might not go if I were washing, or sorting linens, or to another errand back home. Those at-home thoughts, those household thoughts, are disjointed and incomplete and unexplored because there is always something else to do. These walking thoughts are different, for they go on and on and possibly they go beyond truth. They might be just a fancy that hangs in the mind as my body moves forward.

The most remarkable thing I have seen out here is how the distance deceives us. We walk, I walk, and bluffs that appear to be within one mile are often five or seven miles from us. It can take all day to get within proximity of something we have faced and looked at for hours. The rocks seem to hang in the air in front of us, and the air wavers like water or a windowpane in which bubbles remain in the glass. Yet, as much as I walk forward, nothing gets closer until suddenly, there it is, right at hand. I am constantly off balance by this feeling of not knowing what I am walking toward and how long it will take to get there.

At home I walked down streets, or across fields, or to the woods, and in each case I had a sense of the time it would take to get there because there were demarcations. As I advanced, things came steadily closer; I passed over this to get to that; I passed a store and turned a corner; I went up a road and through a gate. This was due not only to the fact that I had walked that way before but also because I could gauge how far away a tree was or how long it would take to approach the riverbank. Distance there, at home, was easily measured in time. Here, however, all those assurances within which I have lived, that knowledge of space and time, are upset, and I never seem to be able to judge where I am on the land. I can start out thinking that at noon we will be beside that bluff, and yet, at noon, the bluff seems just as far away as it was when we began walking . . . and the next day it can be the same too.

Sound is different here, too. Sound is irregular. The tread of the buffalo carries in the ground, and one can feel their approach even before they can be seen. But the calls of birds are only variously heard; some echo from afar, but many birdcalls seem to die in the space where they are uttered and carry across no distance at all. Voices carry, as if they are little packages that skip across the flat land like stones on water, but some voices nearby lose all resonance and drop out of hearing. At night the sounds are even more mysterious, as are the hoots of owls. The calls and songs of coyotes rise in the air and hang there to be heard by all, but the prairie dog yaps are less distinct, as if spoken into the ground holes they create, and the snorts of the cattle are muffled—but comforting. I always loved the phrase "the cattle are lowing," and here they do that and send a sense of peace over us all. Yet, the wolves howling in the night are disturbing and echo over space and time. Out here I can't depend on sound because I don't always know what it means or even where it comes from. Yet, I am glad to be here, for it is God's own beautiful land through which we are passing, and I love its variety.

A white poppy, at least that is what I think it is, growing along the trail, just here on the edge of the river. And ouch! It carries prickles in its defense like a damsel in a tower. It is to be left alone, though I would like to come back to collect its seeds. But we go on.

∗

June 28: Started late drove to the Forts by noon, traviled 10 miles. Found 2 Forts with several men at each whose business it is to trade with the Indians. Capt. H came up, 5 o'clock.
—Medorem Crawford

SUSANNAH COUCH AND MRS. SHADDEN

Susannah appeared suddenly in front of Mrs. Shadden. She had seen that the littlest boy, she didn't know his name, was suffering with the diarrhea. She had a remedy but didn't know if it would be accepted. She had not talked to Mrs. Shadden before, though she had watched the family slip from an initial look of hopeful assurance that they would be able to make the crossing, into some doubt. The first sign of trouble had been Mr. Moss's shooting of their cow; then she had noticed that Mr. Shadden was not much of a hunter and that the family seemed to subsist on scarce greens picked along the way and from flour cooked in fat, both stored in large containers in the wagon.

"Nice to have a rest for a time," she started.

"Mrs. Couch?" asked the weary woman.

"Susannah, is just fine, ma'am."

"That's a nice name. I had thought of that for one of the girls, but Shadden wanted to honor his mother and her sister so we have Cordelia and Amelia. Then we had boys." There was a slight pause. Then, birdlike, Mrs. Shadden chirped, "You don't have no children?"

"None yet," replied Susannah. "I noticed," she hurried on, diverting the conversation from herself to the object of her errand, "I noticed that your youngest seems to be having trouble with the diarrhea."

"That's Thomas James. Named for his father. Willie is the bigger boy, Henry, the oldest one." Mrs. Shadden seemed to have as few words as she had goods, and she used them sparingly.

"Thomas James seems to be having stomach trouble," repeated Susannah.

"Yeah. From the water, I guess. I tol' him not to drink the river water, but the older children do, and he goes along with them. Hard to stop 'em."

"Probably," replied Susannah. She pulled a small paper-wrapped package from her apron pocket and held it out. "This might help. I always used it at home. Though the herbs look bitter, they are pleasant tasting when steeped in hot water."

The older woman reached out, never having declined anything offered in her life and not doing so now. "That is mighty neighborly of you, Susannah. That child needs some relief, for sure."

"Just steep it for a quarter hour."

"Your man out hunting up those cows?" asked Mrs. Shadden with sudden brightness.

"Yes. They should be soon back."

"Shadden didn't go. He was feeling poorly himself. That drink? It would work for him, too?"

"Oh yes, I would think so. I have never known it not to help."

As the two women stood, there was a commotion from a distant wagon, one across the way. Horses came slowly in from the prairie and a woman let out a loud moan. Voices carried across the camp.

"Something's up," said Mrs. Shadden suddenly, her eyes bright with interest in what she seemed to hope was someone else's tragedy, someone else's hurt to stack up against her own. As Mrs. Shadden brightened at the prospect, Susannah backed slowly away, as if keeping bad news at bay. The women separated.

Lorenzo came back to the wagon, where Susannah was preparing food for the evening meal. He squatted next to her by the fire.

"Whatever happened," she said to the flames, "has been tragic."

"Yes," he answered. Then, picking at the edge of a biscuit heating on the little tin oven, he said, "They just brought in Mr. Gibbs."

"What do you mean, 'brought him in'?"

"We were out looking for the cattle that got loose last night, and we came upon them near a butte, off to the south. About twelve had gotten away, or had been led away by the Indians, and we saw ten ahead of us, all tired out, just standing there."

"Well?"

"We went over, rounded them up, and saw that there were more, moving a ways from us. Some of the men rode over in that direction, firing their guns to turn the stragglers, and Gibbs . . . Mr. Gibbs . . ." He stopped talking. She waited for the news that was bound to be bad. "Gibbs got himself shot," he said. "In the head."

"'Got himself shot'?" she repeated, asking, "How does one get himself shot?"

"He was riding along and there was shooting, no telling whose bullet it was, when one of the shots intended to stop the cattle . . . hit Gibbs . . ."

". . . in his head?" she asked thoughtfully.

"There was no helping it. And nothing to be done but bring him back into the camp. The men are telling Allen Davy and the men he bunks near."

"This is a dangerous country we are in, Lorenzo, and it takes its toll. First Bailey, and then the Lancaster child, now Mr. Gibbs. The cost of making this crossing seems high, very high to me." She looked at him as if able to see right through him. In her eyes he could read the worry and the doubt too, that he could prevent disaster from reaching them.

"I take care, Susannah."

"I know. But taking care doesn't seem enough and that frightens me."

"We will get through. I know it."

"I think so too. But I am fearful for you, for there is danger everywhere."

"I know."

They leaned in to each other, not touching, but feeling the air around themselves. The intensity of their feelings cocooned them from the day, from the others.

"You must take care," she said finally. "I am only strong because I have you."

Mary Smith's Thoughts

We all thought crossing the South Branch of the Platte would be momentous, but it turned out to be only difficult. The river is wide, and though not deep, there are large patches of quicksand on the bottom and the water runs swiftly. The men lifted bundles from the bottom of the wagons and placed them on the seat or tied them to the sides, and the women and children rode as high as possible. The wagons were linked together for stability and the horses set in teams. There was difficulty but no trouble, and we all crossed. Dr. White's group crossed south of us, and they all got over also. We camped for four hours to give the animals a rest and to reset the wagons.

We had anticipated this crossing as significant, as a marker of how far we had come, which some estimated is about eight hundred miles from the United States. What the crossing really did was set us into a countryside of rolling land, interspersed with thin clumps of timber growing along ravines between the north and south branches of the river. There is more wood for campfires on this northern side and game is abundant. What the crossing made plain to me was not how far we had come but how far we have yet to go. Ahead is difficult land, and we have the mountains yet to cross, and even then we will not be there. It is not yet July; we have traveled a month and have three months yet to go, and once "there" we will need time to organize for winter. I feel as if we are on a clothing line strung between two trees and we are the lone sheet or sock or dressing gown one-third across and all alone in the breeze. Still, though I tremble, I look forward.

At times with lots of stress, like this, I think of what is happening, but at other times I muse back on what I had, what I left. I think of very particular things, like a coverlet or a baby's toy or even the henhouse. Having left them, I now hold them close to me, remembering what they were once to me.

*

June 29: Preparing carts & disposing of our cattle in order to expedite our journey.
—Medorem Crawford

MARTHA'S SECOND LETTER HOME

Dear Lucia,

Fort Laramy is ahead of us and I am writing to you back in Ithaca so you will know we have come about 800 miles from the United States and are in good health. We have seen a great many interesting things. Jane and I are making quilt squares when we rest and Mother has us reading French, but Jane makes me do all the reading aloud as you can imagine. She sings a lot, which is her forté. Ellen runs about with two young Indian boys who are traveling with us. She does find some interesting things to tell the family, such as the fact that Mr. Moss sometimes leaves bottles behind that the Shadden boy collects and that Mrs. Perry's sister, who is traveling with her and Mr. Perry, is a widow under difficult circumstances, but I don't know what they are. I suspect they hope to marry her off in Oregon where there are very few unmarried young ladies. Of course, she has a baby already. Mr. Fallon said he would take my letter to the fort when we get there because our wagon train will keep on going west and only some of the men will visit the fort. Apparently it is no place for young ladies.

I cannot think of anything else that would interest you, but send you my friendship and hope you will remember your friend,

Martha Tompkins,
formerly of the United States and now going west.

P.S. We have had another death. It was a man named Gibbs who was shot in the head.

*

July 1: Difficulty between Doct. White and Capt. Fallen. Fallen refused to go with us. Remained here all day.
—Medorem Crawford

TOMPKINS FAMILY OBSERVATION

Fort Laramie is just above us, and though men come down from there to talk to Dr. White or to take dinner with us, we are not to go there. I have never seen a fort, so I for one would like to go there to see it. Captain Fallon and Mr. Crocker went, but they said it was no place for a girl much less a lady. Medorem Crawford said that it was really just a trading post, established for the fur traders on their way in and out of the West. Dr. White took up to the fort some letters that people had prepared. Ned says that Dr. White is telling everyone that we are a large and strong party even though we "have foes on every hand." I don't know who these foes are, but Dr. White seems to expect the worst of everything. So while there is some coming and going from the fort, we keep moving westward along the North Branch of the Platte. Went twenty miles. There were many mosketoes where we camped and we are all uncomfortable, even the cattle. We hope for better tomorrow.

It seems there has been trouble again, this time between Dr. White and Mr. Fallon, who refused to continue with Dr. White and came to our camp.

While the doctor was up at the fort, he talked with Mr. Bissonette, who runs the post. Mr. Crawford said that Mr. Bissonette persuaded the two factions of the wagon train to go on together for our mutual protection, as Indians are not far away and they are warring with each other—not something we want to be in the middle of.

The main company protested about joining up together at first, feeling disaffected. Dr. White's party was also reluctant, but the fact is that we either travel as one, remain at the fort, or return to the States. So the company is to become one again.

When Dr. White was leaving the fort, a group of men from Canada who were employed by the American Fur Company came in, along with Jim Bridger, who had a load of furs and who was accompanied by his guide,

Thomas Fitzpatrick. The Canadians decided to travel west with us, and Dr. White hired Mr. Fitzpatrick to take us through to Oregon. He is to be paid $500, charged to the U.S. government because of Dr. White's appointment as Indian sub-agent.

Mr. Bissonette insisted that the company spend some time fixing the wagons and even shortening the larger wagons so that we make better time. Some people exchanged their tired horses for those at the fort.

Went sixteen miles today. I seem to be getting used to writing this Observation and don't really have time to put in all that I observe. I find it hard to decide what is most important. Writing this is certainly better than reading French, as Jane and Martha have been set to do. Mother is in her element teaching us all, excepting Ned and Father of course. Father has been reading a book about telling position from the stars. He thinks it might come in handy. Everyone seems to be happy to have the extra men with us.

The Widow Abel's Diary

Mr. Fitzpatrick is to guide the wagons now. He seems to be famous in the West, and we were told we were lucky to have him with us. He came in with several other men from the fort, men who had been in the mountains and who are turning back to the West. Since Dr. White offered the position to Mr. Fitzpatrick, it seems that he has taken some of the leadership from Mr. Hastings. It will be Mr. Fitzpatrick of course who will be the one in charge.

I would think those men would want to go home, that is, back East, but brother-in-law said they probably had no one to go home to and that they lived rough. Their clothes are a bit raggedy, but all were clean-shaven, having bathed and shaved at the fort. Some of them lean forward when they walk, not a lot, but their bodies are shifted a bit ahead so as to see the ground and forward at the same time. Mr. Perry said it was the Indian way and that some had lived for years with the Indians. And even have Indian families!

Baby has been chewing on a bone from a small antelope that someone shot. The bone is cleaned off, as I boiled it a while. It gives her gums something smooth to bite against, and it is big enough she can't swallow it or hurt herself.

The river is now to our right. Ahead is Independence Rock, a very remarkable mound that rises some two hundred feet high. It resembles a whale, or what I think a whale might look like, or a turtle, which I have seen. I heard Mr. Fitzpatrick say that *he* had named it Independence Rock on a trip into the area some twenty years earlier. All the men wanted to leave their names on the rock, but I didn't care to do so.

We are now at the foot of the Rocky Mountains, ahead of us. The country around is quite romantic, for the rocks, mountains, and plains are all here and the sun beautifies the whole region. The Sweetwater is nearby, so we have a lot to take in. Traveled twenty miles today. Mr. Pomeroy didn't come bothering today.

*

July 2: Joined the other company under Capt. Hastings. Started at 9 o'clock met a company from the mountains near the Fort. Camped at five, good wood and water, poor grass traveled 12 miles through a hilly and barren country.
—Medorem Crawford

What Caroline Tompkins Thought

The past few days we have traveled along the south side of the North Platte with the river to our right. Ahead is Independence Rock. The going is rough on the cattle, whose feet seem to be bruised. The days are hot, so we rest midday. What was interesting to me is that on Sunday there was absolutely no discussion of church or services; we got up early and started off without breakfast until we came to a wooded spot. We camped as one company, all together, in a grove on the side of a hill.

Some people feel very certain about names. Horse Creek? Who named it that, whose horse was it, and why is it remembered? But those who have been out here before insist it is Horse Creek. Is that what the Indians call it? And which Indians? There are many different ones out here. Perhaps it was an Indian horse that is remembered here? It is hard to know, but what I feel is that to us this is a new place because we have never been here before and because Americans have not settled here yet—if they ever will. Will this new land come with old names, and what if they don't make sense to us? Will new people give these places new names? Do we have a right to do that? What about

Independence Rock? Whose independence? And from what I don't know. I see a grove of trees and could call it Poplar Grove, but someone else coming along might call it Standing Grove or something else, so we keep naming anew things that have been here before and that probably have other names. That is an odd feeling. Who has a right to bestow a name, and, furthermore, why does one name stick and another not? There is a question for you.

I was told that unlike us, some Indians have different names during different phases of their life, rather like our calling a boy baby and infant, then young boy, then lad, then young man, I suppose. Curious.

Last evening, about midnight, there was great noise and the horses were very frightened and nearly broke loose. Some people think it was wolves, others think it was Indians. It might have been the horses themselves, getting excited. In the absence of certainty we develop all manner of ideas, some that might be true, others that are surely not real. But the wolves are out there; we hear them or sense them lurking.

We passed two small, rather shabby forts with several men at each whose business it is to trade with the Indians. Why don't these forts have names? They are surely landmarks of sorts, and so one would think they need names to be talked about. "Meet me at the two-forts" sounds vague in this large uncertain country; don't they need to be identified?

One man from the two-forts decided to go west with us, probably being tired of sitting about in a fort with no name. So we have more men with us, and this one looks as if he is useful with a gun. I think his name is Trask—at least that is the way it sounded when Ned told me about him. So here is the question again about names: how did we get ours? Smith is easy, that comes from an occupation, but Trask? Or Tompkins? Or Brown? It turns out that the Girtmans are related to the Gabriel Brown family and some of the others might also be. That would make them another tribe, although out here "tribe" means Indians, not Christian families. But are we not a tribe?

Dr. White is an odd, contentious man. In Elm Grove, when he showed everyone his credentials from Washington, he waved them in front of us and pointed to the signature of the president, but no one read them. Mr. Crawford said his charge was to oversee the Indians, while Dr. White claimed that he was to become the territorial governor when the allegiance of the Pacific

Northwest is determined. He has boasted that expenses for the trip west are to be paid by the government. How much of what he says is true is hard to say.

He had been, however, for a time with the Methodist mission in the Willamette Valley, and when he returned east he was one of the few people in the country who had been to the Pacific Northwest and had knowledge of the Oregon Territory. Now he is headed west again. And we are going with him; I wonder if this is a good idea.

*

July 3: Sunday Entered what is called the Black Hills. Traviled 15 miles over bad road without seeing water. Mr. Fitch Patrick employed as guide came to camp.
—Medorem Crawford

What Mrs. Shadden Had to Say

We have gone fifteen miles without seeing any water. The road is rough and our cart broke down, so we have to find some way to repair it. Those herbs that Susannah gave seemed to have worked. Shadden is feeling better, which makes the going easier on all of us, but he is proving to be a poor hunter and we have to depend upon others willing to share what they get. That Lorenzo brings us some meat and gives some to Mr. Moss, too. Even when the buffalo come near, Shadden aims too high or too low and gets nothing. You would think, well, I think that hitting a buffalo can't be all that difficult as they are so large and stand still for long periods, unless they are thundering by, which they did last night, veering away from the camp at the last moment. What would we have done had they come straight through? I don't know.

We are going along a series of steep hills that require the teams to be hitched together to climb up and then again to go down the other side or else they cannot make it up and they go down so swiftly that they run into the wagon in front or crash at the bottom. And they require shoulders to the wheel, with every man and most boys pushing or pulling at the wagons or at the horses. This is the hardest country we have gone over. I have never seen anything like the mountains ahead. Shadden ain't much help, but my boys pitch in as they can.

There was a second trial of Mr. Moss for not standing guard, but the jury could not agree and so nothing happened. Mr. Moss, a most disagreeable small man, has proven superior to all the organization that was put in place. Shadden said that at the meeting of the company, Captain Hastings and Mr. Lovejoy were reelected, to the great discomfort of Dr. White.

*

July 4: Waggon to repair. Wrote a few lines to my Parents. Started at noon had a very rough road. Came to water 6 ½ o'clock, traveled 11 miles.
—Medorem Crawford

CAROLINE TOMPKINS

Dan mentioned this morning before he went to water the horses that this is Independence Day. At home there would be speeches in the village square, and one of the ministers would offer a long prayer for our veterans. We would have little paper flags to wave and the children would be excited. There would be a parade along the streets and at night suppers in the public houses and bursts of fireworks. The newspaper would have an eagle on the masthead and would boast of what a singular country this is.

Out here we travel on. I wonder what editorial Dan will write for July 4 when we are in Oregon? He will surely attempt to draw the Americans in the Pacific Northwest close together to our common cause, yet not antagonize those who represent Canada or England—that is, until the border between the nations is settled. He seems, it appears to me, to be walking into his future.

DAN AND CAROLINE TOMPKINS

When Dan Tompkins came back to Caroline and settled into their blankets, he looked tired from the day, but not unhappy. Caroline turned to him and asked, "Do you think they mind?"

"Who?" he asked wondering what she had been thinking.

"The Indians—you know, the Sioux, the Crows, and Blackfeet. Whoever is out there on the land."

"Mind about what?" he asked, smiling to himself at the ways this woman he married so long ago could still surprise him.

"Our coming here," she answered quickly. "You know, going across their land."

"Well, why should they?" he answered slowly, wondering if he was about to tangle with one of what they called "Caroline's big questions." He could think of many times she had posed such issues to him, as if he had the answer or could right the wrong. He thought of their discussions of slavery, about which he agreed with her, and about the value of missionary work, about which he disagreed but had not pushed his point. And then there was women's education and voting. This woman he had married had become a complex individual, always challenging.

"Well, they were here first, weren't they?" she asked. "They live here," she said emphatically.

"So?"

"So, that makes this their land, doesn't it?"

"How could it be theirs?" he said. "They move about—they don't have houses as we do."

"But they have families," Caroline said. "They just move about with them."

"That hardly seems like ownership to me, Caroline, and I am a fair man."

"Of course you are a fair man. Who else would listen as I challenge things and who other than you would help me work out questions in my mind? You are my rock," she said, and then added laughingly, "my Independence Rock, Danby Tompkins." She paused, then added, "They don't own the land the way we do back home, with deeds and fences and law, but that doesn't mean it is not theirs."

"Well . . . ," and his voice trailed off. He wanted to sleep.

"They might well have their own ideas about these things."

"Caroline, they are savages. They are not even Christians."

"I know they don't have what we have, but what if they have something else?" She paused and added, "And I don't know about savages."

"They are not like us," he said, thinking it might be the end of the conversation, though his mind had been unsettled about Indians. He had thought some of these same things as he had ridden the horse across the land, but he enjoyed sparring with Caroline, and he was willing to hear her out. "But of course, we have a right to cross over the land. The Indians, well some of them, requested teaching, and we are bringing them education and religion," he paused, adding, "and government. Isn't that important?"

Caroline shifted her body a bit away from him. Then she turned and said, "Perhaps. But walking, I think of these things and think that there are many ways of living." She looked down and saw that Dan Tompkins, after his long day tending cattle, driving the wagon, and dealing with life on the trail, had gone to sleep.

*

July 5: Repaired the cart. Started at noon found good water at three o'clock, had some heavy hill to rise. Buffalo very scarce. Camped early good wood, water and grass, traviled 9 miles.
—Medorem Crawford

CAROLINE TOMPKINS AND MRS. GIRTMAN

"Your dress looks pleated, all spread out around you," said Caroline as she approached Mrs. Girtman, who was sitting on one of the few chairs to be found among the travelers.

"Cynthia likes to do that for me," she said simply. "She likes me to look like a picture when Mr. Girtman comes in for supper." Caroline thought that, for a well-spoken woman, Mrs. Girtman looked somewhat vague.

"You walk always with your daughter," Caroline observed.

"Oh yes. It's my eyes, you see. Everything is just cloudy, so Cynthia is my eyes. She tells me what the path ahead is like and where to step carefully. I have vision, but it is not acute."

"I am so sorry to hear that, Mrs. Girtman," said Caroline.

"She reads to me, too."

"I came over because I had observed you sitting with a book in your hand sometime earlier, to tell you that I have a copy of the *Odyssey*, the Boston printing of Cowper's translation. It was part of my grandfather's library, and he left the first two volumes to me."

"My sister," she added quickly, "got the *Iliad*."

"I will ask Cynthia if she will read some to me," said Mrs. Girtman, looking in Caroline's direction but not quite focusing on her features. She said with a chuckle, "We seem to be traveling with travelers who go into remote nations."

"And both men have trouble getting home."

"Yes," said Mrs. Girtman. Then, "Have you been enjoying *Gulliver*?"

"Yes," said Caroline with enthusiasm. "I read the first book about the Lilliput when I was in school, but I never read the rest. I thought there was a bit of authorial fiddling, in that part, that Gulliver got home at all."

"It is men having adventures that turn out all right in the end," said Mrs. Girtman.

"That is why we are here, isn't it? Men having their adventures." The women smiled, and Caroline handed over her copy of the *Odyssey* and turned to go. "I might be more fond of Odysseus than I am of Gulliver," she said.

"We will see," said Mrs. Girtman.

"I think you are a very brave woman to be making this trip," Caroline said as she turned to leave.

"My family is making it possible. They will get me through."

✷

July 6: Started at six drove on at a good pace until noon found a first rate camping place. Concluded to remain here today as there was no good chance ahead, traviled 12 miles.
—Medorem Crawford

WIDOW ABEL'S DIARY

Traveled over very rough ground today and went hours before finding a good place to camp. There has again been trouble. Captain Hastings heard Mr. Moss say that he was going out to find an Indian horse. That so alarmed the law-minded among us, including those who are led by Dr. W, that a trial was called. Moss was charged with interfering with the Indians and putting us all at risk. Moss argued that he could do what he wished and that he only said he was going after an Indian horse; he didn't do it, so he could not be punished for saying something that he didn't happen. That flummoxed the jury and nothing was done. Moss didn't go after a horse, however.

Baby is beginning to teethe.

*

July 8: Started at 8 o'clock had a very hilly road stopped for dinner at 12 o'clock on creek started at 4 camped on the Platte, good wood and water but short grass, traviled 15 miles.
—Medorem Crawford

MARY SMITH

It is rather nice to see Caroline Tompkins talking with Mrs. Girtman. They are about the same age and they were both schoolteachers. I understand from her daughter Cynthia that Mr. Girtman was once her student, "one of the older students," Cynthia had added. Pity about her eyes, Mrs. Girtman's, that is.

The area we have passed through, along the Platte valley, was teeming with wildlife. There appears to be an abundance here moving unchecked across the land. The buffalo of course are the most surprising, and yet, with all their power, they seem to spend their energy quickly and are soon overcome by the hunters, some of whom are even able to lead them close to camp before shooting them. There are the prairie dogs, small and quick and seemingly alert, with their heads up, and then they disappear into the ground. They are called dogs, my son John said, because they make a barking sound. They are comical to watch: always busy. I like the birds best, of course—the pigeons, plover, and marsh quails that run about the ground. Especially, though, I am always thrilled to see a great blue heron. They look folded up as they fly against the sky, and they land to stand upright in a stillness of their own. The jackrabbits always surprise me, jumping out of nowhere and then racing away.

I dislike the snakes. Are we humans always to fear the snake because of the Garden of Eden? Or is it because they slither, they coil, they strike, that they cause alarm? The wolves break into the quiet of the night, while the antelope are a delight to see as they spring up and away when we come near. The hunters for the most part do not try to take the antelope. The animals move so quickly that it takes a good deal of ammunition and energy to finally bag one.

*

July 9: Very cold, water in the pail froze ice like thick window glass. Started early raized a long hill detained by wagons breaking down 1 hour.
—Medorem Crawford

WIDOW ABEL'S DIARY

Baby can walk, holding my hands. I can see this is a blessing and then not so much of one. Her independence means I need to be more watchful that she does not do something that might be harmful.

The men held a second trial of Mr. Moss for not standing guard. The men sat and talked among themselves, Mr. M. refused to attend, and in the end the council decided it could not agree on a suitable punishment—that is, one that they could carry out. Mr. M., funny little man that he is, seems to have bested them and I suppose will do as he pleases from here on. We walked for five hours today, saw some buffalo. Our hunter killed one.

*

July 10: Started at 7 very heavy west wind yesterday & today.
—Medorem Crawford

MARY SMITH'S THOUGHTS WHILE WALKING

As we traveled out from Elm Grove, I have come to realize how important it is that we work together. None of us could do this trip alone. We need the talents and strength of all of us: some can hunt, some tend the livestock going with us, some provide leadership—well, that has proved to be a problem; others cooperate to get us across rivers and over the hard spots. Gabriel Brown fixes the harnesses when they come loose, and when someone gets cut or sick, Dr. White brings his medicine kit and does what he can. At the moment we are all healthy and moving forward. This country is no place a person or a family can go it alone.

Probably no place is, to think on it. At home, that is, back in New York State, we had schools we all paid for so our children could learn to read; we all paid for bridges and pitched in for road maintenance. Back east, families might think of themselves as being self-sufficient, but we never were. Not in fact. We depended on each other.

Mr. Moss puts all of us at risk. It is a wonder he doesn't understand that. And truth be told, Susannah and Lorenzo do a lot to keep him going, even without his acknowledging it.

*

July 11: Started at 8, left the Platte & Black Hills traveled miles over hilly roads & camped in sight of the Red Buttes good water and grass but no wood. Cool wind.
—Medorem Crawford

TOMPKINS FAMILY OBSERVATION

Yesterday we crossed to the North Branch of the Platte River. Some men went out and tested the riverbed, finding quicksand along the way. They decided that to cross the river safely, they would link the wagons together, have the women and children ride on the top, and have the strong team that belongs to Gabriel Brown lead the way. The river is about three-quarters of a mile wide, but Mr. Brown brought us safely across by going a bit upstream, then downstream, and then upstream again, zigzagging to use the faster currents to aid us across. It took a long time, but we came through safely. We camped on the other side to let the animals rest. I rode near the end of the line of wagons and could see how Mr. Brown tested the way forward with a long stick, looking for the safest way.

Today we left at 8:00 a.m., leaving behind the North Branch of the Platte River. We went over hills and camped in sight of the Red Buttes, which are very different from the green, fertile Platte River valley. Here the ground has spots of alkali and sand. There is good water and grass for the cattle, but we had difficulty finding wood for the campfires.

*

July 12: Crossed some very Rocky Hills said to be the commencement of the Mountains. Stopped for dinner 2 hours. Camped in a little valley surrounded with bushes grass good & first rate water and wood. Traveled 16 miles.
—Medorem Crawford

Susannah Couch to Lorenzo

"I was sorry to leave the river, as it seemed to give us direction as we followed along it. And there were interesting plants to collect that grew near the water's edge. Now we head across the land as if at random."

Lorenzo looked at her. "Captain Fitzpatrick is here to lead us," he said. "He knows the way and gives me confidence," adding carefully, "more so than Dr. White or Hastings, who both seem like bluffers to me."

They smiled into each other's eyes.

*

July 13: Verry cold, water in a pail froze ice like thick window glass. Started early raized a long hill detained by wagons breaking down. 1 hour.
—Medorem Crawford

Caroline Tompkins While Walking

I have never seen such a quick contrast. Everything was green and soft along the Platte River. Then, a mile or so off, we crossed along a path that is sandy, without a particle of grass but spotted with a white substance looking like salt. Alkali. And there are some magenta spots too.

The day also veered from very cold in the morning, with water frozen in a bucket, to very warm during the day. One minute I needed my wool shawl and the next I put it away and opened the top button of my dress to get air.

All this is like the contrasts in *Gulliver* and those between my daughters: two rather nice young women, though conventional, like me, and then Ellen, all angles and curiosity.

*

July 13: Stopped for late dinner on very warm road level and sandy not a particle of grass, passed beds of white substance partaking of the nature of salt and magnetia. Camped at sunset on Sweet Water, traviled 20 m.
—Medorem Crawford

MARY SMITH WHILE WALKING

Men make their own trouble. We camped at the Sweetwater, and ahead is Independence Rock. I learned what was going on when Ellen came running to tell me that a party of our men decided to carve their initials high up on the rock, leaving the rest of us to make camp. They went off, about twelve of them, wrote their names, and returned. All but Captain Hastings and Mr. Lovejoy, who wanted to put their names higher than the rest and were trapped on the rock by a large party of Sioux Indians.

Ellen and I went to the edge of the camp, where others were trying to see what was happening. Mr. Tompkins said that the Sioux had been there at least two hours and that Mr. Fitzpatrick was headed over on a fast horse to see what he could do to save them. We could not see much except for some motion on an edge of the rock; no one could tell exactly what was happening. Susannah Couch came over to ask if we had seen Lorenzo, but we could not assure her we had, as we had just arrived. Then Caroline Tompkins arrived with her daughters and Cynthia Girtman.

Dr. White tried to get everyone to organize guns and told the women to take the children into the wagons, as if he were the captain again, with Hastings and Lovejoy held hostage and Fitzpatrick on his way. White almost looked pleased about the situation, although of course he could not have been, for an attack on our men means trouble. We were all frightened but could do nothing and see little from this distance, excepting for Mr. Fitzpatrick as he rode away from us toward Independence Rock.

Then Lorenzo Couch appeared from the side of the camp and Susannah made a great ado about his engaging in such a dangerous sport. He assured her he had not been with the party that went off, although it seems that Ned Tompkins had gone, as had the Bennett boys, Vardemon and another of the older ones.

We watched as Mr. Fitzpatrick began to climb the rock but couldn't see much but movement along the side. Then he disappeared on the ledge and all we could do was wait.

TOMPKINS FAMILY OBSERVATION

Now I really have something to report! What I mean is something that has happened that is History—with a clear beginning, middle, and end—rather than something I have put together to make up the number of pages that Mother requires.

It took several hours, but finally the Sioux up on Independence Rock seemed to flow down the rock to the land below. They were joined by many other Indians on horseback who came in from the plains. There was a lot of activity, then men on horses galloped toward us, creating a giant cloud of dust. Women retreated back inside the circle and hid the children in the wagons. Some of the men got out guns. Mother, Jane, Mrs. Smith, and I stood behind a wagon and watched as the cloud created by the horses got bigger. Then from out of the dust, quite suddenly, Indians appeared, with Mr. Fitzpatrick at the front. Both Captain Hastings and Mr. Lovejoy were near him on Indian horses, their hands tied with a rope, each man with an Indian who led them forward. These were not like any Indians we had seen before, their faces carefully painted, each holding a bow or a spear.

They galloped forward, and just as I thought they might run right up and into the camp they stopped before the first wagon. There was a sudden quiet with us looking at them and they, I suppose, looking at us. Mr. Fitzpatrick spoke, first in English and then in word-gestures that the Indians understood, as there was a good deal of nodding of heads, a universal language of points and grunts used by men in the West.

I can't remember all he said when he talked English, but he admitted that Captain Hastings and Mr. Lovejoy had gone onto a Sioux sacred place. The two men looked battered; Mr. Lovejoy was bleeding from around his ear and holding his arm carefully, as if it were damaged. Captain Hastings was beaten around the face and head.

Mr. Fitzpatrick began to speak again, to us this time, explaining that the Sioux were willing to exchange our two men for some ammunition. He said the Sioux were on the warpath against some other Indians, and he called for Mr. Smith and others of the company council to bring out some bullets and two guns. Old Mr. Smith at first looked confused, but then he ordered Mr. Moss to get his gun and asked Mr. Brown to get one of his. At first Mr. Moss looked as if he were going to refuse, but Susannah Couch looked hard at him, and he went into his wagon and got that old gun of his. Mr. Brown did the same. They gave the guns to Mr. Smith, who took them forward.

Mr. Smith is pretty old and must have looked as if was our leader, just as the leader of the Sioux looked old to me, worn but alert. Mr. Smith handed over the weapons, and the two hostages were pushed from their horses. Free, they scurried over to our side, each sobbing, not having known until then if they had been condemned to life or death. At that point, something totally startling happened because Jane, my sister Jane, seeing that the men were alive and free and running to the wagons, began to sing a hymn of praise and suddenly there was silence. Her voice carried out across the empty land and everyone paid attention.

Then it was over. The Sioux turned and rode slowly away.

It is all rather like what Mother said about *Gulliver*. Full of contrasts!

*

July 17: Calling on us & receiving some ammunition[,] they left & traveled up the River. We stay to make meat. Very warm. Several men gone hunting. Very difficult to get meat.
—Medorem Crawford

Widow Abel's Diary

The details come out slowly and piece by piece. Mr. Perry told my sister and me that Mr. Fitzpatrick got there—to the Independence Rock—just in time. The Sioux had forced the captain and Mr. Lovejoy to sit motionless on the ground for several hours while the Indians filed by and hit them with sticks or arrows, and even kicked and punched them. A big chief had somewhat shielded Captain Hastings from the abuse he would have gotten, but Mr. Lovejoy was severely beaten and it took Dr. White some time to clean his wounds and set his arm with a slat of wood to keep it straight.

What I noticed, but no one talked about, was how naked the Indians were. Their faces were painted with black and orange marks and some had paint on their chests, but they had no clothing except over their manly parts and a blanket over their shoulders. And perhaps skin shoes or boots, I don't remember exactly, but they had something on their feet. Exposed to view were their most splendid chests and shoulders, although I have not seen many men's chests. I was rather startled, and I wonder what Mrs. Tompkins thought with her young daughters standing there. Or what they thought.

Then, Jane, the one who stutters, absolutely stunned all of us when she began to sing, and even the Sioux were surprised and silent. Can you imagine anything like that?

And then it was over.

*

July 18: We reluctantly remained here today. Several gone hunting slight shower of rain. Considerable of meat brought in today.
—Medorem Crawford

MRS. SHADDEN'S THOUGHTS

We thought it was over, the Sioux coming with Captain Hastings and Mr. Lovejoy and returning them to us. But it wasn't. I don't know the whole story, but what Widow Abel told me is that Mr. Trask, who came in to join the company just a couple of days ago after we left those two small forts, said that it wasn't likely to be over. Not just like that. And it wasn't. There is a large company of Sioux camped nearby, maybe a thousand. No one could count them. We saw only the men, as the women and children hid away from us—as if we would do them any harm.

After releasing the hostages and retreating, for several days small parties of Indians would charge up to our wagons, wave their arrows and spears, and then race back away like little boys daring each other to be the bravest. We don't know what they meant, but they charged one side of the camp and then another, and so no one went outside the wagon circle except to see to the cattle. Some of our party brought their cows right up next to their wagons. A shot went off from inside the camp that grazed the arm of that little Bennett girl.

Mr. Trask said to Widow Abel that we should watch carefully and stick close to camp for a day or two. Hunters went out and brought back some meat. We cured it on sticks over low fires so that we would have food farther on. But we were unsettled, the wagons curled together, the children kept close, and guards set day and night, everyone feeling rather nervy.

Then the Sioux appeared again, riding up in a cloud of dust that fell from them when they came to an abrupt stop, as if they themselves stepped from the invisible to the visible in all of a minute. One moment, they were not there; the next they were, sitting silently on their horses looking into camp.

There were so many Indians that we stood as if frozen as they dismounted and walked about the camp, in and out among the wagons and tents, picking up items and putting them down, measuring the cattle with their hands, touching the horses to see how strong they were. They put fingers in pots and stared at the women and children. They stuck their heads so often in and out of Mr. Tompkins's wagon that he went off to complain to Mr. Matthieu to see if he could do something because the Indians were frightening his wife and daughters.

Matthieu is one of the French Canadians who joined us at Fort Laramie. He moved slowly and spoke to the leader, and everyone became silent. Mr. Matthieu didn't look happy about the way the conversation was going. His body was seeming to say no even while he kept up the palaver.

Finally, Mr. Matthieu turned from the Sioux and walked slowly to the wagon of the Tompkins family. He called out the father, the man named Dan, and with him came his son, Ned. The three stood in the center and talked low so no one could hear, but no one looked happy. I asked Shadden what was going on, but he didn't know.

Susannah Couch

I asked Lorenzo to go over to hear what was going on. He wasn't sure he should show himself, but we needed to know what the Sioux wanted so he went.

Seems on this visit, there were fewer Indians who came, and they brought along a string of horses. Several men from our camp went out hunting and then we moved farther down the Sweetwater.

TOMPKINS FAMILY OBSERVATION

The Indians were here to buy Jane! *Our* Jane!

They wanted to buy Jane as a bride for a great chief. Mr. Matthieu explained carefully to Father, all the while saying, "Do not react, sir, do not do anything to insult these people," holding his arm to steady him, saying, "Softly, sir, softly." We were not to annoy the Indians lest we have the whole band down upon us. Father grew white, and then red, and he tried to move about even while Matthieu held him steady. Matthieu turned to the clutch of Indian men standing at the tent to explain to them that white people, Christian people, American people, didn't sell their daughters—something that seemed to baffle the Indians.

The Sioux pointed out that that was not true. White men who came into the mountains bought Indian women all the time, with pelts and copper pots and even guns. They make families with Indian women. Why shouldn't the Indians do the same?

Why not indeed? Well, there is the question.

CAROLINE TOMPKINS

Mr. Matthieu saw the shock on our faces as he told us what the Sioux wanted. He explained that there was a great chief among them right now and that the gift of the White Girl Who Sings would be highly esteemed. They offered twenty horses for her. Matthieu looked pained as he explained all this to Dan and me—and to Jane, who was standing behind me—while saying to the Sioux at the same time that it was not possible.

Then, like Solomon, Mr. Matthieu attempted to find a way out—without dividing Jane in half of course. He looked at us and knew we could not agree to such a thing, and he looked at the Sioux and suggested calmly and with a certain assurance that perhaps they would like to be sung to themselves by the White Girl Who Sings. There was a pause and then the Indians sat down and looked up at Jane, expecting her to start. Which she did. She sang a new song she had learned just before leaving Ithaca, called "Swing Low, Sweet Chariot," and by the time she had finished our family was in quiet tears and the faces of the Sioux sitting before us were calm and sweet—if *sweet* is a word that can be used with men whose faces were painted and who planned to buy your daughter.

Then Jane sang "Auld Lang Syne," and Mr. Matthieu, reaching out, picked up a container of salt and offered it to the Sioux. They, moved by the singing and the solemnity of the moment, accepted the gift, rose, and left the circled wagons.

The whole time, I held in my breath and only let it out as the Indians moved away. I looked with great pride at Jane, who had calmed the day. We thanked Mr. Matthieu for his intervention. "What would we have done without you?" Dan asked in amazement. "What would we have done?"

Matthieu bowed slightly and smiled. "There is always a way, somehow, but your daughter saved herself." And we all looked at Jane, who seemed amazed at what had happened: she is our wallflower, she, the stutterer, she is the middle daughter, a pale copy of her more beautiful sister, and nothing like her younger sister. She looked around and said, "I was not afraid, Father. I knew you would never let me go." Then she looked up and said, "Twenty horses isn't a bad an offer, is it?" She didn't stutter once while she said that. Then she left the tent to go tell Martha all that had happened.

The Indians came back that evening, perhaps not the same ones, as we couldn't really tell, but others perhaps, looking for liquor of which there was none, we insisted, until a Shadden boy said loudly that Mr. Moss had some and so Moss was made to give up two bottles of his supply. Everyone wondered how much more he might have.

We will travel on in the morning.

*

*July 19: Started at 7 o'clock, followed up the Sweet Water, tremendous
Rocky Mountains on each side. Camped at 12 o'clock, good grass, water
and wood, traviled 7 miles.*
—Medorem Crawford

MARY SMITH

I heard about the Tompkins girl! That was something. John worried when he
heard about Mr. Moss. Was he going to be aggrieved that he had lost a gun,
an old one that didn't seem to work well anyway, and some of his cache of
liquor? Would he now have another grudge against the company or was his
debt paid? Were we all even? John wondered.

And twenty horses! That was quite an offer, even if it was never to be
considered. But we have seen the importance of horses to these people, how
they travel about on them and how they pull their houses along, and how well
trained the horses are to react to the Indians' wishes. Some in the company
traded their own horses with the Sioux to get fresh ones, and the Sioux tried
to steal some horses from two of our hunters out looking for more meat,
which caused Mother Bennett to race about shouting that the Indians had
taken her son Weston, and we had to raise a party to get him back. We hadn't
known his name was Weston.

Twenty horses indeed; perhaps that will give Jane something to be proud of.
We traveled twenty miles and camped along the Sweetwater.

MRS. SHADDEN'S COMMENT

They wanted Jane? She's not the pretty one, Martha is. Why would they
want Jane?

The answer: Jane is the one who sings.

*

July 21: Stay here all this day Brown lost a horse leg broke by a kick. Indians came back before noon a few came near camp & told many different stories. We observed they had more horses than when they went up. 280 were counted in their Party. They passed quietly by and said they were going home. Extremely warm.
—Medorem Crawford

TOMPKINS FAMILY OBSERVATION

Since the "great event," we have had many Indian parties come to sit with us at our campfire expecting to smoke with the men or perhaps they came for more liquor, but Mr. Moss has not offered any. Medorem Crawford explained to me that Mr. Matthieu had smoked the peace pipe with the Sioux and mostly they were the ones who came to visit us. But out there on the prairie there are also Cheyennes, who have come to fight the Shoshones or Snake Indians; there seem to be small war parties everywhere. Mr. Matthieu negotiated with the Sioux over Jane because Mr. Fitzpatrick did not want to be seen by the Indians, with whom he has lived. He didn't want to be known for bringing white families into their country. He seems to have a family or perhaps several families among them.

I walked with Mr. Matthieu for a time yesterday. He thought I should not walk alone because the Indians were still interested in having a white woman, and while I am still young, I could be taken if I am not careful. Mr. Matthieu said he was from Canada, where as a young man he had participated in a revolt against the English government and he was sentenced to hang for treason. A friend warned him to leave the country and not return. So now he is going west to join a community of Canadians at Champoeg in the Oregon Territory.

I have to listen to him very carefully in order to understand his words. His real language is French and some Indian, and both can be heard as he speaks English words with funny inflections that come from his past, he says, from his origins in other places, he explained rather mysteriously. His eyes sparkled as he asked what I am taking with me. I could not answer that because we are not there yet and because I don't really know. I have felt until now that I am casting off some things I don't like, but I never thought about what I was taking with me. Well, my family of course, and the dog, but Mr. Matthieu was talking about in my speech and thoughts. That's interesting isn't it? What am I taking from Ithaca or from the United States or from the time I was young? Mr. Matthieu sees us as a process of accumulation—he said that word making it sound like *ackcumlassasion*, or however he did it in his Canadian accent.

*

July 22: Started at 7, traviled on at a good pace until 10 met a party of Shian [Cheyenne] Indians. Camped within two miles of their Village, about noon the Chiefs together with some hundreds of others came to camp. We made them presents of ammunition, tobaco &c. and smoked with them. Started after dinner passed their village which consisted of several hundred lodges. Several Indians accompanied us to camp. Mr. Fitzpatrick judged they were in the villages of Crows, Shians, & Sues [Sioux] between 4 & 5000. Many of our Company traded horses with them. Camped near sun set on Sweet Water, traviled 15 m.
—Medorem Crawford

MARY SMITH WALKING

The nights are astonishingly cold. I was not prepared for such a fluctuation of the weather. Hot days and cold nights. We piled some coats on us, but Mr. Smith and I are old and had trouble getting warm enough to sleep well. The days, on the other hand, are hot, and we have to protect ourselves from the sun. I made a peak for my cap and wear it pulled down over my face, like a beak, so that in the afternoon the sun does not blind me. Otherwise, facing the sun all afternoon gives all of us headaches. We keep our heads covered and face in front of us—not looking out to the distance but somehow down, into a middle space above the ground but not into the sun. That is one big difference between here and home.

I don't think of home often. My family is my home; like a turtle I carry my home on my back. We had a nice house back there: a large farmhouse, barn, a small cottage where John and I lived, cows, and fields stretching out so we could see Lake Erie—and the storms that came in from the lake. And sunsets.

It was a lovely place to be, but now home is on the trail, with my husband, my son and his family, and these other people I am getting to know. In the end, home will be wherever we settle on the land.

The Indians have surprised me. Not their wanting Jane, although that was surprising, but their very presence. I always thought of Indians as away, as being elsewhere, doing their Indian things, as enemies and as helpers, perhaps. But when a group of Sioux rode up to our camp at a fierce speed, then stopped short and dismounted, they were not only individuals on the piece of land I am calling home at the moment, but they were a very physical presence.

We are not supposed to notice that they are naked! We women that is. Well, not totally naked, but from their hips to their necks they wear nothing but some painted designs; their chests gleam in the sunlight, which seems to bounce off them, making them appear like gods, each with his own aura. I never saw such shoulders, arms, legs, and hands. They have robes thrown around the lower parts of their bodies and they move gracefully. They startle me as I wrestle with a long skirt and long sleeves and a bonnet to shield my eyes, yet I could not go as they. Their skin is so bronzed, so gleaming. I can also see the scars they bear, the ones they make on their skin for whatever purpose and the scars of wounds they have borne. I am very conscious of their nakedness—and I am an old married woman. I wonder what young Widow Abel thinks, or her sister, or Ellen and her sisters. Or what Caroline Tompkins thinks as she sees her daughters look at these men who appear among us, arrogantly walking about—and even wanting to take Jane away with them as a bride for a great chief. What do the younger women think of all this, I wonder.

I know it is something we will never discuss; it is too private to be said aloud or to one another. I would be ashamed to speak of it, embarrassed to think that others knew I had thoughts about nakedness—or even noticed it. So we ignore it, all of us.

Do the married women mentally compare these gleaming beings, albeit without our religion and learning and ideas, to their own husbands? Might those husbands look a bit paunchy and pale to them? Well, probably not Susannah, for that Lorenzo is bronzed, in his own way. But the others: what do they think and why could we not talk about it? Well, of course we could not; it is too private and somehow it is—it is sacrilegious, shameful to even acknowledge it. Yet Jesus is often shown in the same clothing on the cross—without the paint, of course, but He has blood marks on Him. Can we compare these nonbelievers to Him?

All I know is that these young bronzed warriors who frighten us with their sudden appearances and their needs—and their ignorance of who we are and of our ways—fascinate me and stir something in me. Is it their wildness, or their ways, so different from our own, or might it be because many of these young men are marked by life that we know cannot last because this country is ours—or will be? What pleases me is that the older men among the Sioux have great dignity and respect. They are not considered fools or useless because of their age.

People here respect Mr. Smith, but I am sure not one of them would see him as a leader in battle. He is more a wise counselor or someone who speaks with caution and perhaps wisdom. But he could never lead them on a hunting party or on a war party as these older Sioux do. I suspect that, mostly, Mr. Smith is respected by the rest of the members of this company because he is quiet, offers opinions only when asked, and keeps to himself for the most part. They don't know he is nursing his wounds, not wanting to be here at all, resenting being bothered by our yearnings for something different.

We are such complicated beings.

We traveled early today over a long rocky hill and camped at noon. We ate our dinner. When we got ready to start up again, a wagon broke down and we had to remain overnight while the men pulled the axel apart. We traveled ten miles today, some of it in a hard rain, but I walked a long while too.

*

July 28: Started 7 o'clock left Sweet Water crossed the dividing ridge. Camped at 10 o'clock on a little stream running westward, traveled 6 miles. Left the cart here, one wagon left. Snowy mountains constantly in sight.
—Medorem Crawford

Caroline Tompkins

Ahead of us today is a long stretch where there will be no water or game; the land is covered with wild sage. We hope to get to a place called Little Sandy Creek that empties into the Green River. Another landmark. But we climb steadily up now, through this dip called South Pass, and are grateful for it because all around the mountains tower above us and the thought of crossing them is daunting. My legs are now used to walking, even walking uphill, and while I could not have contemplated doing this when at home, I see that putting one foot ahead of the other will get me over this hump.

Last night we camped on the Sweetwater. Ellen tasted the water to see if it was sweet and she said it tasted regular, but the name softens the area and makes it friendly and welcoming. Mr. Fitzpatrick said some trappers had spilled a bag of sugar in the water—or was it people with the great expedition of Lewis and Clark? Were they the ones who sweetened this place? I don't remember. But afterward it was called Sweetwater. Surely, that is not what the Sioux call it; they must have their own name, and do the Cheyennes call it Sweetwater or have they a different name for it, and what about the Shoshones? Possibly all the Indians in the area have a common name for landmarks so they can meet up, but they might also have names in their own language, too.

Yet, here we come along and call it Sweetwater, and the Sioux—I don't know about the others—the Sioux know what we are talking about and they do not laugh at the white people who call it Sweetwater. They must know it as something named by ancient peoples generations ago. Do they call it that still? A horse might have died nearby and they could have called it Dead Horse Creek or something like that. Would we still enjoy being camped here if the name were different? Names. I think they tell us something about the thing or place well before we get there to see for ourselves.

However, Sweetwater fits this place. We camped along the stream that was flowing westward: going in our direction, to the west. I found this a signal that we were heading in the right direction and that the land is moving forward with us. Until now we have been pushing, it seems to me, pushing upward and westward and away. Now, we are going toward—although still upward. I wonder if that makes sense.

We left a cart here at the Sweetwater. It was in such bad shape there was no fixing it, and it caused more trouble than it was worth. The men, those Germans who had been using it to take equipment west, made packs and have tied their tools to the mules and on their own backs. They pulled off useful parts to carry along.

There are snowy mountains constantly in sight ahead of us. I do not enjoy the cold nights. I keep my high socks on and sleep close to Dan, sometimes with one of the girls on my other side so we make a cocoon. We do not emerge as butterflies in the morning, however, but slightly cranky from the rough ground, from being cold during the night, missing our nice bed linens and goose down pillows left at home.

I have changed: I look at the landscape instead of simply passing through it. I see the small hurdles, the rough pathway, the stones, even the pebbles that sometimes slip us up or cause me to slide. I see the trees as places to rest from the sun and the rivers as places to find water and to wash. I sense that I am using the land rather than living upon it, and I know myself to be changed by this journey. We head into the West.

*

July 30: Started early stopped on the creek for dinner 2 hours. Camped near sun set on Big Sandy Creek traviled 20 miles.
—Medorem Crawford

WIDOW ABEL'S DIARY

We traveled twenty miles today, up and over the South Pass. I stood and looked ahead at what we face and back at what we have left behind. The view startles me with its beauty, but I know that beauty can also be cruel. It is just as hard to make a living in beauty as it is where the land is plain. Perhaps even harder. We reached the Big Sandy and face a desert crossing to the Green River.

I dread crossing the land ahead, and, with no water, how can this land ever be used? To be useful to us? We need water to survive, water for crops and animals, and if one person found water, I think others would fight to have a share. Perhaps we are not supposed to be here in this quiet, dry land.

Baby walked some of the way, and then I carried her tight against my breast. As I was walking along, that new man, one of those who joined from the camps back near Fort Laramy, came up and offered to put Baby on his shoulders. I backed away, but he put out his arms to take Baby and she reached out to him, totally unafraid of this stranger. So I walked for a time freely, without a bucket in my hand, or Baby, or any other thing, and I felt my gait shift. I swung my arms and my legs moved easily, my back loose. I moved my shoulders back and forth and felt the muscles ease.

Baby is getting heavier to manage and she wiggles, so I have to keep her tight. But there she was, sitting on that man's shoulders, astride his neck, her back erect, looking forward, holding tightly to his hair. He even reached up and pulled her bonnet down to shade her eyes. When she bounced, he didn't seem to mind but played horse for her for a time. Then he saw that the Germans were having some trouble keeping a pack together on a mule, and he handed Baby back to me and went over to help.

That's a nice man, despite his ragged-looking clothes and his bushy eyebrows that seem to shield his eyes as my bonnet does mine. He doesn't speak much, though. A quiet man lost in his own thoughts, as we all seem to be.

Sister has grown quieter as we have moved west and her belly has enlarged. She seems to be delving into herself for when her time comes. She dreads this, I know, for she left two unborn babies back home. As she walks she pats her belly, and I believe she talks to the baby inside. That Mrs. Smith always seems lost in thought unless she is with the youngest Tompkins girl, in which case they chatter away. Whatever do those two have to talk about?

And Caroline Tompkins, she thinks I don't know, but she talks to herself—and out loud. I can see her lips moving and her head nodding. It was her head, actually, that gave her away. I saw it bobbing up and down, not to the rhythm of her walk but as her lips moved. We all have developed our own walking rhythm. I saw her speaking and realized that she was talking aloud to herself as there was no one else around. Her head moved to the rhythm of her words as if agreeing with herself.

I came across her one day as she moved out from behind her wagon. Her words didn't make any sense to me, but her head bobbed along with the words as her legs moved to their own perambulating gate. She borrowed Mrs. Girtman's copy of *Gulliver*, so I know she is a learned woman. Susannah is heading my way; she is good with Baby too, though she seems very young to have experience with children.

*

July 31: Sunday. Rainy morning Started 7. Commenced raining verry cold & unpleasant. Considerable decending ground. Camped on the creek at 3 o'clock traveled 15 miles. Much talk about dividing the company at Green River.
—Medorem Crawford

Susannah Couch and the Widow Abel

SUSANNAH: Morning, Miz Abel.

WIDOW ABEL: Morning, Susannah. Where there is a Little Sandy, there is bound to be a Big Sandy, isn't there?

SUSANNAH: And then the Green River, but that is a ways off and no water between. Will the water be green, do you think?

WIDOW ABEL: The ground descends, isn't that pleasant? Not to be walking uphill all day long.

SUSANNAH: Just so it is not too steep to keep a foothold.

WIDOW ABEL: Just so the rain is not too cold and unpleasant.

SUSANNAH: I sought you out today because your sister is soon due.

WIDOW ABEL: Yes; soon, I think. The baby seems to have dropped.

SUSANNAH: I do not want to put myself forward, Miz Abel, or to intrude, and I know you yourself have a child, so you are not new to birthing, but I have some experience, if that could be useful in the days to come, though I fear too much boldness in speaking.

WIDOW ABEL: You? But you are so young. Have you a child yourself?

SUSANNAH: No. I am childless yet. But my auntie was an herbalist back in Virginia, where we come from, and she taught me. She taught me many things, and she said I was a natural healer.

WIDOW ABEL: I have seen you collecting plants along the way. Alongside the road and near the riverbank.

SUSANNAH: Yes. I have some experience with plants, too.

WIDOW ABEL: Mrs. Shadden said you cured her youngest—and Mr. Shadden too when they had the diarrhea.

SUSANNAH: Yes, though the diarrhea might have simply run its course. Still, I like to help when I can.

WIDOW ABEL: It is a gift. When I had Baby, a midwife came and stanched the bleeding and got Baby breathing when she was reluctant to.

SUSANNAH: I have helped at births. Were you expecting Dr. White to tend your sister?

WIDOW ABEL: Sister thought it lucky to have a doctor in the company, though he could do nothing to help that Lancaster baby, or Bailey, either.

SUSANNAH: But he is handy bandaging wounds . . .

WIDOW ABEL: But you are the one that healed old Mr. Moss, aren't you, when he sliced down his arm and had all that skin hanging off? I saw that. What did you use?

SUSANNAH: Mostly slippery elm, but some other things to stanch the blood flow.

WIDOW ABEL: Would you come when it is time?

SUSANNAH: Certainly.

WIDOW ABEL: Only if Sister agrees, of course. I can't say for her who she would have, but I would rather have you than Dr. White.

SUSANNAH: Just alert me when the pain begins. I will have my kit ready.

WIDOW ABEL: And if she doesn't want you? What if she wants Dr. White?

SUSANNAH: No harm done. But you can call if you need me.
Lorenzo will take a message back to me. Just you locate him. He
doesn't talk much to others, but he will let me know as fast as he
can get back to me.
WIDOW ABEL: Thank you. So how old are you, anyway, Susannah?
SUSANNAH: Seventeen. I am an old soul, that's what Lorenzo says, an
old soul.

*

*August 1: Monday started at 7. Commenced raining soon rained moder-
ately crossed Green River and camped 11 o'clock traveled 6 miles. Some of
the company preparing to pack from here rainy afternoon and evening.*
—Medorem Crawford

TOMPKINS FAMILY OBSERVATION

I am trying to write about where we are, but other things get in the way. I
mean, the McKay boys and I saw an Indian burial in a tree and we watched
some buzzards swoop around, but they didn't land. One of the McKays said
that was because it was an old burial and the bones had already been picked
clean. We were off a ways from the company, so I didn't tell Mother because
I was supposed to stay close by, but I felt safe with the McKays as they always
seem to know what to do and have interesting things to talk about. I write
about that—even though Mother will know about being out of range—but I
don't think she is reading this Observation each night because she is so tired
she falls right to sleep.

This leads me to wonder about this Observation. Mother said I was to
write what I see during the day. I make a list of things in my head to add to
this history of the Tompkins Family going west. I know Mother thought of
this as a way to keep me writing, and at first I really resented doing it, but it
has become habit now. I keep at it not because Mother said to but because
I see all sorts of interesting things. I don't write everything I see, of course,
because I could not do that: everything is too much and some things are just
too boring to be included. Some are probably interesting, or would be to
other people, but not to me, and some things are too complicated to explain.

Martha, were she keeping this account, would write that Widow Abel's sister is getting near her time to deliver a baby, but that doesn't much interest me, excepting that I would be interested in seeing how it happens. One person would write one group of things and another person would write different things and both of those could be a true account of what is happening on this overland journey. If you read Mr. Crawford's account, as I do when I see him, it is all about the land covered and campgrounds and the weather. That is all interesting, but those are not the things I want to write about. I would like to write about the ospreys we see overhead and their messy nests that Mrs. Smith points out. When I think over my list of things to write about, however, I have other things to comment on. Different people have their own ways of recording this trip, and theirs are not mine.

Right now I am interested in the fact that there is again dissent, and even though I am not part of it, everyone can feel the tension in the air. Some of the company think we are traveling too slowly and want to leave their carts and wagons behind and pack everything they can on their backs to move forward. Others want to keep the wagons going, even though some have been cut down into carts.

It is not the wagons that are the interesting thing but the fact that if the company divides, the family groups will be left behind and the single men will go forward. Not only do they protect us, they also provide us with food as we move along, so a division affects all of us. The problem, of course, is between Dr. White and Mr. Hastings, so Mr. Crawford says. Each wants to rule, and neither one will be ruled by the other. Both, says Mother, are scamps.

If they go ahead and divide, will we be all right? Captain Fitzpatrick said he would take us to Fort Hall and that from there on the Indians are peaceful and would not harm us, though they would charge us for fish and food. I think Father still has money left, although I don't know how much and didn't know how much he had to begin with. Money is not the concern of children, he said to me when I tried to ask, even though I wanted to know for the Observation.

✳

August 2: Cold wet morning some making pack saddles and others repairing
their wagons determined to take them through.
—Medorem Crawford

WIDOW ABEL'S DIARY

His name is Elbridge. Elbridge Trask—such a formal name for such an unruly looking man. His clothing seems to have been put together with whatever came to hand, and his hair is unkempt. A trapper, he was, living by his wits in the wilderness. He said today that trapping was over, the pelts gone, the market for them finished. He said that when he saw our company, with women and children, he knew that the ways of the trappers were over. It was like one era passing another, he said, but he also added that the West was trapped out anyway.

He is looking to settle someplace in Oregon and have his go at being steady. An odd thing for a man to say. Though he is all messy looking and shabby, he is calm with Baby, and she goes to him happily to be bounced and held high on his shoulders. He seems comfortable with her too, as if he is trying out something new for himself that he finds he likes.

Frederick was a steady man. Settled from the start on land in Indiana, in a small house in the village where he worked as a tailor for himself. Men came to him for coats and vests. He had a good business and we had no real wants. But the steadiness must have been a sham, a cover for something deeper in him that churned and churned, so that one day he went out to the barn and hanged himself. How could he do that?

How could he just go out and do that?

How could he cut cloth one day for the minister's new coat and minutes later go into the barn to hang himself? Why did he do that? Was he crazy? Never a word to me about things not being right; never to anyone else, either.

He just went and did it.

Having a dead husband is not so unexpected, though Frederick was only thirty-six. Still, there were many widows who lived around us. That is a final thing and sad. It can be lived with. But I have a husband dead because he rejected me and he rejected life—or both. It is so unresolved a feeling. There was never a word of explanation, of compassion, and people know. Everyone in our village knew. The newspaper said that "Tailor Able suicided." People talked about it but not to me. They looked at me and didn't know what to say. I am sorry for your loss, they murmured to me, but they don't understand what I lost—and I didn't lose him like a pair of sewing shears; he lost himself somewhere in the midst of what I thought was a normal way to live, and me with a baby coming on. What I lost was my life, or what I had always thought would be my life—the two of us marrying, earning a living, setting up a house, digging a garden, having a baby, maybe more than one. Making a family is what I thought I was on this earth for, and he took all that away.

I was glad when Susan and Mr. Perry decided to go to Oregon and insisted I go with them, they making the choice for me. They thought they were taking me away from the horror that Frederick has left in my mind; they thought I would find a new life in Oregon. I protested but not so much about making the trip because, in truth, I didn't care it if was easy or dangerous, if we made it or we died trying because I didn't really care to live at all.

"For Baby," Susan said. "We go west for Baby to have a good life," and I nodded yes. I sold the house and the cloth still in the cutting room and set off with them, but I was numb. I walked when they said walk; I fed Baby when they said it was time to eat. I slept at night, but I was numb, all the time unfeeling, not tasting food or feeling drink go down my throat, not really caring if the Indians attacked and killed us all.

Now, I go west for Baby. I know that. For her to have a good life. I worry about the Indians, and the lack of water when we cross over parched ground, and about getting up the hills and back down again. It is as if I am coming alive from my little toe upward, flesh slowly coming back to feeling, working from my legs to my thighs and into my body. I see things differently now. I feel old, for one thing, or experienced, and I am frightened, too, of what the future holds. But I have some money and I am strong enough to walk along with the company. I have made friends with Susannah and her Lorenzo, and sometimes I talk to Mrs. Girtman, and I have Susan and her husband. My life is slowly expanding, but now, it is life on my terms, or because of me, not because it is Frederick and me, or the Abel family. We are no longer those nice people down the street. I am beginning to think about the future again, and I think this is good.

*

August 3: Capt. Hastings with 8 waggons started at 8 o'clock. Meek Pilot. The best wagons were taken on, 2 were left standing the rest destroyed to repair others. In our camp there is 27 men. Mr. Fitzpatrick Captain and Pilot. Finished making packsaddles cashed [cached] goods and preparing to start tomorrow.

—Medorem Crawford

MARY SMITH'S RUMINATIONS

I think about those at home. The ones we left behind.

I know what they said when we announced that we were going west. Most thought we were out of our heads, that we should remain where we were, with family and church, with a local newspaper to read, a thriving town. But people have always been leaving, even just after John and I arrived at our farm in the 1820s. Some left for opportunities in Cleveland or Chicago, others went for land that they believed would be more fruitful in Indiana and Iowa. Some went because they didn't have much of a place where they were. Or they had fought with families over money or who to marry. The church congregation always had people leaving and then it would increase in size when a new preacher arrived to enthuse folks. The newspaper announced houses or farms for sale. Everyone seemed to have a price for just about anything, to be ready to move along to something better. There was a restlessness among people at home.

But what about those who remained? Did they think they had been abandoned or that they were the wise ones with a stake in the future? One editorial in the local newspaper urged people to be content with a modest living rather than racing after something that seemed spectacular, that old "bird in a hand being better than two in the bush" saying. Did some think our values were lax or that our morals were wanting if we raced away rather than making things better where we were? Who can judge if it is a good move? If we didn't move, we wouldn't know which was better and it might be the same: a decent living in either place. How can we know? Many of the people we knew at home—back there—thought that country living was far superior to anything else because we owned land and had a place in the community.

But we can have a place in the new land too, and we would not know which is best if we don't try. Anyway, who are they to judge us or we them? We just do what we feel the need to do, what is best at the moment, for the family.

If we are abandoning them, back there, then it is up to them to make improvements, as we will have to do when we get to Oregon. Some of us are restless; some are content or too frightened by the unknown to try.

What I couldn't explain to them is that the going is not easy. We leave everything known behind. Some things we regret, like the family stones in the cemetery. We couldn't say that of course, because if we admitted there were hard decisions to make, they would say, "So stay."

But perhaps staying is also difficult. It is hard to watch others leave for opportunities, while those behind have to cope with family and failed crops and the need to put a new roof on the henhouse. To put up with what one knows. Is that easier or harder to do than to find new things to put up with? Do they envy or pity us? And what about us? Do we scorn their lack of initiative and adventure or are we grateful they will take care of Grandmother Dunning in her older age or to see that the bridge over the creek is made safe? Is anyone ever really right or wrong? Is anyone ever satisfied? I wonder about this and, looking about, I think that Susannah and that Lorenzo might be the only ones who are truly forward going while the rest of us have regrets along with expectations. Those two seem so focused on what will be, and whatever it will be they will face together. They were not a particularly interesting couple at the beginning: too young, too raw seeming. But they have a depth about them that I find compelling now that I know them better.

There is division in this company that had pledged to remain together all the way to Oregon. Hastings and White are at it again. Dr. White is in a hurry to get to Oregon first, to announce our coming, to be the harbinger of an increase in population. Dr. White has gotten Mr. Meek to agree to lead his faction forward, and then he left this morning with eight wagons at 8:00 a.m. We are left with twenty-seven men and all the women and children. Mr. Fitzpatrick is to lead us, as he agreed to do.

We lightened our loads and even cached some items with the idea of returning for them. But will anyone actually do that? Would it really be worth it to come so far to recover grandmother's clock or a couple of pieces of silver? I would guess that once in Oregon there will be replacements, or they will be found to be not all that important anyway and the things left behind will rot where they are—or the Indians will find them. Can you imagine some old Sioux chief with Grandmother Smith's clock in his tepee?

We are camped amid a growth of trees of a type I have never seen. The bark is heavy and seems broken into pieces with moss growing between, and there are stumpy branches a ways up the trunk covered with moss. There is a lovely breeze blowing the laundry drying at the back of our wagons.

We are high up; to the southwest there are mountains covered with snow.

*

August 4: All started with pack animals at 8 o'clock had very little trouble on the way arrived at Ham's Fork of Green River at 4 o'clock. Camped good grass and wood traveled 20 miles in a different direction from that which the wagons took. We saw high mountains covered with snow to the south west.

—Medorem Crawford:

MRS. SHADDEN'S COMPLAINT

We were supposed to stay together. At least that was the compact that Shadden signed at the beginning of the journey. Dr. White was to lead us into Oregon. Now he has gone on ahead to herald our coming, so he says, but really, Shadden thinks, White wants to get there before Hastings to claim all the credit. Both of them are snakes!

I saw Susannah over by the Widow Abel's wagon. She's fairly young to serve as midwife, but I might prefer her to Dr. White. When I saw him about this cough I have, he kept pressing my chest in a most uncomfortable way, all around my breasts and onto my belly, too. I didn't tell Shadden, who wouldn't have liked to know that. I am sure the doctor only wanted to be sure I was not sick with consumption. Still, his probing around my body felt odd.

*

August 5: Mr. Crawford has gone off with Dr. White so I will no longer know the miles we travel unless he comes back to see how we are getting along. I will try to put in what Mr. Crawford would were he writing. We crossed a considerable hill during a cold and rainy afternoon and we got very wet.
—Ellen Tompkins in Mr. Crawford's absence

MOTHER BENNETT

Fine thing to do, to collect us together into a company and then go off like that. That Dr. White is a strange government agent, but he says he will be the first territorial governor of Oregon and so is not someone to cross. We are going on anyway, not staying in Oregon. Bennett agreed that we should go to California, where there will be lots of opportunity for Vardemon and the other boys. We want them to have a stake in the land, something we didn't have and couldn't give 'em in Georgia—or elsewhere in the States either. And Oregon ain't yet an organized territory.

Some thought we were outrunning the law, but we wasn't. Just trying to do the best for ours, even the girl. There will be lots of opportunity for her there, even at her age, as the place is full of men needing wives. Even Spanish ones, and they can't be all that fussy as there ain't many white women in the area. Not yet, anyways.

We are still on the banks of the Green River, two days west of Ham's Fork, that's what Vardemon said today.

*

August 6: We traveled about six hours before dinner and went over very rough mountainous country, going along a narrow path. Stopped at sunset.
—Ellen Tompkins

MARY SMITH

We camped with good grass but little wood for our fires. We watched the sun as it went down, a cloud of haze cutting it in half and the sky looking like a paint box smeared with pinks and yellows and some smoky gray. Trees poke up against the sky, limbs akimbo, some with fronds, some with puffy ends of dark green leaves in clumps.

I like to watch the ends of the day and the starts, as they reverse each other. In the early morning vague figures appear in the mist, moving among the cattle or around the side of a wagon. Then as the light lifts the figures become more distinct, their actions more clearly defined: a boy collecting sticks for a fire, a woman bending to cook something, a man twining rope to be attached to the back of a wagon, the animals moving into teams.

At night it is as if the picture unwinds. There are people in the clearing between the wagons, some talking, some just sitting in silence after the exertions of the day, a few younger people singing, first hymns and then popular songs, usually with Jane at the center, Martha sitting in the front of the circle and talking earnestly to whomever she is sitting with. Then, as the light dims, the figures grow less distinct and people move away, some to the animals staked nearby, some to the wagons, disappearing around the ends, or over to see if the clothing set on bushes has dried. Mothers scoop up children and lull them to sleep; Widow Abel sings softly to her little daughter until she is quiet; a few linger near the fire to exchange a last word or two.

These are the soft times of the day; fear is gone; but we are weary. Shoulders pulse forward and back, easing the muscles. Each day we are twenty or so miles closer to Oregon Country. The next day and the next will be the same, as we still have miles to go, miles to go, before we are there—and then, of course, the real work of living begins. This, this walking west is the hyphen between the two parts of our lives. It is a transition from what we knew to what we will face once there. It is everything, of course, while we are doing it, walking it, living it, but this hyphen is nothing in itself.

Except, perhaps, it is everything for those who die along the way.

Part 4

GETTING THROUGH

August 7: We followed the creek and crossed over to a hill when it began raining again. We stopped for dinner at the side of a high mountain and crossed what felt like two tremendous mountains. We camped near sunset.
—Ellen Tompkins

CAROLINE TOMPKINS

We started early, but we had rain and then hail. We crossed a large freshly made Indian trail and had mountains ahead of us. Stopped for dinner, but I could see immediately that something was wrong. Ellen, usually so strong and interested in things, was slow to eat and then slow to rise from the ground, holding onto the side of the wagon as she got up. Very unlike her. I went over and immediately put the back of my hand to her forehead and realized she had the fever. I alerted Dan and we made a bed for Ellen in the wagon, and she gave us no resistance as we carried her over the side and laid her down. Ellen! My dependable, active, curious daughter; my strong daughter. What ails her? How serious is this?

Ned rode ahead to the other company and asked Dr. White to make a call to see about Ellen, which he said he would do a bit later when his duties as captain were completed. He is an odd, self-important man, liking to call out "Halt!" and "Go ahead!" I know he does more than that, but I hoped for a quick response from him about Ellen, given that he knows us from home. He disappoints.

In the meantime, word spread that Ellen was ill and Mrs. Smith came running, while the McKay boys hung back, away from the wagon but near enough to learn what was wrong. Mrs. Smith came in and touched Ellen's forehead and nodded "fever" and then said, "No knowing what kind. Has she been drinking river water?" Haven't we all, I wondered, haven't we all? Then Dr. White appeared and cleared the wagon so he could examine Ellen, touching her head, feeling her wrist. He asked that we loosen her bodice so he could hear her lungs and he put hands on her body and his ear down on her chest to listen. "Lungs okay," he said, lifting his head. "There doesn't seem to be tightness there."

At that point Martha poked her head between the flaps and asked, "Is she going to be all right? Will she die?" and "What do you want me to do, Mother?"

Martha has a head for many things, but not for a crisis. She excels in languages and reading, is good at handiwork, is a good friend to those she likes, and has fine social graces. She has no head for sickrooms, where to her everything is life or death with little room in between.

"No," replied Dr. White. "She is not going to die, but she is sick." He looked up to me and said, "Give Martha something to do," and without a thought, but knowing what the family Observation meant to Ellen, I said to Martha, "Go take up Ellen's Observation, so that she doesn't miss a day."

Martha looked startled. "You mean, write today in it?" she asked.

"Yes, Martha. Go see that it is kept up while Ellen is ill." And off Martha went, shaking her head. I knew what sorts of things Martha would write but giving her a task was a good thing to do. Jane can take over tomorrow if that is needed, if Ellen is not yet well, though I knew what sorts of things Jane would write too. When Ned came by, I asked for a bucket of water to be boiled over the kitchen fire and he went off.

I told Dan that Ellen had a high fever, though we didn't know from what. "It could be river water," he said immediately, "or something from that cow she sometimes rides like a horse."

"You mean cowpox?" I asked.

"Don't know, do I? Shall I get firewood to make her sweat it out?" We looked at Dr. White, who nodded his head, at which point Susannah Couch appeared at the wagon flap, looked at Ellen, felt her forehead, and said, "No sweats," saying she needs to rest and to drink this tea.

Dr. White looked daggers at Susannah, but she held her ground. "No sweating. Just make her comfortable while I brew up this tea," and when we nodded in agreement, Dr. White frowned and said, "If you care to follow the instructions of this child, I will withdraw from the case, but I guarantee nothing. Nothing," he said as he stormed out, his own forehead alive with perspiration.

"It's the fever," explained Susannah. "We need to keep her cool and give her as much boiled water as she can hold down." When no one moved, she said firmly, "Now," and we scattered to our tasks.

Ellen lay as if in a grave, even as the wagons moved forward, but she was never alone. Mrs. Smith was there, as was Susannah, and her man Lorenzo, who came and went, usually with a potion cup in hand. Our family was there, even some Indians who materialized from seemingly nowhere. They hung back but were a presence, quietly watching.

*

August 8: Two accidents this afternoon by falling from horses not serious.
—Medorem Crawford

Tompkins Family Observation (Martha)

My pink frock is still damp from washing, so I needed to wear the yellow today. I put some green ribbons in my hair; I have few ribbons left so was glad to have the green. We ate the same thing for breakfast we always do. Jane let Wooley lick clean her plate, which I was sure to wash most carefully. I am used to my boots but don't think they look all that good with the yellow dress, but they make walking easier and provide protection from snakes that we see now and then. So I am content to wear the boots that Father had made for me. Mine have a tiny embossed rose on the ankle, something Mr. Frost always did for my shoes as a way to know mine from others. No one else has a rose. Jane has a cloverleaf, which is nice, but it isn't a rose. I think Ellen just has an *E*, which is boring, but fine for her.

Well, the drama of the day is that Ellen is sick, so I am taking over the Observation. We have moved today from the level of the river, with a very high mountain on each side. Father said the soil here is very good. We stopped for dinner for two hours and went on.

There were two accidents today caused by falling from horses. Neither was serious, but people should pay attention to where they are going. Ned caught trout for dinner, in a stream we passed, a great treat after all the dried meat we have been eating. Went twenty miles according to Mr. Crawford, who rode back to inquire about Ellen. I invited him to eat with us, but he said he had duties that Dr. White had assigned.

*

August 9: "I found another bottle than Mr. Moss tossed out," called a Shadden boy to his mother.

TOMPKINS FAMILY OBSERVATION (JANE)

Mother said I needed to keep up the Observation for Ellen while she recovers from her fever. Susannah Couch has been with her almost the whole time, sleeping at the foot of her bed and giving her a special tea that her husband Lorenzo brings after it has brewed long enough. No one knows the cause of the fever, but it seems to be lessening somewhat and Ellen is drinking tea and eating a biscuit that Susannah baked in her little tin oven. She says Ellen will be sick three days.

She says she had a lot of experience tending the sick back in Virginia, but I wonder how she knows what she is doing. There is something mysterious about her. And that Lorenzo, he is a puzzle.

There are Indians around too, not the Sioux who wanted to buy me, but people called Poncas. They are moving in our direction and traveled along with us until we got to the river, where we camped. Some people traded with them, Father said on reasonable terms, getting horses, as many of ours are very worn from the trip. I am not totally comfortable with the Indians all about, but these seemed friendly and only wanted to see what goods we were taking west. They had women and children with them, the women in long dresses of deerskin, beaded in pleasant designs. Their dresses hang straight down from the shoulders and do not hinder movement, and are modest. Their dresses, unlike ours, with darts in the bodice and a waist and petticoats, seem easy to move in—and they are durable. I think mother would look just fine in one, and Ellen when she is well. Martha would stick to her laces and taffetas, liking to be in fashion—or even to lead it.

After moving about, the Poncas came and camped all around us.

I don't think much of this is what Ellen would write. I am glad to keep this account going for her, but I want her to get well quickly.

*

August 10: "We are moving along," shouted out Mother Bennett to her family. "Not so long now."

LOUISA GIRTMAN AND CAROLINE TOMPKINS

"The end of the day is so welcome, isn't it, Caroline?"

"Yes. Peaceful, even with our cattle making cow noises and the Indians' horses moving about where they are staked. The children are quiet and the cranking noise of the wagons moving forward has stopped for a time." She paused, "I was thinking just now of *Gulliver*," added Caroline.

"You were? Just what?" asked Louisa Girtman.

"About being civilized."

"What do you mean?"

"Remember the part where Gulliver realizes that the creatures that looked like horses were cultured and civilized . . ."

"And the others, the people who looked like us, were Yahoos?" observed Louisa.

"Yes. At home I thought we Americans were civilized. We had education, churches, written laws. And I thought, from that viewpoint—from home— that the Indians out here were without culture because they didn't have those things—our things."

"And now you question that? Don't we bring culture or civilization with us?" asked Louisa.

"Yes," said Caroline slowly. "Yet, Swift has Gulliver see that the creatures that looked like horses were those to be admired," said Caroline. "They had a culture that included kindness."

Louisa added, "And humans were not to be admired?"

"That is part of it. But here, out here, I begin to wonder who is civilized," said Caroline. "Yes, I know that the Indians don't have writing and our legal system, but what if they have something of their own that fits being on this land? Something that we cannot see or understand."

"Well, I don't know," said Louisa cautiously.

"It is just that Gulliver has made me think differently about the people riding horses, who dart about, who have their own ways."

"There were good Yahoos," Louisa reminded her. "Well, one. Remember the Portuguese ship captain? He turned out to be wise, courteous, and generous."

"Yes. And there are good people among us. And we go forward, I think for the right reasons, for us. But I wonder about the people already here. Don't they have rights too?"

"Gulliver's horse people?" asked Louisa.

"Yes. I think they have something we cannot see, even as we walk straight through and past them. So," said Caroline, "I wonder out here, who is who."

"You mean to say, we are the Yahoos?" asked Louisa, with mirth in her voice.

"Well. I thought about it the other way: that they, the Indians on their horses, have knowledge of the land, while we . . . perhaps not Yahoos . . . are feeling our way forward like persons walking in the dark. We don't know what is ahead, we only know where we have come from."

"I am not sure," said Louisa, "that I want to be a Yahoo."

"We are not really the people on horses, however. Just think about it."

*

August 11: "Ellen is up and walking," called Martha to Jane.

Susannah Couch

Ellen is better. She is moving around and will probably go out of the wagon tomorrow. She will be well pleased to see where we are.

The McKay brothers come every day to check on her, and they said we were camped at a great natural curiosity where there are soda springs and boiling springs that Ellen will want to see. Now on to see how Widow Abel's sister is doing. Her time is close and birth is a difficult time for some women, she having already lost two babies.

*

August 12: One McKay brother called to the other, "She's gonna be all right, that Ellen is."

CAROLINE TOMPKINS

I walked Ellen over to the boiling springs this morning, holding her arm, and she did not resist. She was so helpless while ill that she frightened me. She looked unnatural lying there in the wagon, as she is my child who is always up and running about, discovering things, looking at stones and bugs and anything she comes upon. I am always so confident about her that to see her lying on a pallet without energy was frightening.

Dr. White sent back a question about how she was doing, tho' he was not willing to come to see for himself. Susannah would not leave Ellen's bedside until she knew that the fever had broken and Ellen would be well. So who is the healer—the one with training or the one with the hand on the forehead and the stamina to sit through the night watching?

The boiling spring is a small hole through which the water spouts up. The hole is only about one foot in diameter, with the water flinging itself up through it. It goes about three feet off the ground. It is said that sometimes it can rise much higher. The temperature is blood warm, and it has a sulfur and mineral taste. Around the hole is growing collar of white rock, considerably elevated above the ground. The minerals that fall back to earth create this strange formation.

*

August 13: It is good to be better. Two men from our company left to go up to Fort Hall. The fort shows on Reverend Parker's map, north of Salt Lake.
—Ellen Tompkins

NED AND CAROLINE TOMPKINS

Ned approached Caroline as she leaned against the wagon after a long day walking. She looked tanned from the sun and tired, but she also looked different to Ned from when they started the trip. Her hair, clipped back for the trail, sailed away from her face in the breeze, and she stood straight as a woman who used her body and was strengthened by that use. She was certainly leaner than she had been; that showed in the folds taken in her dress.

"There is going to be a caning," said Ned quietly to his mother so he would not be overheard. "We need your help, you women, that is."

"Of course. But a caning, Ned, whatever for . . . and who would do it?" She was alarmed. At this, Ned looked down at the dirt and the long tufts of grass in which they were standing as if to speak was going to be difficult. Caroline, seeing this diffidence in his stance, also looked down, so as not to make him speak directly to her face but rather to her boots.

"Who is to be caned, Ned?" she asked quietly.

"One of the Frenchmen traveling with the Canadian, Matthieu. One of the younger men in the party."

"And why?" she inquired, to help him say whatever needed to be told.

"For being among the cattle, Mother."

"Is that his job on this trip, as cattle herd?"

"Yes," answered Ned carefully.

"So what is the problem, Ned?" she asked gently. He turned his face slightly away, not knowing just how to inform his mother. How does a son tell a mother such things?

"For caring a bit too much for the cows, Mother," and when she looked baffled, he added, "especially for one cow."

Caroline felt her stomach churn. She bit her lip. "Oh, Ned," she said, glowing red with understanding. This seemed a big thing. She felt grateful that Ned would bring it to her, would trust her with such a thing. But such a thing!

"Nothing much to be done, Mother. The caning has started. Matthieu himself is inflicting the punishment with a branch from a tree we happened by." Caroline listened, and from across the camp she could hear and see nothing.

"Ned, when done," she said, "take the young man to . . . ," and she paused. Who would be best? Who would understand and not judge? Who could ease the pain?

"But there is other pain, too, Mother, having been caught with the cow. What others will say and how they will treat him."

"Most," she said, "won't know. Others will ignore him for what he did. Some will snicker—and don't you be one of the young men who do that," she added needlessly, as she knew he would not.

"I wouldn't, Mother," he quickly added. "He is a lonely sort. He doesn't understand English so travels west unable to talk to many people. Yet he is among families, while his is far away and probably never to be seen again. He is lonely. And he knows it a sin, too."

"Ned, I think about sin a great deal while I walk, and I am not sure I really believe in it at all. Well, murder is a sin, of course. Some things are. But we are also human and we seek ease to make our way in a harsh world—and I am not talking about the hardness of this trip west but about what we face as individuals in a landscape that is hostile, among people we don't know who might harm us, among others with whom we cannot find the words to talk to or the words to make others understand what frightens us. We all need comfort."

"Take him to Susannah Couch. She will help. I will go and warn her of what has happened. Shield him from those who might snicker. In this world we all seek connections, and, lacking them, we find whatever else we can find for comfort. While what he did was probably wrong, he is just a young man, frightened as we all are."

"Are you frightened, Mother?"

"I don't know that I am, Ned," she said, surprised at her own answer. "I question what we do and wonder if it will be worth it. But somehow I am not afraid. I worry for you and the girls, and for your father, too. But he seems strengthened by this journey. I am not frightened; at least, I don't think I am. We can do this, but it is not easy."

She looked puzzled about her feelings and sharing them with Ned, then she added, "And don't tell others about this. Keep it quiet, if possible."

She turned before Ned could speak and went to the Couch wagon, a democrat modified with a panel side. Its frayed roof was held up by poles at the corners, and flaps came down on one side, with a panel on the other, to keep out the rain. It didn't look capable of getting through, but with Lorenzo always making little adjustments it was still with them.

"Susannah," Caroline called. "You are needed." When Susannah appeared from the side of the wagon and heard what had happened, she began opening jars of salves and oils she had stored in large canvas bags on the wagon floor. "I will attempt to heal his body, Mrs. Tompkins, but I cannot speak his language to help his soul."

"I can speak to him," said Caroline. "It is one of the things I learned in school, although the vocabulary we memorized will hardly help in this situation. If you apply your healing salves, I will attempt to draw him out and show him we do not judge—nor will we talk about this with others. It will be easier for him if few know."

"Especially the men who could make him feel small—and Dr. White, who would make him stand and publicly confess his sin. We can trust Lorenzo, as we know how to keep secrets, and your Ned seems a solid fellow unlikely to belittle others."

"He is a good man. I am proud of him and so grateful he chose to tell me of this directly and not shield me from the act or the punishment. But it was not easy for him, either. Look, here he comes. Can we lay him in your wagon?" And with that, the two women went to work, Caroline with her dainty French taught at the Academy by Mme. Grébarde and more suited to requesting a pen from her *tante* than establishing rapport with a damaged boy. Susannah applied a poultice she had brought, used last on the Virginia plantation where she had learned from Auntie Beechy how to doctor those in need. She also applied some salves she had used to ease the sting of the lash and some creams she had made, some smooth looking, others vile concoctions with acrid odors. Soon the boy was lying on his stomach, his back bare and showing large welts but only a few, for Mr. Matthieu had shown restraint.

"On ne te juge pas," said Caroline haltingly to the boy as she pulled strips of cloth away from the red welts appearing on the Frenchman's back, worrying about the placement of "you" within the verb. This seemed no time for *vous,* anyway. *Tu* was right. "Dors maintenant," she murmured.

When a shot rang out later, Caroline knew that the cow was dead.

They put out the word that the Frenchman had caught the same fever from which Ellen suffered, and most of the company avoided the Couch wagon and forgot about the boy—few having noticed him in the first place. F. X. Matthieu came to call daily and watched over the young man. Matthieu's gray eyes were sad, the corners of his mouth pulled down. Even his mustache drooped.

"*Mon pauve jeune homme,*" he said. And in English, "Life is a lonely business. *Moi,*" he said, pointing at his chest, "*moi,* I take it easy and try not to be caught."

*

August 16: "Some of the men went to the fort to have a bath and a shave," *said Gabriel Brown to Reuben Lewis. "I'll wait until we get to Fort Walla* *Walla."*

TOMPKINS FAMILY OBSERVATION (JANE)

Ellen is still unsteady but recovered. Yet not so much that she wants to take up the pencil again to write our Observation. I read what Martha wrote, about her dress and all.

What I have to report is that our part of the company moved on down the river, which we crossed in several marshy places. It has been a very warm day and I thought the river water would be cooling, but it was sluggish and seemed thick with mud. Some people who had lightened their wagons had to retie the packs on the horses because they kept slipping off. Not enough rope, I suspect, and some tied hastily.

The little children set off each morning as if going to school, trudging forward but without a desk and teacher at the end of the trek. I think Mrs. Abel has been trying to teach her daughter her letters because when I walk

I sometimes see an *A* or an *M* written in the soft ground. It looks so funny to me, letters for a language that only we speak out here. What must the Indians think of these signs? Do they think they are magic marks or do they understand that we use letters to tell each other stories?

Martha is writing another letter home to leave at the fort: she is worried that her friends will forget her. I am not so concerned because I always hung back, letting Martha go first and be in front while I stood back in her shadow. The experience with the Sioux, though, them wanting to buy me for their chief, makes me think somewhat differently about myself, as if I have something of value, just as Martha has her good looks and fine sense of style.

I am worth twenty horses! Imagine.

I can sing. And I love singing and I like people hearing me. It is as if singing has given me a voice; well, that's a silly thing to write, but in singing I become Jane and not Martha's other sister and faceless. So I sing during the day as I walk, just as Mother talks to herself as she walks. And out loud. She doesn't think we know, but of course we do. We have heard her talking to herself all our lives, and when she isn't around we laugh a bit about it. Her talking makes her seem to always have a friend with her, while I always felt I needed Martha to stand up to everyone for me. Now I don't feel that way. I feel like . . . what? Like Jane the singer, the one who comforts, and leads others in song, and the one who sings sorrow when there is pain and the one who gives voice to joy when joy is wanted.

The one worth twenty horses.

I did not want to come on this trip. I think I didn't want to come because Martha didn't want to come—and I understand why she wouldn't want to be here. This is nothing that she likes, nothing at all, and I know that Grandmother Fitch has told Martha that if she does not like Oregon, she can return to Ithaca and Grandmother would pay. But Grandmother didn't offer me passage, and I don't think I would take it. I find I like this walking, my singing, and I like the Indians who seemed to approve of me for myself and not because of Martha.

I was scared, I admit, when I thought the Sioux were going to take me away, even though I knew that Father would never allow that to happen. It is just I didn't know how he would manage to block their request without all of us being killed. But Mr. Matthieu managed to talk to the Sioux. We gave them sugar and blankets and Mother's opal necklace, too, and they went away happy. They did hang around for a few days, as if expecting more, or expecting me to decide to go with them, but then they left and Mr. Fitzpatrick said they had gone off hunting buffalo.

When all that was happening, time seemed very slow; the Sioux came slowly up to the wagon. We watched them approach, then they sat down on the ground to show they were not hostile and explained what they wanted. Then time stopped because it was so startling that they would want me for their chief—as if I were a prize to be wanted. Everything seemed to last forever, but now looking back, it feels as if that day happened in a flash: that they were there and there was excitement and then they were gone. So looking back makes all that seem only a part of this trip west, not a giant stoppage of the journey that had great consequences. Perhaps the kidnapping of Captain Hastings and Mr. Lovejoy on Independence Rock also seemed that way to them: a giant event with great consequences but now only something to look back upon as a good story to tell.

And now I am glad that it happened with the Sioux because I feel I have a worth all my own, if that makes sense. I sing more and loudly, and people look pleased when I come by singing, and babies stop crying and shoulders on the men ease back a bit from the strain of moving forward and being alert. So while that day was awful while it was happening, it was also a very good day for me. Since then, I have opposed Martha in some things, such as wearing my boots, and cutting my skirts to above my ankles, and putting my hair in braids. This is not a place for frills but a place I am happy to try to match—to fit into and not look as if I were walking down Seneca Street to music lessons or to church. I would wear a skin dress that falls from the shoulders if Father would let me, but he would think that was "going native." But I would wear it because it is sensible in this land of dust and things to walk over and past without being caught in branches and prickles, and it would not tear and would give me even more freedom of movement than I have even with my skirts cut up. Martha would be horrified and think I had become Ellen, but that is not true. I am not interested in the exploring that she does, or hanging out with the McKay boys, though they are nice young men. I am interested, I think, in being Jane. That is what going west has done for me.

*

August 18: A warm day. We kept to the river, crossing several marshy places.
—Ellen Tompkins

MARTHA TOMPKINS'S LETTER TO GRANDMOTHER

Dear Grandmother,

We are at Fort Hall, where I will post this letter to you. We have seen
the fort ahead of us for a time as we walked to it, its walls whitewashed
and a flag that says H. B. C. for the Hudson Bay Company. We will
wait a while here readying for the trip along the Snake River and then
into Oregon.

I am so tired of all this walking. While the scenery could be called
enchanting, I am definitely not enchanted by stretches of desert, rocky
peaks, or the long ascents through the passes in the mountains.

What has happened is that Father is working hard to get us through
to Oregon and he talks about topics for the newspaper he plans to
publish. He has a letter ready to send from the fort to tell the San
Francisco shipping company to send the press to Oregon City. He is
all set to become an editor.

Mother seems to enjoy all the walking and she continues to talk to
herself, out loud, as if someone else is there. The most interesting thing
that happened is that some Sioux Indians came to our wagon to buy
Jane to give to a chief—as if she is a prize. For twenty horses! We were
not amused. Father and Mr. Matthieu, a Canadian man, prevented
that from happening, but in the process we had to give the Indians
something and so Father handed over your very lovely opal necklace
that you gave to Mother, that I had hoped she would give to me, as it
would go so well with some outfits I plan to have made when I return
to Ithaca. And yes, I hope to return as you and I discussed.

Ever since the Indians offered to buy Jane, she has been singing
nonstop, and while it has not stopped her from stuttering, she has
made a number of friends among these people traveling with us. They

seem to like her singing. The other thing that has happened is that Ellen became ill, possibly from drinking the river water, and so Jane and I had to continue writing in her Observation so that it would be complete when the family gets to Oregon. I cannot tell you much about Ned because I don't see him often. He manages the cattle and sets up the wagon each day and has become friends with some of the other young men on this journey.

One whom you might know of is Medorem Crawford, whose family live in Havana, New York, and who started out this trip with Dr. White. The doctor is an odd man, very self-important, but he is also to become a figure in the territorial government and carries with him a document from the president of the United States. Mr. Crawford is very nice and will carry my letter with his to Fort Hall. The fort is no place for a young woman, I am sure, as it is where mountain men bring in their pelts to trade for liquor.

I try to say my prayers every night and I am halfway through the French book you gave me. There are some French Canadian men on this trip, about four of them, but their French is nothing at all like that in the book, so we do not converse.

I hope you will remember me to all my school friends, who by now are graduated, and to your friends who visit with you, and to our pastor and Mrs. Elmer who taught me piano. I very much miss my piano and hope to resume lessons when I am again with you.

Your very loving granddaughter, who is currently near Fort Hall out in the wilderness.

Martha E. Tompkins

PS. I am wearing those boots that Father had made because the way is rocky and uneven and there are snakes out here and I certainly do not want to be bitten. M.E.T.

*

August 20: We are near American falls, not a perpendicular fall like the ones at home, but more like rapids interspersed with large rocks.
—Ellen Tompkins

AT THE PERRY WAGON

Susannah moved quietly to Mrs. Perry's side and held out her hands. "Mrs. Perry," she said softly. Widow Abel said to her, "Susan—she is Susan. My sister is Susan."

"Ah," replied Susannah, "then we have our names in common." Susan Perry looked up, her face contorted, her hair wet with sweat. Her back arched up as if to push the baby from her own navel, her clothing pulling every which way. There was water at Susan's feet, more streaming down her legs.

"Susan Perry," said Susannah in her slow southern voice as she took Susan's hands into her own, cupping them together, holding them safe. "Let us push these skirts away to make you more comfortable." Susan nodded but looked at the opening of the wagon.

"The doctor was to come," choked out Susan.

"He is with the other company, several miles ahead," said Widow Abel. "Susannah is here to help you," and then seeing the panic in her sister's face, she said quietly, "I know she looks young, but she said she has had experience."

"I have," said Susannah quietly. "Much experience, since I was eight years old and accompanied my auntie all around. We delivered babies for the women who lived in the area. At first I just carried baskets and boiled water, but Auntie taught me and at times I took over. Trust me to help you," she said, and at that Susannah pulled from her basket a stack of white linen cloths and some jars of healing herbs. She began chanting, slowly, quietly.

"There was little Ezra, and Sally, and Amanda, and Polly. There were the twins and Felicity, along with Benjamin and Charles," she intoned.

As clothing was pulled gently away, Susannah put a large white linen cloth across Susan's belly, the cloth draping gently across her body like the finest tablecloth. Then Susannah opened one of the jars and took out a cream, slipped her hands beneath the cloth and gently massaged Susan's belly, barely touching the flesh but filling the air with scent. She sang easily: "first there was Sarah's baby in the big house; then Eliza's out in the east yard; then Biddy's baby in the back forty; then Maud's baby named Ezra in the loft of the barn."

The chant would ease Susan's mind, she hoped, until another wave of pain caught the young mother in the chest, moved to her back, and burned through her belly. Susannah could feel the pain beneath the skin. She put her hands gently on Susan's thighs.

"Breathe," said the girl. "Breathe deeply."

Susan yelled again in pain and then looked to her sister. "Hannah . . . ," she gasped.

Susannah leaned into Susan's body and said, "You have walked half a continent and are strong." Susannah's hands never left Susan's legs, gently circling and creaming them with her poultice that smelled of gardens in the East: of rose petals and verbena and peonies and lavender. "Out of pain," she said, quietly, "comes life."

Under everything there was the thrumming of Susannah's quiet chant listing the babies that she and Auntie had delivered back in Virginia.

"The baby!" yelled Susan.

"Not yet," replied Susannah. "It will come, but not yet. It is getting ready to meet the world but needs some time."

"No!" yelled Susan again, as if speaking from above the pallet on which she lay, as if out of her own body. "Hannah's baby? Where is your baby? Have you lost Baby?"

Hannah smiled. "No, Susan. I was walking with Mr. Trask when I heard your call, and he said he would take Baby to old Mrs. Smith. She is cared for. Now: let's get you a baby."

Susan lurched forward in pain and grasped her belly, staying Susannah's hands. "Help me!" she yelled.

Susannah reached over to the pan of clear water, rinsed her hands, and pulled another cream from the basket. She rubbed the lard over her hands and reached down, between Susan's legs, and pulled them far apart. "Now, just pant a bit, Susan, pant like a kitten licking a bowl of milk, quickly and lightly." Sweat poured from Susan's head as pain racked her body.

"I am going to put grease on your legs," she said as she pulled Susan's leg upward, creaming Susan's taut upper thigh, indicating to Widow Abel to take the other leg. "Push when the pains come," she instructed. "The pains will come, faster and faster. Push the pain out."

Susan recoiled as a fresh flash of pain came on quickly.

"You are strong, Susan. You have walked half a continent," said Hannah. Susan winced, tears rolling across her face.

"Babies are born in pain," said Susannah. "It is women who bear the pain to populate the world. It takes courage." She paused, then said, "Now push! I can see the baby's head."

A spasm that about ripped the young mother apart suddenly eased as Susannah reverently withdrew the baby from within and placed the newborn in a cloth ready at the end of the pallet.

"It's over? Is the baby here?"

"No. Not yet. We need to cut the cord. And there will be the afterbirth. But we will give you your baby." And Susannah did these things. Hannah wiped her sister's face with a clean white cloth and combed through her tangled hair: and so a baby was born.

*

August 21: It is Sunday, according to the chart I kept in the Observation.
—Ellen Tompkins

A BABY

The company had stopped when Elbridge Trask alerted them that a baby was to be born. The wagons pulled into a square, the dogs fled into the shade, women and children stopped walking. Everyone could hear the mother's screams. The men looked uneasy, some even guilty for having had their pleasure, this woman's screams reminding them of the price to be paid. Some scuffed their boots into the ground, while others went off to manage the cattle or tie a pack more securely. They didn't look at each other.

The women reacted in a concert of remembrance. Then there was quiet and the weight of expectation settled on the company. Was the baby alive?

The mother? Was it a boy or a girl? What would it be named? Was this place, along a river, in the middle of a giant continent, a place to be born?

"Mr. Perry!" sang out Hannah Abel, "Mr. Perry, come up and see your daughter." There was collective relaxation, shoulders came down, relief showed on every face: a daughter, a girl, a baby had been born in this unlikely place—or was it unlikely? Generations of people had been born here, others might yet be. This emigrant train was only the first of others that would follow. It was only an unexpected place to those in the wagons making their way west.

"W. T. Perry, come along now," called Hannah Abel happily.

William Perry looked down at his wife, exhausted but happy, and saw the bundle on her stomach, the two breathing together. His eyes misted, and slow tears made their way down his face. Susan reached for his hand: "I know, William; after years of trying and losing two before they could be born, how extraordinary to have a baby here, on the trail, in a wilderness." He looked at the three women. Their efforts to bring a new life into the world showed in the droop of their shoulders, the disarray of their clothing. "All three of you," he said. "You all did it," and the women shook their heads slightly.

"We should name her Marie for your mother," he said, "and Susannah for the three of you: you are Susan, and Hannah, and Susannah."

Susan nodded but said, "Susannah first, and then Marie, I think. She will need a strong name in this harsh world. Sit with me while I sleep, Mr. Perry, and watch your daughter's first hours."

∗

August 22: We will rest for a day, said Capt. Fitzpatrick, for the baby. The ground is very rocky but everyone seems happy.
—Ellen Tompkins

Mrs. Shadden

So she got a baby girl. A comfort for life, a daughter is, not like sons, who never look back when they are leaving, even though I stand there and wave and wave until they are out of sight. Different creatures they are, sons and daughters. And that Susannah did all right, it seems, young as she is.

I wonder about her and her Lorenzo. So secretive, yet so competent in some ways. They kept Mr. Moss alive when he was causing all that trouble, and they helped with Shadden's diarrhea and that was a blessing, for washing clothes along the trail ain't the easiest thing to do, much less getting them dry again, especially when Shadden ain't got but two pairs of trousers to his name.

We are putting all our hopes in this Oregon. For us and for our kids. If it don't pan out, there is nothing beyond but ocean and no one is going to get Shadden into a boat heading into the ocean. He don't like a little boat on a small lake, much less something bigger. He don't like fishing either. Question is, what is Shadden gonna do in Oregon? We will get some land, but he ain't much of a farmer either. Not wheat and those crops, but he does know trees. I know he put some whips from the cherry tree in Kentucky into the wagon, but I don't know that he kept 'em watered. Wouldn't Kentucky cherries taste good in our new place and maybe they could make us a living for once. And I can keep chickens; I know chickens, if we can get some starters. Do they have chickens in Oregon?

It's best to try, for us to try. A new place might be lucky for us this time. I'd like a house of our own, with a lilac and perhaps a rosebush outside for the chickens to nest under. A rambler. Yellow. Yellow would be best, I think, but I wonder if we can do it, if we can make it this time? We are making this trip with so many hopes, so much pushing us away from the old. Perhaps this is our time.

Dr. White's company is ahead of us again, and we are camped on the river. It's been a hot day and a good one to rest, so I am glad for that Susannah Perry being borned, as everyone agreed to wait a day to give her a good start. That Jane, the one that sings, that the Indians wanted, is going over to sing for the baby, and Mr. Smith, the old one, is going to say a blessing and baptize her in the name of the Lord. This has gotta be a first out here in the middle of the country that a little white baby girl is born.

*

August 23: We started out early. Capt. Fitzpatrick told me that the Snake River was to have been named for Meriwether Lewis, but that name didn't stick, so it is the Snake we are traveling along.
—Ellen Tompkins

TOMPKINS FAMILY OBSERVATION (JANE)

We had a baby born and everyone was happy, so we rested another day but started up. We are traveling behind Captain Hastings's company, but we can see them ahead and I have found things on the trail that they drop. There was a bottle, and I found a piece of a buckle, I think. It is hard to tell exactly.

We drove as quickly as we could over very rocky land that is hard on the oxen still with us, and the horses. The countryside is covered with sage. To the north there are snow-capped mountains. Overall we traveled thirty miles and landed with good water and grass, having suffered with much dust. Mr. Crawford came back to see us and gave me the figures.

We came close to the river and camped on Goose Creek. It feels comfortable to be on a creek with a name we know. It is even marked on Reverend Parker's map. Having a name on a map makes it feel as if we have come to a certain place, not just any place. A party from the Hudson Bay Company came up from behind us, but we could not keep up with them and they passed us by and joined with the company ahead. According to Mr. Crawford, Dr. White wants to leave the first company to travel with the men from the H. B. Company, intending to get even more quickly to Fort Vancouver. The first company now travels without a pilot and with only eight men left.

✱

*August 24: Camped on a very pretty Brook after a long day. I don't know
the distance because Mr. Crawford is no longer traveling with us, but he
rides back now and then to see how we are doing.*
—Ellen Tompkins

MRS. SHADDEN

The Hudson Bay Company traveled quickly past us, four wagons, but as
they did their leader jumped down and spoke with old Mr. Smith and then
left two bundles for us to take with us. And they were two women! Imagine
that! Now I suppose someone is going to have to take them in and give them
food, because they didn't seem to have anything much in the way of luggage.
Just two bedraggled women: one fairly old, the other young. What were they
doing traveling with the H. B. Company? And who are they anyway? If they
have been traveling with the trading company, they are certainly not a polite
sort of woman, if you know what I mean. And they looked tattered. Why
should we have to take them in?

I am not all that happy when unexpected things happen and we have to
look out for more than our own, and that's the truth. Our own is enough
work as it is, and we Shaddens don't have much extra to share anyway. Why
do we have to give up something? What right does old Mr. Smith have to
make decisions for the whole company? He might be the eldest among us,
and served to baptize the baby, but it is the men with shares in our company
who have the power to decide, not him. We Shaddens have to hang on to
what we have, little as it is. This is all very upsetting.

I'll go see what is going on.

MARY SMITH

As the trading company pulled up to us, their leader jumped out to talk to
Mr. Smith, and faster than a tick they hauled two women from their wagon
and set them down in ours. Then the trading company moved on. It took
only minutes. My John reported that the company leader had said to him
that coming up from Santa Fe they had recovered two captives from the

Comanches, but the company wagon was no proper place for them to travel. They need woman-comfort, he thought. Would we take them?

John explained to me that the women had first been taken captive somewhere down in the Missouri country, where their family had been killed. They have been with the Indians for some time. A trading caravan of men is no place for them, the leader had said, and Mr. Smith agreed. They don't much care where they are headed but didn't want to be with the Indians and are glad to be free.

They have nothing but the rags they were in.

We can provide food and they can ride in the wagon until they are well enough to walk, but they need clothing and possibly some aid. I went to Caroline Tompkins, who said she would find clothes, and Susannah came running with her basket of salves.

Our company passed an old campsite, replete with garbage and fleas and then found a clean place farther on to take stock of the situation, because the way ahead is steep. We can see a deep ravine from here, all rocky with a stream running at the bottom. I think it is the Snake River; it's where we have been heading.

The Women Confer

Susannah and Mrs. Smith moved to the two women, huddled in the bottom of the Smith wagon. Caroline came soon after, bearing several dresses, some stockings, and shoes, donated mostly by Jane, who was glad to see them go. "Ned is bringing heated water," said Caroline, "so you can wash."

"Are you injured?" asked Mary Smith, wrapping her arms around the younger woman.

Susannah reached out to the older woman and gently held her arm to steady her. "We are here to help you," she said quietly. Slowly their story came out. They had been visiting neighbors and were returning in the family wagon when they saw their house on fire, their men dead in the yard. The Indians, they were unsure of which band, were quickly upon them, dragged them to horses, and took them away.

"Months," said the younger woman. "We were with them two months." Mary Brown explained that she and her daughter, Adeline, had been badly treated by the Indians, she as a slave to an old Indian woman. Adeline had been thrust into a different household.

"We were used," said Mrs. Brown simply.

*

August 25: We descended into a tremendous valley with banks of perpendicular rock at least 200 feet high on the north side. Water spills out on the north side of the rock. We camped on a large stream formed mostly around a spring.
—Ellen Tompkins

MOTHER BENNETT

I know what it is like for those women: everyone here is wondering how they got here, what happened while they were with the Indians, what's the state of their virtue. No one person would say that, but it is what they are thinking—and why the trappers wanted to give them up to us. I think the trappers didn't want to be thought the reason for the women's troubles. Not at all a nice situation to be in; I know that. And if they were with the Indians, they didn't leave those women alone to do chores, or not only to do chores. Lucky to be alive, but now they are in some sort of living hell with everyone wondering what sort they are. The older one, the mother, not so much, but the daughter; people will have questions about her, they will. Won't ask them, neither, but will think things every time they see one of them.

They cleaned up nicely. People from the company made reasons to walk by the Smith wagon to take a look at 'em, to see what survivors of the Indians looked like. That Mrs. Shadden was there, shivering, thinking about what happened to them as captives and worrying that she would have to give something up because they are in need. I understand that too; poverty makes you think about conserving what we have, not wanting anyone to get anything offa us or for free, yet these women, they have nothing. I can bring an extra blanket, as I still got one not filthy from lying on the ground.

We think so many things that we don't talk about because they are considered not to be polite. I know about that, too. But minds are nasty things, full of ideas, like spiderwebs that link together into patterns that might or might not be true. Feel sorry for those women. And the young one, especially; she must feel unclean.

Now that we are off from Fort Hall we are descending very steep ravines, going through banks of perpendicular rock. We had to slow the wagons as we went down, putting logs behind 'em to slow the descent, with the men on each side guiding the mules. We went twenty-one miles, said Medorem Crawford, who keeps track of these things and who came by to see the newly released women. Probably so he could report back to Dr. White. Camped midafternoon on a large stream formed mostly by nearby springs.

✳

August 26: We traveled down a swift creek and then descended a steep hill. We passed some Indian lodges, where we traded for fish, both fresh and dried. Then we worked our way up a hill. Camped at last on a miserable sandy and rocky place. I didn't see Mr. Crawford when he was with us yesterday.
—Ellen Tompkins

Widow Abel

We stopped along a swift creek after slowly coming down a hill so steep we feared the wagons would break apart. Now that we are on the western side of the continent, it is as if we are tilting down instead of always climbing toward, as we were before the pass through the mountains. But then suddenly there appears a hill in front of us and we have to climb again. The Snake River is rapid and the water dark green in color, not at all like the Platte. We passed some Indian lodges, where we traded for fish, and left the river, going up a tremendous hill looking for a good place to stop.

Elbridge Trask came by today, looking for me, he said. He had a question to ask, he announced, and suddenly I was nervous. I don't want to make any big decisions right now, at least not until we get to Oregon. It is too soon, anyway, I thought.

Then Mr. Trask asked his question and it was totally unexpected. In his own funny way, he screwed up his face, almost into its own question mark, and said, "Ma'am, this has been worrying me, so I need to ask you something.

If I may?" I nodded and he said, "I am confused about your child." I had not been expecting anything like this.

"About Baby?" I asked him back.

He nodded yes, and then said, "Why doesn't Baby have a name, or is Baby her name?"

I laughed, and he became all embarrassed and looked down at his feet. "That's so easy a question," and then I realized it was not at all easy. To explain about Baby I might have to explain about Frederick. I was not sure I wanted to do that. "Baby was born after my late husband died," I said simply. "If she turned out to be a boy she was to be named for Frederick. If a girl, she was to be named for Frederick's mother, Agatha. But to me," I explained to him, "she was simply Baby and the name stuck. It was easier than pulling the Abel family along with me."

"A girl's name, then," he said simply. "You need a girl's name for Baby."

"I suppose I do."

He surprised me by saying, "My mother's name was Arabella and my father's mother's name was Lucy. Might one of those do? Being so bold as to suggest it," he said modestly. "I am right fond of Baby, you know, and she likes me, too."

"My mother's name was Susan, and we have far too many Susans around for my taste," I said. "Susan won't do, I think. Arabella is nice, but a bit fancy for a fatherless child going into the wilderness."

"It's not wilderness out there," he said most earnestly. "It is a beautiful country, Miz Abel. A hard country, but a beautiful one." Then he said forcefully, "She needs a name of her own, Miz Abel. To carry her into the West."

He got me thinking that evening as we camped.

*

August 27: We followed a narrow path along the Snake River and found good grass. We decided to remain a day to let the animals feed. We traded for fish with some of the Indians who live along the Snake River. According to Reverend Parker's map they may be the Shoshones or Snake Indians.
—Ellen Tompkins

TOMPKINS FAMILY OBSERVATION

I am glad to have my Observation back. Jane gave it to me, and she is right. I would never write what she and Martha wrote, but I guess they have their own versions and none of our versions have to match. There are many things that happen, and all can be true at the same time. I really liked what Jane had to say about her finding her voice. That seemed very true, and she has been different since the Sioux came for her. She stands straighter, though she still stutters, excepting to Wooley, who seems to be holding up on the trip despite Dr. White's insistence that dogs would go mad in the mountains and become rabid. The only change I see is that Wooley likes to sneak a ride in the wagon when no one is looking, and he didn't do that at first. Perhaps his paws are sore. I am glad he is still with us.

And here we are on the Snake River. To think about it, we are on the western side of the continent and the water runs west. Think of where we have been: from Ithaca down the Ohio to St. Louis, to Elm Grove, and then across the plains, along the Platte, across the Rockies through South Pass, down the mountains that are now behind us, and coming up along the Snake River. We are way more than halfway there, I think, though I will ask Medorem about that when I see him. I hope the next part of the journey is easier than what we have come over.

I saw Mr. Crawford talking to the captive woman brought in the other day. Jane thinks he likes Miss Brown. I don't know what Martha would think: she only wants to get to Oregon in order to go back home. Even Mother and Father know that now. But Ned is happy. He likes this trail life, though he admitted he will also be glad to be there—to have a bath and proper shave, to wear clean clothes, and not to have to deal with the mules any longer. They are a trial. Everyone hates the mules, but we need them to get through.

Father keeps talking about his newspaper, what a newspaper means to a place, and to people. He seems even more excited now that we are getting closer.

Yesterday we started in the morning and kept on moving along the river on the side of a steep bank where we were obliged to follow a narrow path through a deep ravine. One of the hired men lost a pack as we went down, and it fell into the water and disappeared in the rapids. We camped on an island in the Snake River with good grass and decided to stay another day to let the animals eat heartily. Today we kept along the river along a sidehill and saw many Indians, some on land and some in boats. Mr. Fitzpatrick said they live mostly on fish, and we traded to have fish for our dinner.

*

August 29: There are fewer plants on the ground and not even much sage. The going will be hard on the animals. We camped on an island in the river.
—Ellen Tompkins

MARY SMITH

I am amazed that we have gotten this far, or perhaps I am amazed that at my age I have gotten so far. As has Mr. Smith. He seems finally to have found a niche for himself. He's not a company member, our son John is that, so we travel with John. But Mr. Smith seems to have become company elder; baptizing the Perry baby, making decisions about the two women left with us. He has even taken them in as family, without any fuss or bother, just pulled them close as if it was meant to be that he would become a family caretaker again.

He hasn't been in that role for some time; I made the decision to come west and he had to follow. I look to our son as the family leader, and perhaps that left Mr. Smith no role in the family at all, so when the two women arrived he had someone to look over, to decide for. It's good for him. He was a good father when he was young, but in giving up the farm and then coming west he hasn't had much of a voice. Now he is the company elder and people look up to him for that. He looks happier, too, and orders people about, but he also joins in. It has taken two-thirds of this country to get him to this place, but it is a good place for him to be.

I am finding climbing the steep hills more and more difficult. I pant at times and hang back when I can so that no one notices. I loved walking along the Platte where the way was smooth and Ellen and I could watch the birds and look out for flowers. Now, however, it feels harder to get myself up and down, and I think I am shuffling a bit. Being with Ellen, now that she is well, is very good for me because we talk about everything and that takes my mind off walking. Sometimes she gets way ahead, but I catch up after a time. Out here the air feels so thin that I have to take several breaths to full my lungs.

John and his family are just fine. They seem to thrive on this constant moving and living out of doors. Even Sarah, his wife, doesn't mind the cooking and treats the easy days happily, and the harder ones like something to overcome. She has gotten leaner too, with all the walking. She came to me one day, about three weeks ago, to say she was thinking she might be carrying a child, as her time of month had not come in a long time. If I judge by the small number of buckets at the back of wagons where the women wash their cloths, many of these women have stopped having a time of month too. Maybe it is the exertion, or perhaps they are all expecting children, though to be quite honest I don't see how they could get a child with the lack of privacy we experience. We are all on top of each other all day, one wagon tailing another, children going from one woman to another, and at night everyone is so tired, I can't imagine anything much happening on the hard ground, sleeping with others nearby.

I told Sarah that if a baby were to come, we would all rejoice, and we have Susannah, who seems to manage child birthing well, so there should be no worries, although I would think that if Sarah is with child that baby would be born in Oregon. That's a sure way to increase the population. It is rather pleasant to think about another baby in the family, especially after all these years, but I tend to doubt it.

*

August 30: We walked along the river and finally camped on a beautiful little branch of the Snake River in a valley surrounded on three sides by hills. Rather like home, in a funny way, where our little village was enclosed by three hills.
—Ellen Tompkins

Mrs. Brown

We are going where we never thought to be, but then we were where we never wanted to be. Our lives, Adeline and mine, have been turned upside down with the attack on our farm, our time with the Indians, and now in a company of people going to Oregon. I didn't protest when the wagon master handed us over to this company, and Mr. Smith has been most fatherly, caring for both of us, giving us food, the women finding clothing. We both feel safe, although Adeline is a bit skittish around others, not knowing what they are thinking about her, not wanting to explain, for they don't deserve an explanation, do they? It's our tragedy—with the death of my husband and the hired man and our being taken. We don't have to talk about it, but we both know that they are all curious and they probably say things. Mr. Smith did say it was a good thing that Dr. White was not traveling with us, he having gone ahead, because he might have made a public display of our arrival and need for care and about our circumstances.

I wonder what I think about Oregon. I heard a lot of talk about it back in Missouri, but I never wanted to go there, nor did Edwin. We were both content to make our lives on our little farm. But there is no one left in Missouri. We moved there from Tennessee some years ago. Now, anywhere is probably as good a location as any other.

In Oregon we will have to make a living for ourselves, and I think we might one day claim land, independent of each other, some acres between us, and we can sell some and set up a seamstress shop. We both sew well if we have the supplies. I think we could support ourselves, although two women alone will be unusual out there, as we would be anywhere. Perhaps a little wagon with our supplies and we could make calls on remote houses to sew clothing.

We know that there are many more men out there than women, so our skills should be welcomed and we can settle someplace. Our circumstance will get around, of course, our having been captives, so there is no hushing up the outlines of our story.

I mourn for Edwin. I hope when the Indians came he died quickly and without undue pain. He was a good husband, though a quiet man. I read to him, he being not well educated, the Bible mostly. We went out to services now and again, but not often. We kept mostly to ourselves, though we did worry that Adeline needed to be in society more to find a husband. That Medorem Crawford comes by, sometimes with a bit of fish, always with news of how many miles we have gone for the day. Eighteen today. We are camped on a beautiful little branch of the Snake River in a valley surrounded on three sides by high hills.

*

August 31: We followed the trail down to the Snake River and finally found good grass. There were Indians there too and we camped near their village.
—Ellen Tompkins

WIDOW ABEL

Elbridge Trask came by as we were resting today at noon. He said he was sorry he had been so cheeky as to suggest a name for Baby, and he went on about how he knew he was out of his place but was concerned about her. I let him talk on for a while as it was nice to have someone to talk to other than my sister and brother-in-law, who are now all wrapped up with their child.

Then I said, "You needn't feel you were bold, Mr. Trask. I thought a lot about what you said and think you are right. Baby does need a name, and if you will allow it, Lucy would do just fine. It's a pretty name."

He got all red, under his beard that is, and poked his foot on the ground and then asked if he could take Lucy for a little walk, which I allowed. He will walk her along the river and won't let her climb on the rocks. For a mountain man he is very gentle. The two laugh together, her little bell-like laugh and his growl-like chortle that comes from his throat and through his beard. Even though Lucy doesn't talk yet, he and she seem to carry on quite a conversation of grunts and chuckles, both pointing here and there.

The river is now going through some high rock banks, but even so there was a long hill and when we came out of the rocks there was an astonishingly barren country. We stopped where there was some tolerable grass among a group of Indians who had already made a camp on the flat ground. We are all more or less at ease with these Indians, as we have been assured that they are only interested in trade and are not at all warlike. We have left the Sioux far behind.

*

September 1: We came to two small streams which are said to be hot water and when some of our party attempted to drink they said the water burned their hands.
—Ellen Tompkins

MRS. SHADDEN

Those Indians came in to camp to trade or sell fish to us. They don't seem to be asking much for the fish, but Shadden don't have much money. We are gonna need a bit for setting up in Oregon City. I tried to give one of the Indians a pot I didn't need, but he pointed out the crack on the bottom and refused it. Can you imagine: not having anything like a nice kiln-made pot and not wanting a perfectly good pot for a little fish?

We crossed two streams that run hot water flowing into the Snake River. One of them Frenchmen cooked a fish in the hot water; said it was good too, and didn't need no salt.

I watched as that Susannah sent her man over to get some buckets of the hot water but don't know what for. He took down a skinny box that fitted into a side of their cart, opened the top, and poured the water in. Then he went to get more.

There is poor grass here and our mule looks peaked. He gotta hold out, though, to Oregon. We went a long ways today. The going was over hard rocky ground. I get tired in my back from the walking and my shoes are giving out, not being of the best when I got 'em, in Independence. That was three or more months ago. Imagine.

*

*September 2: We camped today on a branch of the Snake River named
Warrior, but it is not on Reverend Parker's map. The way was hard.*
—Ellen Tompkins

SUSANNAH VISITS ADELINE BROWN

"Come with me, Miss Brown, if you will. I know you need bathing, and I can
help you out with that. Lorenzo is getting the water now." Susannah pulled
Adeline Brown slowly forward to her cart, where the bath-box sat to the side,
water steaming from it. "You sit in it," explained Susannah, "and we close it
up and you can wash inside and out." She cocked her head slightly to see if
Adeline understood what she was saying. "I have salves and bath soaps for
you," she said, holding out her basket and showing its contents.

Lorenzo poured the last bucket of boiling water into the bath-box and
tested the temperature. "In a bit," he said. "It is still fairly hot." Then he moved
away, standing alert and facing outward as Susannah pulled Adeline to the
bath and tugged at her dress.

"Inside," said Adeline. "Inside needs cleaning." Susannah nodded. She
handed her a jar of salve and indicated she should use that. Then as she pulled
off Adeline's dress, she pushed her firmly into the bath and snapped the side
closed, with only Adeline's head appearing above.

"I hope to get this bath-box all the way to Oregon. Lorenzo is committed
to trying to do that for me, but if we can't, he will make me a new one. It
is modeled on a French bath I once saw back in Virginia." Then Susannah
pulled from her dress a packet of dried rose petals, which she pushed down
into the water. "Enjoy," she said. "I will come back when I hear you call me."
She moved away, listening to the movement of the water in the box and the
sounds of contentment that came from the tattered Miss Brown.

As Susannah joined Lorenzo at the end of their small wagon, she saw Mr.
Crawford come by, startled to see Miss Brown's head bob up and down and
in and out of the bath-box.

*

*September 3: We arrived opposite Fort Boyzea. It is not marked on the
Reverend's map. Only some of the men will make the trip across the river
to visit it.*
—Ellen Tompkins

Tompkins Family Observation

Ahead is Fort Boyzea, a new trading post where we hope to get some fresh
supplies before heading into the Oregon Territory. Everyone is on edge as we
are getting close, and people are tired. We camped on the south side of the
Snake River, and the men prepared to go over to the fort. Mr. Moss wanted
to go and Father said he would too, along with Mr. Brown and Mr. Lewis.
Father put on his wide-brimmed hat and took a bit of money with him. A
couple of others got ready. Mr. Matthieu was eager because the man at the fort
is known to be French and Mr. Matthieu was going to *parlez* with him: that's
French for speak to him. Mother set us to washing clothing in the water, and
I was told to set out the wet clothing along the side of the wagon so it would
flap in the wind and dry. I don't see the need to enter the Oregon Territory
with clean clothing, but that is Mother's way.

We all headed to the river.

I will finish this later because I want to write about the Salmon River that
enters the Snake at this point, and from here the water of both rivers flows
on into the Columbia. The water here is swift, bubbling, and pushing around
large rocks. This is no river for a boat to travel down.

Adeline Brown

Mr. Moss came over to talk to Mother in a more than friendly way, saying how
difficult it must have been for her to have been with the Indians. He asked
did she want him to bring her anything from the fort. She and I backed away,
partly because of his more than familiar way and partly because he smelled
so bad. He seems a nasty little man.

Susannah saw him with us and came over, suggesting that if he was to cross
the river with the others he should be on his way. Susannah and I talked some.

She is an easy person to be with because she can talk, and she can be very silent, too. I don't feel the need to have to explain anything to her.

We stood quietly together for a time. I thanked her for the bath. She smiled nicely and said she was happy to be able to make it happen and wasn't it fortunate that we had come upon some hot-water springs.

We stood and watched all the activity at the riverside, the men getting their horses ready, the Tompkins family washing, and Ellen running back and forth from the water to their wagon with wet clothes. That family always seems to be washing, the missus having six people to see to.

We watched birds circle about the high cliffs on the other side, and the H. B. Company flag flapping above the fort, which we could see from where we stood. Behind us I could hear Mrs. Shadden complaining about something. Mother Bennett was getting ready for the ride across the river and was giving instructions to her family as to what to do while she was gone. Some other men in the company tended the horses. I could hear the Frenchmen talking away in their funny language, speaking so quickly and with their hands flying about as they talked. Wooley, Jane's dog, belched while he slept just under the wagon. There was the usual noise of horses entering the water, of clopping against stones, of men yelling directions, of people on the banks sending last-minute requests.

Then, there was chaos.

Gone. The word echoed around the people at the riverbank, through the trees nearby, up the cliffs, down into the water, splashing hard against the rocks, and flying off into the sky.

Gone.

SUSANNAH

I looked up from my conversation with Adeline to see the men on their horses enter the river going in a line, one after another. Then Mr. Moss's mule bucked and bit the horse in front of him, setting off a chain of hooves in water, men yelling. Mr. Moss attempted to control his animal, but he was not much good at that, and in front of our eyes Moss yelled out something, a horse slipped sideways, and Mr. Tompkins went flying into the deepest part of the water right into the rocks and was—before our eyes—carried away. Once his body went under the water, he was not seen again. He was just gone.

Behind, him floating serenely on the surface like a small sailing ship, was his broad-brimmed hat, following him downstream.

There was silence on the riverbank: a silence that comes of seeing what is happening and then absorbing it, understanding it, and of being totally incapable of doing one small thing to make it stop. There they were on their horses; there was the usual yelling and sound of horses working hard in the water, men above managing them, and Mr. Moss yelling at his mule.

Then Mr. Tompkins was gone.

I looked at Adeline to see if she had seen what I had witnessed. Her face was ashen with horror. Mr. Crawford appeared at her side and took her arm. Then the others, all frozen in their places, seeing and understanding the event, jumped into action, running this way and that, pointing to where the body might again appear, for no one could survive being jerked backward into rocks in the rushing water. Someone jumped on a horse and followed the river downstream as if to pull Mr. Tompkins from the flow; others yelled.

The small company moved to Mrs. Tompkins and her family standing frozen at water's edge and surrounded her with their concern, their sympathy, and, in their silence, their sadness. She stood stunned in the center of this choir of pity, unable to cry or to cry out, unable to move. Her children ran to her and someone yelled, "Get Ned!" But we all knew, every single person there knew that once in the rapid river amid all those boulders there was no hope: that within seconds Mr. Tompkins had drowned and was being swiftly carried downstream.

Gone.

Gone?

Gone!

Gone. Gone. The word reverberated at the riverbank; it echoed among the stunned people on the shore.

"Gone," said the men on the horses heading to the fort.

"Drowned."

"Gone for good."

It was the most horrible thing I have ever seen, and though young, I have seen a good deal. There was fright and terror and horror and immobility. Then everyone hugged someone near, holding them as if holding up the earth, as if holding up the sky, even. Happy we were to be living flesh in the face of one so quickly dead.

Later that day, as we camped in sorrow, Reuben Lewis came back upstream holding Mr. Tompkins's broad-brimmed hat in his hand—an offering to Mrs. Tompkins. She accepted it as if it were a precious stone or a newborn baby: tenderly, quietly, with tears running down her face, her family at her side. Each reached out to touch the brim of the sodden hat. She turned it round and round, feeling its edge, smoothing the water from the brim, holding it quietly as tears slipped down her face and onto the hat.

Mr. Smith, the elder one, announced that he would hold a service for Danby Tompkins at sundown. The camp was quiet. I am not sure anyone at all ate supper. Everyone knew Mr. Tompkins, knew about his plan to open the first newspaper in the Oregon Territory. And everyone liked him.

From somewhere a bird cawed.

Then in the gloom of the camp, with the sky mellowing in the west, Jane began to sing:

> Fairest Lord Jesus, ruler of all nature,
> O thou of God and man the Son,
> Thee will I cherish,
> Thee will I honor, thou, my soul's glory, joy, and crown.
> Fair are the meadows,
> fairer still the woodlands,
> robed in the blooming garb of spring.

Everything stopped while Jane sang, everything excepting the tears that swelled from her eyes and that ran down Caroline's face. Caroline did not cry aloud, she did not move. She stood like a statue, her eyes fixed downstream.

*

September 4: Our family stood at the river's edge for what seemed forever.
—Ellen Tompkins

MRS. SHADDEN

We remained in the camp today to let the horses and cattle feed. Two young men became impatient traveling with us and decided to ride ahead to join Dr. White's party. Everyone was quiet. I wonder, if Shadden had been the one to go, would there have been the same concern? Everyone is looking at Sidney Moss, who caused the accident to happen. We could all see that: we saw it happen, what Moss had done, his dumb actions with that mule, and the moment when Mr. Tompkins went flying into the swift-moving stream.

We will move on tomorrow, no matter what grief anyone has. We have to keep going. That is what we do, have to do.

Mrs. Tompkins seems rooted at the river, looking west, as if she could pull her husband back again and rewind the spool of events that happened before her eyes but without her being able to do anything at all. Jane stands with her and sometimes sings but is mostly quiet. The smallest of them, Ellen, is with Mrs. Smith, who is talking to her about the cycle of life and all that. She should be telling her about going home to our Heavenly Father, but she is not doing that, from what I hear when I walk near.

It is not so much the death of Mr. Tompkins that is so horrid—that is hard enough. But how do we contain grief, especially knowing that we have to move on? We cannot stay here; we have to keep going west. It was just as bad for that Mrs. Lancaster when her baby died the first week of the trip; she had to bury the baby and go on—which for her was going back east. For young Bailey, too. And Mr. Gibbs, now hardly remembered. For Mrs. Tompkins there will be no grave to mourn over, but at least she is not wailing as the Lancaster woman did, lying in the dirt and making a spectacle. Mrs. Tompkins simply stands silent at the river as if she were a stone waiting for the water to come lap at her feet. Her shoulders sag and she looks worn down.

Now, the whole rest of this journey will be on her. I hope her mister didn't take all their money with him to the fort. They had such hopes. Shadden said that Mr. Tompkins was shipping a printing press to Oregon City to start a newspaper.

In the evening Ned, their son, walked up to his mother and gently took her hand. I was close by and heard him say, "Come, Mother. Susannah has prepared a warm broth for you." After a time the two of them walked quietly away, she holding his arm, her face like a stone.

*

September 5: Mrs. Smith took my hand and asked me to walk with her a bit.
—Ellen Tompkins

MARY SMITH

Ellen asked me if I believed in heaven. I paused a minute, wondering if she was too young for me to speak the truth—my truth—or if it might offend her mother if I discussed my views, which are certainly not those of the Methodist Episcopal Church, or any other church, for that matter.

I chose the truth. But I explained it was my truth and might not be, most certainly was not what her mother or her sisters or she might believe. She nodded and said, "Tell me what you think." This put me on the spot because while it is easy to disdain a belief, it is far harder to explain one, especially one I have held without ever having to put it together before. We hung back from the others, and I said that while some people believe that they will go to heaven and be whole people again, others do not think that.

She nodded. "So what do you believe?" she asked again.

"Ah. Well. I believe in life," I said after a time. She screwed up her face at that, as it sounded like a dodge. "What I mean is that I think life goes on and on."

"Like reincarnation?" she asked without much interest. "Being born again in another body, like one day you are Mrs. Smith and in some other life you are Mr. Jones or Mr. Jones's dog?"

Her voice was full of contempt.

"Not quite," I said. "I believe that we are created; we live in our mother's wombs and then are born. Then when we die," I hastened on, "when we die, we molder back into the earth."

"Whatever does that mean?" she asked.

"Well, like with plants, we set seeds—children you might say, or things we do—and then our bodies just become part of the earth again—like the husks of corn that we don't eat and throw on the refuse pile to be dug into the ground next growing season. We are part of that."

"No Jesus?" asked Ellen.

"No," I said firmly.

She paused, thinking.

"No God?" asked Ellen.

"Well, God, yes, or more probably the Holy Ghost. Something greater, but I don't quite know what." I tried to explain that it would be "something unseeable and all around us." I dug my shoe into the ground in front of me. "Something of nature."

"Reverend Wisner would certainly not approve of any of that," Ellen said tartly but also with a sparkle in her eye. She didn't think highly of the minister at home and had complained of his barking at the congregation about God's laws.

"I think, Ellen," I said, starting over, "that we are part of the living world and that when we die we go back into the plants and flowers of the earth."

"And what about Father?" she said bitterly. "The fish will eat him? And then," and here she began to tear up, "and then we eat the fish? What a dreadful thing to think."

Then the absurdity of all that struck Ellen, and she smirked. I smiled softly until suddenly Ellen began laughing wildly and we laughed together until we cried at the same moment, our eyes full of tears, faces shining with wet. I was hardly able to breathe and I could feel my face turn red as I tried to catch my breath. As Ellen wept. I said to the grieving girl "You needed to cry, Ellen. For your father."

We walked a bit, Ellen rubbing the tears from her face.

"I don't know how to talk about this with you, Ellen," I confessed. "I don't put much stock in heaven."

Ellen looked up. "Well, I don't either," she said, rather fiercely. "The idea of everyone in white robes singing hymns sounds positively like a daydream to me."

"We are two wandering souls," I offered. "We are born, we live, we do our best. And then for us, I think, it is over. It is," I hesitated, "it is just as it was before we were born, when we didn't know we were to be born or that we were the unborn. Our goal while we are living is be kind to people, try our best. And then, we—or the thing that pastors call our soul—just floats away, perhaps like a dandelion seed in the wind. Then it is over, and we are as unconscious dead as we were before we were born. Does that make any sense to you?"

"Martha thinks that Father is watching over us to make sure we will get to Oregon City," Ellen said. We both struggled to keep back a giggle, our laughter of minutes ago erupting again.

"That's a nice thought, Ellen. I don't know that I believe that. I think when I die, that is all there will be for me. We have to make the most of what we have, who we are. So I am going to Oregon and so is your family, and we will do our best there, as we would have at home."

"I don't want you to be sad when I die. I am sixty-two this month, and I have seen a lot. I have helped my son pursue his dream, and I have seen my husband take on a new role, as elder of the company."

"He speaks at services and helps people, like those women in from the Indians. I've seen that," she said.

We walked on, mostly in silence, looking at the plants along the trail, the ones that managed to grow between the rocks or on the hard ground. Suddenly I pointed up as a great blue heron, its neck curled back on itself, its wings open, flew close overhead. "Look at that," I said, at the beauty of the bird flying so near. "Possibly we scared it from the riverbank."

"That, that is a gift to us—to see such beauty and grace."

"Yes," Ellen said. "I understand that."

*

September 6: We walk along a ledge and one mis-step would be fatal. We finally came to a good camping ground and rested.
—Ellen Tompkins

Cynthia Girtman

She still doesn't cry. I sobbed when Mother's sight began to dim. I cried when our dog at home died—and again when we left home, just because of the leaving. And again, when the kitten died on the trail—and no one even knew I had a kitten with me.

Caroline Tompkins goes about the camp quietly, tears streaming down her face but without making a sound. She sees to her children, eats when food is offered, goes to sleep. But she makes no noise at all. It is as if her insides have erupted but she has no voice.

Her face, though, grieves. One can see it, and it is more dreadful than sobs.

Widow Abel

Elbridge came and walked with us, drawing his horse behind him as we followed the Snake River, moving downhill and then across a mountain. He put Lucy on the horse so I could navigate the rocky path along a series of frightful precipices. In many places the path wound along the side of a mountain, and if we or our animal made one misstep it meant certain death. We camped early in the evening. Elbridge talked about the West, about his time with the Indians, and about his hopes to have a house and small farm. He hasn't seen his family in the East for many years and doesn't know if his parents are still alive. He wants to make a new family, he said.

I sense what this is leading to. My sister encourages me to think about marrying again. That is what she and Mr. Perry expect to happen, although I am not sure they would have selected Mr. Trask, he being a mountain man for so many years, roving about among the Indians. He is not at all like Frederick, who was very tidy but impatient, and sometimes short-tempered. He even slapped me once when I didn't have dinner on the table when he returned from his shop. Although Mr. Trask is a man used to physical danger and is courageous, I don't think he would ever slap me. Just look at him with Lucy, upon whom he dotes.

I don't know a better man. He did say he wanted me to take up my land portion when that is possible so that I would have something of my own, even if I were to marry. Marry him, is what he means, I know that. The question is, do I want to marry him, or anyone? Is being a wife what I want most? I cannot live with my sister all my days, and Lucy does need a father to see that she gets to school and finds a husband of her own.

But I am not a maiden. I know what marriage is all about. Marriage is a curious state: we all grow up, we girls, expecting marriage as our proper course in life. No one doubts that fact, but none of us really knows what it entails. My sister has a good marriage, I think. But my experience was not so very good, and that was probably as much my fault, because of my expectations, as it was Frederick's fault. I expected what? I expected that I would have a husband who would always put me first, who would give me what I needed and some of what I wanted, who would be a father to our little ones, and who would provide. A man who would head our household and also be part of a community—that Frederick was not. He was not a social person, although he liked the part that said he was the head of the household. He expected things to run his way.

But now that I have experience with marriage, and was not all that happy in one, do I want another? Mr. Trask doesn't seem to have any money put aside, but I know him to be a hard worker and not one to give up. He is kind to me and he loves Lucy. I believe that he would be good to me, but from my experience with Frederick, I wonder if we would have things to talk about besides Lucy's schooling and the bills that need to be paid. Would he, dare I ask it, enrich my life—not with wealth, I don't expect that—but with companionship? Mr. Trask is not a steady talker, but on the other hand, he took initiative when he thought that Baby needed to have a name of her own—and we were not as well connected to each other at that time as we are now; that is, we hadn't talked all that much. Mr. Tompkins's death seems to have changed how I and perhaps others view things. Life is to be held to, acted on, not to push important things into the future. Elbridge is gentle with Lucy, I can see that, and he said he wanted a family—to create a family after all his years wandering.

He is old, however, at least thirty-seven, while I am only twenty-three. Does that matter? There seem to be so many questions to wonder about, some that are rather unseemly for me to even consider, but having been married I know that it is far better to live with someone who is personally clean rather than not so. I cannot judge this well here on the trail, where none of us is very clean or tidy as much as we want to be. I would want someone gentle at the physical parts of marriage; I wouldn't have known that had I not been married once before, which makes me wonder at all the dither girls go through to get married without knowing much of what it entails.

Marriage is surely what is in my future because living alone with Lucy would be hard, and possibly unseemly. Perhaps even dangerous for both of us. Marriage provides shelter as well as companionship and family; I would also like laughter. Is that too much to hope for?

Mr. Trask has a comfortable shoulder for when Mr. Tompkins died in the river; I was standing nearby at the time, and Elbridge took me in his arms so that I could cry over the awful events, and he held Lucy too. Elbridge is quite a bit taller than me, too, and that feels good. Frederick was just my height or slightly taller, and he always stood straight up when we were out together so that he would appear to be of greater stature.

It felt good to have Mr. Trask's arms around me at the riverbank. I am going to have to come to some decision about this and soon, I think, so that I do not hurt him or myself. I had not expected this when we set out from Indiana, not at all.

*

September 7: We move forward, but I think about Father a lot, too. Today there was a most tremendous hill we had to cross and I stumbled on a rock, hurting my foot some.
—Ellen Tompkins

MARTHA TOMPKINS

Dear Grandmama,

By now you have heard about Father and grieve as I do. What happened was just awful. He was always a good father to me, and I miss him a lot. He would let me sit by him to talk about Ithaca and you and the house we left behind. He knew I wanted to, he knew I would return to Ithaca and so he was sorry he had brought me here. He would say "Oregon Country really isn't for you, is it, Martha-berry?" He always called me Martha-berry, you know. He said he left some money with you for my education, and I am happy to hear that.

I am sorry to leave my family, as Ned is a dear brother and Jane a good sister. Ellen is as we both know her to be, but, I must say, she has kept up the Family Observation well. I would not write about birds and flowers, but it gives her pleasure to do so. And she keeps at it.

I am thinking that before I get back to Ithaca, you might have the front bedroom, the one with the sycamore tree outside the window, painted a light yellow with white trim. My blue bedcover is packed in your basement, and that would look good. I would like a session with Mrs. Elmer about my piano work and one with Mrs. Hurley to have some hats fitted in the latest style. The going has been rough on my shoes too, so I would like to see Mr. Frost about having some new pairs made.

I will bring you a small series of watercolors that I did. They are not the best I could do but will have to serve until I can do better.

With much love,
Your granddaughter Martha

*

September 8: Some horses strayed from camp and delayed our start this morning.
—Ellen Tompkins

Ellen Tompkins

Medorem Crawford came to our camp today, and when I asked how far we had gone, he pointed to my Observation and said he would write today's report. I don't know what Mother would say about that, but he went ahead.

Mr. Crawford's contribution, just as he wrote it:

Thursday 8, Sept. Horses strayed far from camp and instead of an early start as we intended we got off at 9 oclock we left the Branch and gradually rose a long hill. Stopped for dinner on a small stream at 12 oclock started at 2:½ & continued to rise by degrees.

The country over which we have traviled today is mostly covered with bunch Grass which the Horses are very fond of. The Blue mountains are ahead and they struck us with terror as their lofty peaks seem a resting place for the clouds. Below us was a large plain and at some distance we could discover a tree, which we at once recognized as "the lone tree" of which we had before heard. We made all possible speed and at 7 ½ o'clock the advance party arrived at the Tree nearly an hour before the cattle. The Tree is a large Pine standing in the midst of an immense plain entirely alone. It presented a truly singular appearance, and I believe is respected by every traveler through this almost Treeless Country. Within a few yards we found plenty of water and we soon made ourselves comfortable by a good fire. As soon as we arrived at the top of the hill in sight of the Blue Mountains we felt an uncommon chilly wind that increased so as to be uncomfortable before we arrived. As soon as we reached the valley we found our old friend Sage, flourishing in a most unwelcome manner. The grass about camp was not good, traviled 18 miles.

I think Mother would have Mr. Crawford rewrite his entry to correct his spelling, but this is what he wrote, truly.

*

September 9: There was frost on our beds when we woke this morning and a cold wind from the Blue Mountains, their tops all covered with snow.
—Ellen Tompkins

CAROLINE TOMPKINS

I walk with grief, but I keep my feet moving. Otherwise I would be left behind because this company is determined to get to Oregon City before the weather turns. I leave my dear husband behind, ungraved but not unsung. Jane has been a great comfort to me and sings when she sees me tiring. What sort of a monument can we make for Dan? I could ask his mother to have his name etched on the family stone in the cemetery back in New York, but that gives me little comfort, though it might give her some. I could make a grave for him in Oregon but he would not be there: that feels like an empty gesture. Nothing of course can be placed along the Snake River as he was snatched at the falls of the Salmon and he—his body—was raced away downstream. I dread to think that as we are traveling down the river we might come upon him, in fact that is my greatest fear, to see him hooked into a tree or stone. Yet, do I want to think that he is traveling forever, from the Snake into the Columbia and from the Columbia River into the Pacific Ocean, never to be at rest?

If I think of this in a rational way, he is being returned to the earth. I can't think happily that way because wherever he is, he is not with me, nor I with him. We are separate for all times unless of course, there really is a great choir in heaven as the preachers say. If I hold that idea, that we will be joined together one day, it feels fine, but it doesn't hold up well for long. Would body parts also be in heaven waiting to be put together? Would pieces find their rightful owner? In my grief I smile at this idea, which is far-fetched.

I need to learn to live in peace with the fact that he is gone, that I cannot go to a place to mourn, that I need to keep walking for my children so that they have a future—because we cannot stay here. I long to leave the Snake River and never see it again, with its dark green waters and swift current. How different will the Columbia be?

What matters is that the children are healthy and I need to take charge, as Dan had. I look to Ned for help but must not lean on him too much, not give him too much of a burden to carry. He will represent us in the company meetings, although those seem to have dwindled with the company split and the cattle dragging on some miles behind us. We are less a company than a string of travelers, in all sorts of arrangements: Dr. White aiming to get to Oregon before Captain Hastings; the young, unattached men eagerly riding on ahead to find the best work; the wagons in various states of disrepair; then the cattle behind. We are at ease here, at least, with no worries about the Indians. Yet, the way west in this part is more difficult than we anticipated, as we all believed that once we were over the Rockies, it would be as it was along the Platte—a flat and easy walk—which this most certainly is not. The weather has changed too, with a cold wind from the Blue Mountains, their peaks covered with snow. This terrifies me, as does the uncertainty of having water.

Dan would expect us to carry on. That is what I tell myself. He would say, I think, to stay together, get to Oregon, make a home. And then what? There is the printing press. Do we carry that on? Can we do that? I don't know.

Part 5

BEGINNING AND BEYOND

September 10: A very cold morning. The mountains on our left are covered with Pine Trees. Our descent lasted for near an hour, but midway there was a small stream and we rested there. I noticed White Pine and the Spruce Pine, some very tall & slim. We ended in a beautiful valley with good grass and water and much wood for fire.
—Ellen Tompkins

Susannah

It is very cold in the mornings now. We cannot always set off immediately, because sometimes the horses wander from camp in the night; they must be collected before we can start. So we stamp our feet and drink hot water to warm us. Today we walked steadily uphill and then at midday climbed a tremendous hill, which took us more than an hour and three-quarters to descend. The near mountains are covered with white pine trees. We rested and then resumed our descent, sliding along the rocks. Sometimes I slid along on my bottom, as the slant of the hillside was so great it was hard to gain a foothold. We aimed at a beautiful valley below where we found good grass and even several paths leading into a camping place.

After dark two Indians came into camp on horseback. They were from a different tribe from any that we have yet seen, and they carried fish traps. They were dressed more soberly than those Indians of the plains and mountains, where the men were without much clothing, their bodies shining in the sunlight as if polished. I did not think much about them, but I did watch some of the women when they first appeared. The women did not seem to know which way to look, or where, so most looked directly at the faces of the Indians and nowhere else, as that seemed safest.

∗

September 11: It is Sunday. We are all short of food and hope to trade with Indians along the river and found that they had plenty, so instead of starving, or eating from the bottom of our sacks as we expected, we have now enough fish to last us to Dr. Whitman's mission.
—Ellen Tompkins

TOMPKINS FAMILY OBSERVATION

Last night two Indians came into our camp and told us that we would be in Walla Walla in three days. We are so tired of these mountains and find little to soothe us on this high desert where nothing grows.

Walla Walla: that is the site of the mission station created by Dr. and Mrs. Whitman, the place that Reverend Parker, of our town in New York State, decided would be a good spot for missionaries to settle. It feels in some ways as if we have come full circle, from looking at a map in Ithaca that Reverend Parker published in his memoir of going west, our going into the American West, and now to the actual mission spot he selected that is marked on the map.

Father traveled with a copy of Dr. Parker's book, and we have been using the map tipped into the back cover as we travel along. Dr. Parker was a kindly old gentleman when I knew him, but others talked of him as being stern. I know that he sent Dr. Whitman back from the Rocky Mountains to New York State to marry Miss Narcissa Prentiss and then to go west as a missionary couple. They left from our church in Ithaca. Dr. Parker even told Mary Dix, whose family I knew, that she should marry William Gray and leave the next morning for the West. That's something, because even though they did not know each other before, they did as he said. Mother said it was a shame, but I didn't understand why.

Dr. Parker first went west in 1835 to find mission sites for the missionary society—I like to say the letters: ABCFM, the American Board of Commissioners for Foreign Missions. Dr. Parker returned to Ithaca a year or so later.

On the trip back, sailing from the Hawaiian Islands, he wrote the book that was published in Ithaca. In it was the map. His book and his speeches caused a good deal of interested talk about the West. Now we are here, following his map, fulfilling his dream.

It is hard to know how to talk about Father. What I mean is, it is hard to change from "is" to "was," because I still think of him as "is." But it is definitely "was" now: we all saw it happen—right there in front of all of us. Mother mourns but keeps walking. I know she is worried about what to do, how we will manage. I think if we stick together, even though we know that Martha is going to leave, we will do all right. We will have the printing press after all, the first in the Oregon Territory, and there will be a need for things to be printed, like announcements and sales and laws because soon Oregon will have laws of its own. I plan to learn to set type, my fingers being small and agile, even though my spelling is less than excellent.

✻

September 12: Our Indian guide showed us the way to leave the mountains and camp by the water where there was some grass. It was cool and cloudy with rain after dark.
—Ellen Tompkins

WOMEN WATCHING

CAROLINE

I have been standing by the wagon with the warm September sun on my back. Were we moving about it would be hot, but when we stand still, the sun bakes into my skin and helps me relax. I am grateful for the pause, even though I know others are anxious to get going. As we waited, Indians came bringing back our horses that had wandered in the night and had mixed among theirs, showing what Mr. Crawford, who had come back for a time, said was "moral honesty."

These are very different people than those we encountered earlier. They seem used to us white people and speak some English words, like "large boat" and "many years ago," and "white men with us in wintertime." I wonder if these are memories of Meriwether Lewis and William Clark on the expedition that President Jefferson sent out in 1804. That seems like a very long time ago and these Indians are not all that old. But it might be that they passed down a memory of them, or of Astor and his fur trading company, or of others who sailed west and stopped at the mouth of the Columbia River. It is hard to tell. Unlike the Sioux or the Snakes, these Indians seem like . . . like shopkeepers.

MRS. SHADDEN

I stood by the cart this morning and listened to Mr. Brown and Mr. Smith, the old one, talk. They were wondering about the condition of slavery in the Oregon Territory, which Mr. Smith said should be the same as that of the Northwest Territories, that is, no slavery would be allowed. Mr. Brown said that he had heard back in St. Louis that Negroes would not be allowed in the Oregon Territory. Mr. Smith looked surprised. "Not even the free?" he asked. Mr. Brown didn't think so but was not sure. Such a law would only be possible after a territorial government was established, and that wouldn't be for a while. Mr. Smith said that in talking with Dr. White, he learned that the doctor thought he would be appointed acting governor, but Gabriel Brown could not believe that. White, he said, is such a difficult man to get along with.

"Well," said Mr. Smith, "Washington would not know about that. It seems that people in the State Department have high regard for the doctor because he had been in the Oregon Territory and knew something about it. They had not."

"We'll see," said Gabriel Brown.

SUSANNAH

I noticed Mrs. Shadden listening to the men talk, so I went closer and heard their opinions about allowing free Negroes in the Oregon Territory. Or rather, disallowing them. That might mean that we would have to move on shortly after getting to Oregon, yet another move to contemplate.

Caroline Tompkins surprised me when she asked from behind, if there was a problem. She said quietly, "You look worried, Susannah. Is something wrong?" I jumped slightly and replied, "Oh, no," and she moved back to her wagon. I watched her go over to speak with Mrs. Shadden.

"What did you hear, Mrs. Shadden?" Caroline asked with concern.

"No Negroes to be allowed in the Oregon Territory," she replied with a downward smirk. "I always suspected that Lorenzo," she added, "Right from the start, I wondered about him," she said.

"Oh, no need to worry about him," Caroline said. "He is from an old Virginia family with a large plantation near the Carolina border. His mother was from Portugal, I think Susannah said."

"Portugal," snapped Mrs. Shadden. "Ain't that in Africa?"

"Oh, no," replied Caroline softly. "Next to Spain, in Europe."

"Papists?" asked Mrs. Shadden, eager to find some fault.

"Most probably," responded Caroline as she walked away. "Most probably they are Roman Catholics, but they could also be Jews." She could hear Mrs. Shadden muttering that they didn't need "papists or other foreigners here no more than Negroes."

✱

September 13: We keep walking, up and down, around large trees, avoiding rocks. While I walk, I also think about the people with us, and what we will all do in Oregon City.
—Ellen Tompkins

Mary Smith

Mary Smith walked through timbered land along a difficult trail that required descending and then rising up again on the next hill. She walked carefully around rocks in the path, and she watched with awe as a great blue heron, its neck curled, feet trailing behind, flew past.

Mary Smith looked ahead through the trees. The way looked long. She put her right hand gently on her chest to quell its rapid rising and falling and to tamp down the cough she could not shake. It was from the exertion of walking, she knew, from going up and up and up. She thought she might sit, and she remembered sitting on the bed that she and John had taken across New York State in which they had warmed each other, comforted each other at the loss of infants, and then in which they had created Young John and his sister. Anthea still had that bed, back in New York. Would it pass along for generations, she wondered? Might it be known as Mary's bed? Wouldn't that be splendid!

Mary thought about the bed of her childhood, the narrow cot in the room with her two sisters when she was young. She had carved her initial on the bedpost, to the astonishment of her father that she, so young, could do such a thing. He had punished her for putting an *M* on the post, but she had always liked seeing it there and knew it would always be. She thought of the family on this journey sleeping in the wagon and then on the ground and of sitting on the ground, an effort for such an old woman, but overall the trip had not been hard. She and John still warmed each other, their old bones needing all the comfort they could get, especially as the nights grew cold in the mountains.

Mary felt tightness in her chest, causing her to lean hard against a tree. She wobbled, and things near her, like the tree, became fuzzy. She reached out to feel the rough bark against her hand as she pushed into the tree trunk. Yet another mountain to climb, she thought to herself as she slumped slowly to the ground. She placed her hands as a pillow between her cheek and the bark, the tree holding her upright. She thought to herself, "We have gotten to Oregon; I," and she hesitated, "I got them here." Then she corrected herself: "We have brought the family—John, his wife and two children, and my John out here, and all are strong and eager to take up land to begin again. Everyone is well. We have made it to Oregon."

With several gasps for air that could not fill her lungs and looking toward the west, almost without a sound, Mary Smith slid to the ground and died.

*

September 13: Our path today is through dense trees. We found water near the bottom and camped.
—Ellen Tompkins

In Camp

She was not missed, not until Ellen went looking for her to show her a flower she could not name. "Have you seen Mrs. Smith?" she asked around, but no one had. One man, traveling with the cattle, said, "She is trailing along behind us, as she has been lately. Takes her time, but for an old woman, she is a marvel. She always catches up."

Her son John called out, "I'll go and walk back with her to the camp." And off he went. Ned went off in another direction with the horse, Caroline prepared some warm bread for lunch, Jane went to see Susannah, and Mrs. Shadden watched everything, greedily wanting to be in the center. After a time, there was shouting from below the camp: John calling up "hullo, hullo, hullo," and a number of people walked back downhill to where he stood over his mother.

"She just died," he said to the first who arrived. His face contorted as he said, "She just lay down and died here, against a tree, on the road into Oregon." He laid her gently on the ground.

Mrs. Smith was well loved among the company and women cried out how good she was, and men nodded in the face of death, yet another death. As everyone looked down at the woman lying so still in the middle of the pathway, a ball of wool slowly spooled from her pocket.

Her son said, "She looks so small."

"She looks peaceful," said Caroline. Old Mr. Smith finally made it down to his wife, his face covered with tears. He lay down on the earth next to her and cradled her frail body in his arms.

The company watched and mourned. Mrs. Smith had been well liked, but she had also been admired. She was an older woman making a trip that they all had found difficult; she had guts, some thought. Others wondered if she had been wise to set out, yet who could know who would reach their destination and who might not. Caroline said quietly, "She might have died at home just as easily as out here. She was brave."

Then Ellen stepped forward, Ellen who had never talked to a group, who looked small among all the adults. "She didn't want us to mourn," she said. "Mrs. Smith told me that life was a journey and hers had been an interesting one. She was raised along the Hudson River, went as a bride to the Lake Erie area, and now was on her way to Oregon." Ellen looked surprised at herself speaking to these elders. "She said she believed that when she died, she would be returned to the earth that she loved." Ellen came to a complete stop, not knowing how to express Mrs. Smith's ideas about life and death and the afterlife. "We laughed as we talked. We laughed until we were both red in the face because she was . . . she was joyful. She was," and Ellen paused, "she was not afraid."

Ellen stopped, and just as the silence began to feel long and with Ellen having no more to say, Jane stepped forward and began to sing:

Hide me, O my Savior, hide,
Till the storm of life is past;
Safe into the haven guide;
O receive my soul at last.

It was decided that this was no place to bury Mrs. Smith because the ground was hard and the trees dense and they needed to move forward. She could be carried in the last remaining cart to Walla Walla and put in the little cemetery at the Whitmans' mission house. With her final resting place there, she would have made it all the way into the Oregon Territory.

*

September 14: We got to the mission where we will bury Mrs. Smith. What else is there to say?
—Ellen Tompkins

Mother Bennett at Walla Walla

Mother Bennett watched Caroline Tompkins as they laid Mrs. Smith in the ground in the mission cemetery. A small white fence enclosed the area containing several graves. Mary Smith would have company, as there were the graves of several Indians who had died there and one for young Clarissa Whitman, who drowned when she was barely two.

Dr. Whitman, a Presbyterian missionary, had been at Walla Walla with his wife, Narcissa, for six years. He maintained a large farm and was as much a farmer as a missionary, but he sold his produce cheaply. People from the company bought fresh vegetables from him at reasonable terms. It was Dr. Parker, who had drawn the map the company had been using, who had sent Dr. Whitman back to New York to marry Miss Prentiss and to set out for this mission station among the Indians.

Mother Bennett thought to herself, "Others won't think it, but Mrs. Tompkins surely sees this burial is different, perhaps even difficult. There's no comparison between putting someone in a cemetery next to a drowned infant and having a husband hurtling down the river, never knowing if he was gonna stop or just keep on and on. I know Mrs. Tompkins liked Mrs. Smith—and appreciated her too, for her wisdom and for walking so much with her daughter Ellen. Those two talked. I saw 'em looking at things, turning over rocks, wondering about birds. They were a pair, one so old on this trip west and one young and eager. Perhaps they were both eager to know everything about what they saw and could understand. Now, Mr. Smith, who didn't want to go to Oregon at all, will be there, and she won't. Odd, that."

ELLEN

Ellen smiled softly to herself as they laid Mrs. Smith's body, wrapped in clean linens, in the ground. "Just the way she said it should be," she thought. "Just the way." She kept her smile small and private, as it was between old Mrs. Smith and herself alone.

MRS. SHADDEN

I watched Mrs. Whitman at the cemetery. She stood very still and her dress hung about her, something like the angels on the tombs back home, the ones the rich people put up. Her face, covered by a bonnet, was chinalike and unmoving. I was surprised at her glowing red hair. Mourning she was, and not for Mrs. Smith, I bet, but for her little girl, buried nearby, a victim of drowning in the river when she was just a little thing. Her grave was neatly trimmed with small yellow flowers up against the fence rail. There she stood, Mrs. Whitman, going through the motions of mourning the newest arrival, but I saw her red hair swing around to look at her baby's grave.

LOUISA GIRTMAN

Dr. White told me, back a ways on the trail, that we would come to Walla Walla and would meet Narcissa Whitman at the mission. In going west to create missions, she and Eliza Spaulding were the first white women to cross the country (for both, the journey was a wedding trip). Mrs. Spaulding and her husband are at a place called Lapwai, somewhere north of here. They left from the church in Ithaca, New York; most probably Mrs. Tompkins knows about that. It was a Mr. Gray who guided them.

Dr. White said that his wife, who is named Serepta, and Mrs. Whitman had corresponded, especially after the death of tiny Clarissa Whitman, for the Whites had also had a child drowned, theirs in the waters of the Willamette River. This Oregon, so hard won by all of us, getting there, and being there too, will extract a toll. I don't wish I were Gulliver, but I would not mind a giant eagle landing here to take us on his wings the rest of the way.

I grow weary.

WIDOW ABEL

Dr. Whitman held a fine service for Mrs. Smith, and Jane sang Psalm 100. We all joined in on the refrain. Mrs. Whitman seemed a nice woman but distracted, deep in her own thoughts. Dr. Whitman said that Dr. White had stayed at the mission several days before but had gone on to Oregon City. We got ready to leave the mission when some of those with the cattle traveling slowly behind us came in, so we are now a larger force excepting that the Bennett clan is talking about going on ahead. The Hudson Bay Company fort is about a day's walk west from the mission at the joining of the Snake and the Columbia Rivers.

We are not much of a company at this point. Our wagons are gone, broken down for faster travel. Along the way we have dumped a chair, a grandfather clock, dishes, a tea set, some old wooden chests. Susannah and Lorenzo took apart their wagon and left the bath contraption behind, it being too bulky to take forward, and we have all left clothing and boots and other personal items, like breadcrumbs trailing out behind us.

We have also gained some things—well, people. Mrs. Brown and her daughter, Adeline, are now with us. That daughter looks a lot livelier now than when they first arrived. We have a real sense of which people we can trust and who we don't or can't. Mr. Moss still galls all of us with his cranky ways, and we blame him for Mr. Tompkins's death at the Salmon River. He can't but know that.

We know who will come when there is an emergency, with whom to leave a child for a couple of minutes, who will share meat or fish, who looks out for all of us. And young Lucy has a cousin named Susannah, whom we birthed along the way.

We have lost people too: the Lancaster baby, Bailey who was shot, Mr. Gibbs, Mr. Tompkins, and now Mrs. Smith. They are all gone. And then there are those who have gone on ahead: Dr. White, Captain Hastings, some of the trappers who joined us near Fort Hall, a few of the young men, and now the Bennett family is talking about going off to California.

Elbridge has just brought Lucy back to me for dinner. He relieves me of her each afternoon when we camp. They go off to enjoy the woods. He and Mr. Perry get along and Elbridge chucks baby Susannah under the chin, but it is Lucy he dotes on. He brings us game or fish and eats his supper each day with us, which seems to me to imply some sort of unspoken understanding. Is that understanding enough or do we need to speak out our intentions? I don't know, but I think for now it is enough. I am in no rush, but at the same time I am anxious. Anxious to have things settled, for one thing, and anxious too about how do I say this, about the marriage part of being married. I like Elbridge's arm around me, comforting me. I hope more will also be pleasant.

Mr. Crawford is now traveling with our company, tending Dr. White's cattle. He eats each evening with Mr. Smith and Mrs. and Miss Brown.

There was laughter from the Tompkins family at dinner last evening. That is a good thing, for what happened at the Snake River is something they will never get over. How could they? They will see forever the image of Mr. Tompkins going head over his horse into the water. They will see Mr. Tompkins's hat, sailing down the water, as if going after him, as if he would need it.

*

September 17: Drove to the Fort found Mr. McKenly from home not to return until evening. Could not get the Doct's Things drove down the river and camped, traviled four miles. The rest of the company went on. The Banks of the River on each side present tremendous pinnacles of rock mostly perpendicular. We find considerable of sage yet in places.
—Medorem Crawford

CAROLINE TOMPKINS

"There is something I want all of you to know," Caroline said to her family as they sat to eat. "When Oregon becomes a territory it will be governed under the laws that were in effect in the Western Reserve, you know, Ohio, Illinois, Indiana, Michigan, and Wisconsin—those states gained after the Revolutionary War. Those laws prohibit slavery. At home we were an abolitionist family, against slavery existing in our country, and there is no reason for us to change our thinking even though we are heading for the west coast. The problem is that Oregon Territory is poised to exclude all Negroes from living within it."

"So?" asked Ned.

There was a pause. Then Martha pounced: "That Lorenzo Couch. He's a Black man, isn't he?"

"No," said Caroline, quietly. "Lorenzo Couch is from an old Virginia family that married into a family with whom they had trading agreements. His mother was Portuguese," she said.

"Then what is the problem, Mother?" asked Ned.

"The problem, as you call it, is Susannah Couch, whose father was a white man but whose mother was a slave on the plantation."

"But she's white, Mother," exclaimed Jane, without stuttering, jutting out her arm. "She looks totally white, like us. I'm darker skinned than she is!"

"Race," said Caroline, "turns out to be a complicated thing. Susannah's mother was also the child of a white father and a Black mother. Susannah appears to be white to us, but according to the laws of some southern states, she would be classed as Black or mulatto. Her situation is that she was born a slave. I don't know what her standing will be in Oregon. Nor does she."

"They are running off," said Martha, with a great burst of romantic enthusiasm.

"Indeed, they are," said Caroline. "There was some threat to Susannah, and she and Lorenzo took off. Now they face possible discrimination in Oregon."

"Well, no one need know," said Ellen.

"We know, Ellen. And we can keep it to ourselves. But others might not. There are Virginians in this company, and others who will come to Oregon."

"We will vouch for her," said Ned, without hesitation.

"We could," replied Caroline evenly, "but that doesn't change the truth of the situation."

"Are they married?" asked Martha.

"Yes, at the cathedral in St. Louis," said Caroline, satisfying Martha's long-standing curiosity about the couple.

"So what do we do," asked Ellen, who looked questioningly at her family. "What do we do?"

After a moment, Caroline said, "We stand by them, for one thing. And we work to change public opinion and the law."

Martha, looking at Ned, said, "Well, Ned can vote, but we can't."

"Shouldn't we be able to?" asked Caroline evenly. "Shouldn't women also have the right to vote? Didn't we all make it over the mountains, men and women both? I will be subject to tax when we get to Oregon, but I will have no voice in what taxes I will be required to pay."

"Of course we should vote," said Ellen. "No taxation without representation," she recited. Caroline looked pleased that Ellen had paid attention in class.

"But until then," said Caroline, "we must use whatever means we can to promote the vote for women and equality for everyone living in Oregon."

Ned smiled. "Spoken like a newspaper editor, Mother. You are going to do it, aren't you?"

"I think so. I think we can. We have a lot of causes," said Caroline, "and we have a printing press and an order for paper and ink. I think we should, but we will all have to help. What do you think?"

"Well, I'm in," said Ned. "I don't want to be a farmer."

"And I," said Jane.

"May I be?" asked Ellen.

"We all are then," Ned said, and he looked at Martha.

"You have to decide, dear, what you are going to do," said Caroline gently. "You can stay and make the Oregon Territory a state or return to Ithaca to your studies. Both are good options, but it is for you to decide."

Martha looked confused. "I don't know, Mother. You and Father have always decided for me. I don't know yet."

"Take your time. Meanwhile, we need to get down the Columbia River. That is the next step."

"To Oregon," they said in quiet unison.

*

September 18: Went to the Fort and got our things. Started at 9 o'clock lost two animals went back and found them and kept down the river, the most of time a steep bluff of rocks was on our left with occasional spots of grass sufficient for camping. Traveled 12 m.
—Medorem Crawford

MARTHA TOMPKINS TO HER GRANDMOTHER

Dear Grandmama,

We are near the Columbia River. If you look at the map by Reverend Parker that Father gave you, you will see an "F.W.W.," which means Fort Walla Walla. We are headed from the mission that Dr. Whitman and his wife Narcissa Prentiss run. It is the mission that our church— your church on the village square—collects money to support. We buried Mrs. Smith there, in the small cemetery.

I think travel from here on into Oregon will be difficult, but we might be able to find some Indians with a boat to take us down the river—and wouldn't that be grand? We have cut apart our wagon into a pull cart that one horse can manage, so we are able to move a bit faster. A wagon would be difficult on this road along the high riverbank, anyway.

If you look in Reverend Parker's book, the one with the dark cover, about his time in the Pacific Northwest, you will see the only picture is of the rocky walls, which are near. That way, you can know where we are almost exactly. While I have not enjoyed this trip, I do like seeing on the map where we are and seeing what progress we have made. Mr. Crawford, the young man from Havana, New York, keeps the daily mileage, but I am not quite sure how he does that.

What astounds me is Reverend Parker's map. He was not a cartographer. I am sure he had someone else's map to go by when he went west in 1835, but he has all sorts of up-to-date things on his map, and he also charts places he surely didn't go. So how did he do that? So making a map is an interesting and complicated thing, especially for one untrained to do so. Mr. Crawford said that there is also a map by a man named Mellish, but I haven't seen it and don't know if Dr. Parker's is like that or not.

The big news is that Mother is going to take up the printing press to publish the first newspaper in the Oregon Territory. I am sure it will be a smashing success. Well, I hope so. Ned and Jane and Ellen are going to work with her, Ned saying he doesn't want to farm. Ellen's spelling will have to improve for her to be a typesetter, but she is avid to be involved. Earlier Father had said she might write short notes on nature, which she would like to do. I don't know what Jane will do. Nothing is figured out yet, but Mother already has some causes she hopes to promote.

Would you believe, she is going to advocate for woman suffrage in addition to abolition of slavery. Now whoever thought of such a thing, but Mother thinks with so few people in the Oregon Territory there will be a need for women to vote to make Oregon a state—in due time, of course. So now she is looking forward and not acting numb all the time. And she cries less, though I know she misses Father.

Perhaps Ned will be the publisher and Mother the editor; they are working this out.

They offered me a place in the newspaper business and said that it was my choice to return to Ithaca to study or to stay and build a state. This leaves me confused, but I am still hoping to return to live with you and to see my friends.

With all my affection,
Your granddaughter, Martha

*

September 19: Started at 8 o'clock drove on at a good pace very warm day camped in a good spot on the river traveled 15 m.
—Medorem Crawford

TOMPKINS FAMILY OBSERVATION

I need to take this Observation even more seriously if I am to become a newspaper person. That makes me feel odd about writing. It makes me self-conscious. Writing for the family was one thing, and after a week or so I was writing for myself, but to write for a paying public is a different thing altogether. I need to know what I am writing about, for one thing, and I can't assume that what I think is right. When I had questions before, I went to Mrs. Smith, who usually had answers about plants and birds. Where do I get my information in a place with no Mrs. Smith, no libraries, and no newspaper but the one I am writing for?

I know that I can ask people—if they will take me seriously. But I have also learned from writing this Observation that people can have different opinions about things, such as what happened or why. So I guess I need to ask several people and then figure out what to believe. Do I state what I believe? I don't know. I asked Mother, and she didn't know either but said there are various types of articles in a newspaper, both factual and opinion pieces.

It seems what we need, more than articles, is advertising to support the paper. It was decided that Ned would look after that, getting people to advertise. Jane will take care of billing them and keeping accounts. She liked mathematics at the Ithaca Academy and said she can figure out bookkeeping, especially if we get someone to show her how to start. It should be an easy thing, money in and money out. It is the money owed and the interest part that I would not like, but Jane says that she can do that.

When we started this trip, we looked forward and it was interesting. Then Father drowned and we didn't look anywhere except at the ground in front of us for the next step we had to take. Now we are looking forward again, and I think that's a good thing.

＊

September 20: Kept down the river very sandy barren country destitute of
timber (crossed the Unadilla). Cold wind & little rain. Mr. Gray called
at camp on his return from Vancouver.
—Medorem Crawford

MRS. PERRY, WIDOW ABEL'S SISTER

Elbridge Trask has been courting Hannah and takes supper with us. I
don't know that I would have selected Mr. Trask for Hannah, but he is
kind to her, makes her laugh, and he loves Lucy. Mr. Trask seems a bit
rough around the edges, that is, not a neat and tidy man, but his good
qualities are ones that matter. Frederick was neat and tidy and look how
that turned out.

I am sad that Mrs. Smith died on the trail and that Mr. Tompkins
drowned, but it is good that we are now going forward and our family is
healthy. Baby Susannah seems to thrive with the jiggling of the cart or on
Mr. Perry's shoulder. But the company has come apart, with Dr. White
somewhere ahead crowing about his achievements, Captain Hastings coun-
tering everything the doctor has to say, and now Mr. Force is angry about
something. Mr. Moss, of course, is always at odds with everyone. We are a
string of people, with some cattle to the rear. We are walking more easily
as we are not bunched up or smothered with dust. The way is rocky and
narrow, and it is up and down. Today we crossed the Umatilla River amid
a cold wind and some rain.

We also met up with Reverend and Mrs. Spaulding, the other missionary
couple who traveled with Dr. and Mrs. Whitman to the West six years ago.
Mrs. Spaulding is a lovely woman and we talked for a while about setting up
a household out here in the wilderness. She said that Oregon City is new but
quite civilized, with streets and shops, but she lives at a mission called Lapwai
somewhere north of here. Then to our surprise a man named William Gray
appeared on the trail. He was on his way back to Vancouver. Suddenly, this
was like an Indiana turnpike.

*

September 21: Started at 10 o'clock and parted with Mr. & Mrs. Spaulding. Traveled 20 miles.
—Medorem Crawford

Widow Abel

It is most curious having a life to start over. I come to Elbridge knowing so much more than I did when I became engaged to Frederick, and I think I am wiser about myself. I know more now what I want. Frederick was a handsome man and I thought myself lucky. Now, I look at Elbridge, who is a large man and somewhat shaggy, and find in him things that I care more about than a smooth face and tidy clothing. Elbridge touches my arm most gently when he wants my attention, and he looks to me for my opinions, as he has never had a home of his own excepting in the mountains, where he lived rough. So I feel valued, if that is the right word, or appreciated, or a person in my own right and not just an appendage. I am sure Elbridge is not perfect and I know myself not to be, but I think we can adjust to each other. I know he listens to me and he is kind to Sister and her husband. He brings in meat when he can, although there has not been much game along this rocky trail along the river. But there is salmon that the Indians know how to catch and cure.

What I feel is this, and it is hard to put into words. In my marriage with Frederick there was a right and wrong way to do things, but that was back in Indiana. Here we are dealing with different things, and while there is certainly a wrong way, one that could be dangerous to us, the right way is something that has to be figured out as we go along. I am not trapped, dare I say that, into the way things always were but can make new decisions, and consult, and figure out what is the best thing to do. Everything feels very new and even exciting.

*

September 23: Started late, lost my horse last night, Indians brought him into camp this morning. Traveled 11 miles
—Medorem Crawford

THE BENNETT GIRL

My pa bought two mules at the fort to carry our goods, and they have been a great trial, as we have to keep them going in the right direction, without losing them in the forest or over a cliff. Ma keeps us fed, even shooting game along the way, but now we are eating fish. Sometimes eating outside is fun, but today there is tremendous wind and food whips off our plates unless we turn our backs on the gusts.

I am the youngest of the family, and we are all well. My brothers have enjoyed this time, as they want to be farmers and to go hunting and trapping. We aim to go to California. If each of my brothers receives 640 acres, they will be richer than the men back home.

My pa calls me the Belle of the Pacific and says I will be the prettiest young woman there. I wonder if Belle is gonna be my name, or something else. I can't remain the Bennett girl forever. Since I know myself to be plain, the scarcity of females will be good for me. As it is, several men call at our wagon, but I am not yet much interested in marriage. I seen it with Ma and Pa. As an unmarried girl I seem to have gotten a status I never would have had at home. Here, I have that choice.

I heard that Mrs. Tompkins is going to set up the printing press and put out a newspaper herself. She plans to campaign for women voting, but I didn't mean voting when I said I have choice. I don't care about voting. But when the time comes, I do care to pick out a husband that pleases me, and that is a vote I look forward to. I don't know if I will choose well. I will talk it over with Pa and Ma, but I do get to choose.

*

September 24: Came to a tremendous rapid Creek, obliged to take all
over in a canoe which was dangerous. Large Indian town, traviled 6 m.
—Medorem Crawford

MRS. MARY BROWN

Adeline and I could not have fallen in with better people. Even though this company is pulling apart, with the more able going faster and those tending the cattle and with families moving more deliberately, we have been welcomed. Mr. Smith is kind and solicitous; the Tompkins family, even with their own grief, are caring; and Susannah and her odd husband, Lorenzo, are thoughtful about our needs. I talk a good deal to Susannah and enjoy her company. She is very hopeful about the future, and we both talk about the way that Mr. Crawford has been courteous to Adeline. He eats supper with us sometimes, but he also has responsibility for the cattle following along and is, in some ways, the clerk to this rump of a company.

I regard Mr. Smith as the leader, but Mr. Fitzpatrick is the trail boss, as he knows more than anyone about the country we are entering. He said he would leave us soon, however, and Mr. F. X. Matthieu plans to go on ahead to join fellow Canadians at a place called Champoeg.

The names on the land here are difficult and reflect the native presence more than the names back home in Missouri or before that in Tennessee, where names were mostly of the families who settled in the area. Of course there are many Indians here; we see them daily now, and they do not frighten me. One brought a canoe to help us cross a very swift-running stream. It was precarious, though, with goods in the canoe, and then people. The boat was hard to manage.

I am so very conscious of water here. I never really thought about it before, but now, there is the Columbia River along which we are traveling, and the streams that flow into it, each needing to be crossed in some way. Today was a trial. We lost a box of linens that belonged to Susannah Couch. She seemed sad to see them go but then said, "Better linens than one of us. I can weave more," and so they were forgotten. Will someone downstream pick them up and use them? There are many waterfalls, small streams that spill long distances down the sides of the rocks.

*

*September 25: I feel bad this morning in consequence of getting wet yester-
day and my eyes are much affected by the flying sand. Started at 11 o'clock
traviled over hills, saw a high snowy peak which we understand to be Mt.
Hood. Passed the Dalles or rapids of the river which is a singular sight.
Arrived at Mr. Perkins who preached in camp this evening.*
—Medorem Crawford

Susannah Couch

This is nothing at all like Virginia.

We are all affected by the flying sand. It gets in our clothing and especially
in our eyes. We suffer blindness from time to time, even when it is dangerous
not to see what we are doing or where we are going. The way is very rough.
To the south we see Mount Hood, a high snowy peak. It is majestic, and we
are so glad we do not have to climb it, as it juts way into the sky; the snow
looks like cream dripping down the sides of a sweet. We have traveled over
hills and steep places where we slid down the hillside. We also passed rapids
at The Dalles and have gone to the mission run by Mr. Perkins, where we met
up with others from our company. Mr. Perkins preached in the evening and
everyone attended, glad to be together, to sit on benches and not the ground,
glad to hear a preacher in such a place.

Lorenzo and I have got to figure our next steps. We planned to settle in
Oregon, but if there is a prejudice we might have to go on to California or
even to the islands. I would like to overwinter here before we have to travel
any more, as I am weary and running out of my supplies for healing. My
innards are rumbling, especially in the mornings when I cannot keep down
what we call coffee but that isn't more than warm water with a touch of tea
leaves. I would like to rest a bit and care for Lorenzo and me and not have to
tend to everyone else, at least not all the time.

Baby Susannah had some trouble keeping her milk down, but I think
that problem has eased, and she is now gaining weight and looks healthy. I
went over and rubbed her all over with salve to oil up her skin. She seemed
to like that.

*

September 26: Mr. Perkins rec'd and hospitably treated, got potatoes &c.
The day is very pleasant indeed and the tall trees through which we are
passing adds much to the beauty.
—Medorem Crawford

Mrs. Perry

We traveled today up a long and tiring hill, leaving the river behind us, moving into the most romantic country I have yet seen. The day was pleasant, and Mr. Perry walked along with me, carrying baby Susannah. Our goods were on a fairly sure-footed horse we got from the Indians trading for the last of our cart and what was in it. We have lost just about everything we thought dear: our family Bible, christening clothing for Susannah and other children we are yet to have, the silver spoons that my grandmother gave me, Mr. Perry's best tools, and most of our clothing. We carry along food enough to get us through—we are still saying that, getting through. The way does not seem to get easier.

What we have lost seems little, now, even though we thought those things so necessary in Indiana when we packed for this journey. Things we could not be without, things from home. Things that meant home. But here we are feeling richer than ever. We have our health and feel sure we will make it to Oregon City. We have our child, something that we could not succeed in doing in Indiana, and we have hope for the future. So the things we carry now, that seem most precious to us, are weightless. We have a family, and Mr. Perry will help build up Oregon.

We carry other weightless things forward with us, too: the memory of our parents and of our home in the East, relatives we have left behind, and we carry forward the burden of Frederick's suiciding in the barn—of Hannah finding him hanging from the beam, the bench he climbed on and then kicked back, his face blue. That will never leave us. As we moved forward, after Hannah met Elbridge she was able to stop looking back to Indiana and to look ahead to Oregon. Frederick hangs like a shadow, however, but the hurt he gave her is fading; the future she thought she lost is appearing before her, though differently than she might have imagined. She seems to be able to remember Frederick without hating what he did to her and to the life she expected to live. He'll always be there, of course, in little Lucy's flaming hair and her darting eyes, but Lucy never knew her father and she is very attached to Mr. Trask.

We both know that this is not a happy ending but a new beginning. It won't all be easy, and who knows what occupation Mr. Trask will take up, but I think he will prove to be a gentle husband and a good father. Already they talk of children they might have of their own. She is over the worst, but the pain is not gone and never will be, I think. At least, not totally, but she is whole now or as whole as one can be on the verge of a new life.

On our left arises Mount Hood with its snowy peak glistening in the sunbeams. On the right and about the same distance from the river is Mount St. Helens, which resembles Mount Hood very much. As we descended this evening we saw far below us the mighty Columbia River flowing forward to the sea, dividing the two snowy peaks. We went down a considerable hill and found the pleasantest camp, the best wood, grass, and water we have had in a long time. Though the way has been hard and long, I feel a peace within myself and with the world around me. Yet, we are not there. We have days to go.

WHAT CAROLINE OBSERVED

Watching as people unloaded their treasures along the trail, Caroline marveled at what people had kept with them and hauled over the prairie, along the Platte, and then, even when the going became very rough, over the Rocky Mountains and beyond. Left along the way there was a Watson shelf clock, made in Cincinnati, and a Bible; a box of fine linens; a yellow hat with a feather; a tangle of shoes; a crock from home cleaned of the butter it had once held; a burned cooking pan; various undergarments; a heavy lock; and a lady's silk shift that Caroline watched Adeline Brown pick up as she went by. There was a French spyglass and its leather case; extra tackle for the oxen; a small chest of drawers that had been fitted into a wagon; a large carpetbag; several heavy coats; part of a wagon bonnet that had torn in the wind and no longer provided protection; a single candlestick; some twine; various tools— from the Gabriel Brown wagon, she thought. There was a dog lead; an extra axel, unused; several buckets; a long whip for oxen—and one ox itself. There was a small pile of books and even the tablet that Ellen had been given for botanical drawings that she had not used. There were cut nails with hammered heads in a cloth bag, some large wooden screws for wagon beds, and even a wagon seat that had been dismantled to lighten the load. There were two Bennington glazed pottery bowls, a Cantonware dish that had come by ship to the East Coast as ballast in the previous century; a ladder-back chair that had hung on the side of a wagon—the other had been jettisoned days earlier in a pile of leavings. There was a battered wood and bristle hairbrush with some long strands of hair still attached, and there were peaches that had not been sufficiently dried and had spoiled and smelled of rot. There were some odd pieces of wood; a hunting horn inscribed with the initials J. M. C. A. that someone had thought would be handy; a bedpost, but no headboard; a pile of laces now seen as unnecessary in the world they had entered. And there were broken parts of just about everything, things kept because they might be useful, or things kept to repair later when there was time but were now seen as too cumbersome, too heavy, too unnecessary to put on a mule or in one's sack to carry.

Caroline reached into one pile and from it pulled a book that she slipped into the large pocket of her apron.

*

September 27: Mr. Crawford has gone back to find his missing horse.
—Ellen Tompkins

Adeline Brown

Mother tires of being on the trail, of the walking up and down, of the cold, wet rain and then the parched places. The rocks are especially hard to walk over and around, and small pieces jut from the ground to catch our feet. Mother and I have cut our dresses way above our shoe tops to make it easier to walk. We are not able to wash our clothes, having little beyond these borrowed dresses and the shifts we sleep in. Mother, who came from a good family in Tennessee, has had a life of toil. When they were young, she and Father moved to Missouri, where they set up a farm, away from those who favored slaves. They thought they were doing things in an honorable way:

not causing trouble with neighbors, hating slavery, being kind to those who came in need.

But then the Indians came and changed our lives forever.

I try not to think of our time with them, but memories come. The family that took Mother was kind to her, in their way, and gave her the lighter chores because she was elderly, but still she was a slave for them and given little to eat. She collected wood and packed up for each move they made. I was treated somewhat more kindly because I was younger and probably seen as someone who could bear children.

I have not been able to talk about my time with the Indians with Mr. Crawford. He does not ask, but he calls daily and brings Mother and me, and Mr. Smith, game and fish when he is not chasing horses that have gotten loose. He pays me attention, but I am not sure I am ready to have attention paid. Mother says, however, to think carefully before sending him away. He is a good man, I know. Steady. But I feel clouded by what has happened even though I want to be happy and someday to have a family.

It was Susannah Couch who understood that I needed to feel pure again. I know the hot water and the herbs she put in it helped ease away the past and made me feel clean. Still, I cannot block out the fact of our captivity, because it happened. The cruelty of it is lessening; I think of it less.

We were lucky to have found ourselves with this group of people, as mostly they have been kind. I know some of the men, and possibly that Mrs. Shadden, still look at me as having secrets they think they should know. Mostly people just accept us as we are—poor women traveling west, with nothing to call our own, not so far different from any of them. Those we are traveling with, this small part of the company, have almost as little as we. The wagons have been given up, and the carts too, and we travel with packs on the horses or on our backs. We all have our own pasts, but we also have our own hope for a better future.

Although Mr. Crawford takes my arm now and again, I am not yet ready for more than the daily walking. I shall need time before I can trust in the future.

*

*September 28: Mr. Crawford comes and goes, but he always stops to see
Adeline Brown.*
—Ellen Tompkins

MARTHA TOMPKINS

Dear Grandmama,

We are walking through the most beautiful country, with large snow-
covered mountains to the north and south and the Columbia River
below. The way is rough, but I am used to picking the path between
rocks. I am writing this as we are camped and will carry this letter to
Oregon City, where it will go into a boat to San Francisco and then
down the coast to Panama, where there is a land crossing over to the
Atlantic Ocean, and then by ship up to you in New York. The letter
will travel farther than we have gone, and we have been walking since
mid-May and here it is almost October. We have crossed the continent
and I feel strong, able to do things that I would not have imagined
back home.

Yet, I want to return to you to continue my education. I have
thought about the newspaper business, and I don't want to do that.
I don't think I want to sit in an office and wait for people to come
in to take out subscriptions, or to take money for ads. I could be a
newspaper-woman with a pad and pencil going up the street to a fire
to see what is happening, or to ask people for their views. But none
of that really suits me: I don't like talking to strangers, or interrupting
people; I am not keen on asking the same question over and over, and
I certainly don't want to keep accounts of money. These are not what I
want to do, and what else would there be?

I should like to study music and perhaps become a teacher. I like
painting and perhaps could attend school in Brooklyn, living with
Mrs. Brewster, of course, for a term. These are the things that attract
me. And Grandmama, I like my friends at home and miss them and

you. I think I am a settled person, not one who likes upsets—and we have had many upsets on this journey west.

Mother is willing to send me home if it is my desire. She will consult with people at the Methodist Mission so that I might accompany a missionary family returning to the East. It might take a while, and I might even follow the route my letter is to take, returning by sea, perhaps by way of the Hawaiian Islands, where there is a large mission school from which, she has been assured, people come and go all the time. This sounds so much more a pleasant trip than the one we are currently on. I would have time to read and even write up important events or paint sea birds as they land on the ship.

I won't be home soon, but do know I am coming back.

With my love to you,

Martha Tompkins

*

September 29: We lost another mule today. Our party gets smaller and smaller.

—Ellen Tompkins

Widow Abel

Indians came into camp today after a most uncomfortable night. Lucy cried in the cold, and I could not quiet her though we slept close together under our blanket. Our party grows smaller as Mr. Fitzpatrick has left us, and Mr. Crawford has gone back after some horses that were left behind. John Force, who started out with us and went ahead some time ago, came back looking for horses of his that had gotten away. I wonder if we have gotten sloppy knowing that we are close to our goal, or perhaps there is a lack of rope to tie all the horses at night.

Everyone is edgy; I do know that. I think some worry that something might happen within days of our being in Oregon City, or that we won't be received well, coming as we are at the beginning of the winter season with so little, or that we will be disappointed by what we find. No one wants an accident at this point, as it would all seem so senseless to have come such a distance and not reach our destination. It would be like being killed the last day of a battle or a war—having gone through everything but not living to the end. I trust nothing will happen and we will get through.

Elbridge is aiding us. He brings food and carries Lucy when he can. He and Mr. Perry talk about what they will do in Oregon. Mr. Perry is a skilled carpenter and will want to use his skills, while Elbridge wants to settle down and farm. After so many years of traveling, he wants to have land that he improves, perhaps with an orchard, and something to leave to his children at the end of his days. He has become so very dear to me, I shudder to think of his end of days, and wish him a long life—wish us a long life. He wants to go a ways from Oregon City. When Oregon becomes an official territory of the United States, he will qualify for free land. As will I.

✳

September 30: We camped in a most dismal place, but we are getting closer and closer.
—Ellen Tompkins

MRS. SHADDEN

I don't want to be bragging too soon, but judging from what has befallen others, the Shaddens are doing fine. All the children are well, excepting for the ringworm that the youngest has caught. Shadden himself is steady, though he has the piles and complains every time he needs to go, but that could have happened even at home and is probably his own fault anyway. But we have enough food to get us through; the elder boy trades for fish, and we have much of what we started with, excepting the wagon, which is now gone. We started with much less than most of the others, so we had less to lose. We are survivors.

Our mule died a while back, and of course that Mr. Moss shot our cow a long time ago and still hasn't compensated us and probably won't ever. But he isn't doing very well either. His liquor supply is gone, he ain't got no tobacco left, and his horse and cart fell over the cliff a day or so back, not that anyone noticed. It just went. So he is walking the rest of the way, begging bits from that Susannah Couch and hanging around her Lorenzo, who is a dark-looking man if I ever saw one. I doubt either one of them is up to much good. The

Couch wagon is gone too, so we are all walking together. The animals that still live are lean and weary. It seems to me that the children on this trip have come out stronger than ever—and resourceful. They don't need to be told to mind. They see how things are and what dangers are nearby. They all—well, those that are old enough to walk on their own—seem fine to me.

We all had services back at the Whitman mission for Mrs. Smith and Mr. Tompkins and then again at The Dalles, where Reverend Weaver gave the children a special talking to about our Lord and our duties. They listened to him, not having been in school for a long time, and seemed pleased to have been singled out. The smaller children, Widow Abel's and her sister's child, are still in arms, the one an infant, the other getting carried everywhere by that Mr. Trask on his horse or on his shoulders. What do you think those two are cooking up?

The roads we are on are not roads but ways to go along, around the rocks and through groves of trees. Some places are bad and some are worse. We have come almost to the Willamette River and are not far from Oregon City. Some of the young men have gone on to Fort Vancouver with the McKay boys, and some have simply gone ahead and who knows where they might be. We have no company to speak of but are, in fact, a group of traveling families, a few of which are still together.

There are all those traveling with Mr. Brown. There is the Tompkins family, without the mister of course; there are those two young'uns from Virginia: Couch. The Perrys are intact, with a new baby. Mr. Smith, whose wife died on the trail, is still with us, even at his age, along with the two Indian captives. I would like to know what happened to them while they were with the Comanches, who are not known for their polite ways. Those women, Mrs. Brown and her daughter, seem skittish around the rest of us, but Medorem Crawford, the young man Dr. White brought on this trip, pays them attention and brings food when he can. He has other duties, though, keeping track of the horses and I guess reporting to Dr. White when we get to Oregon, but it is my guess that he will break with the doctor and stick with the young woman to whom he pays a good deal of attention.

We set out in such an organized fashion, with a constitution even, and then fell into pieces. Captain Hastings caused trouble, and then others battled with the doctor. Everyone dislikes Dr. White, who, once he smelled the Columbia River, had little time for us anyway. A grasping sort of man he is, and not a trusty soul. What was our government thinking by making him a captain of an overland company I do not know. He is no leader of men—or women. He got himself in a lot of trouble over those dogs, and yet there are a number of dogs still with us. Some have suffered on the trip; one or two died. That Wooley is still going but is acting old, yet none of the dogs got rabies or went mad, and to be truthful, none warned us of the Indians because, by and large, the Indians were more helpful to us than threatening. Of course there was the time with the Tompkins girl, when they wanted to buy her, but they went away without doing so, and what family would do such a thing anyway?

I think, and I say this carefully, that my children have benefited from this trip. They are stronger than they were, and self-reliant, though they could hardly rely on Shadden, who never was good for much but making children. He is one sad man, though not as bad as Mr. Moss, who has traveled all this way alone, and the whole trip he was angry with the company. He is even sadder, to my mind. I'm getting through to Oregon City, but I'm worn, I know that. I might only be thirty-six years, but I feel like my elderly aunts, and all they had to go through was a poor childhood and sad marriages. I have been through a great deal more, and now just look where I am.

We all anticipate Oregon City. It will be so good to actually get there.

*

October 1: We are all worn and my left boot is giving me some trouble, as if there is a stone inside, but when I reach into it I can find nothing.
—Ellen Tompkins

Susannah Couch

We have been meeting people on the way into Oregon City. There are men traveling back and forth, going here and there. After so long on a lonely trail it is pleasant to see other folks. We have been greeted in a most friendly manner, they being happy to see more Americans arriving to vote or fight for the land. Most of the people we meet up with, excepting for the married missionaries, are men making their way in a new place. They each say that

Oregon City is quite up to date and nothing like it was when they arrived. Now, they call it a city.

They look at us as additions to make the area stronger, I think. To build up a real city with families, schools, and churches. They seem a hearty group of people, coming and going, knowing what they are about. To them, we must look like innocents, not knowing what we are getting into yet lucky to be here now, rather than when things were just starting up. I think many of them have Indian families, there being few American females here. I see them eyeing Cynthia Girtman and the Bennett girl, and one asked her age, which is thirteen. They nod in approval. Adeline Brown, the woman who joined us with her mother, is most often on Medorem Crawford's arm and appears to be spoken for.

What this country needs, one said to me, is families, and you folks will be welcomed. Another warned us about the weather, which will soon become rainy. Get your houses made quickly he said, or you will grow moss on your legs, so wet it gets. One man asked if we knew about the mushrooms, which were safe and which not, and one man said that we should take care around the boats, as they can be dangerous. People fall off and are drowned. So we get a lot of advice but also encouragement, and I think we will do well, or well enough.

*

October 2: The families are all walking together now, as if making friends at last—or perhaps saying good-byes. The path we are on is well worn.
—Ellen Tompkins

CAROLINE TOMPKINS

Ned came to me today to say that he had had a talk with Reuben Lewis, the man traveling with Gabriel Brown, who had been supplying the company with meat. Would I talk to him about our plans for the newspaper?

"We should talk to him together," I told Ned, who went to get his sisters. He brought Mr. Lewis over.

Mr. Lewis said, "Would you put out your hand, Mrs. Tompkins?" He hastened to add, "I know it is an odd request and at a very awkward time, but I have something to show you." I put out my hand, and Mr. Lewis placed on my palm a small piece of lead.

"What is this, Mr. Lewis?" I asked.

"It is a printer's plug. It is 20 point, for a headline; it is an ampersand. I carry it with me because I was once a typesetter and always liked the ampersand because to me it stood for the possibility of something else, sometimes something known and sometimes something quite surprising. I once set type for a small newspaper in Hudson, New York, and laid out pages for printing. Your boy says you have a printing press, paper, and ink waiting for you in Oregon City and that you plan to start the newspaper your husband hoped to operate." He hesitated. "Might I offer my services?"

I stood with the piece of lead in my hand but had to say we had no way to pay a salary. Then Mr. Lewis took something from a small bag hanging from his neck and said, "This is an 1842 gold eagle I bought at the United States Mint in Philadelphia before I left the East. It was just cast when I was there. I have carried nine of them sewed into my pack. I brought them all across the country as my stake in Oregon. It is what I have from home, just about all I have. It is to buy me a new life. I would like to be a partner—a junior partner to the family."

"What if we do not succeed, Mr. Lewis?"

"I think we will, Mrs. Tompkins. Ned has a good head on him. We have tended the horses together for this entire trip. I know him to be true and steady. I know the newspaper business, and Ned tells me you have some crusading ideas. This is a new country, and we are all making new lives for ourselves. It is a place for a newspaper. A newspaper will become necessary for the creation of a territory and a state, a place to publish legal notices, advertise sales, give the news. A newspaper is important for business and for people to know about each other. For obituaries: people like to know who has died and where they came from. A newspaper speaks to and for a community, and you have no competition." He smiled at that. "We will succeed."

I explained that I needed to consult with the family, but I already knew the answer, for we have known Mr. Lewis to be levelheaded. He wants what we want, and that is a place for ourselves in Oregon. We all know it will be a struggle.

I had thought with the loss of Dan that we were diminished, but an ampersand stands for something more.

＊

October 2: We can see the Willamette River from this hillside.
—Ellen Tompkins

CYNTHIA GIRTMAN

Cynthia Girtman pulled her mother closer and said quietly near her ear, "What can you see, Mama?" Louisa Girtman shook her head back and forth slowly. "Not too much. A lot of green on the edges. Trees; surely trees."

"And in the middle space?" asked her daughter.

"Nothing much, Cynthia. A blur." She paused. "Maybe of blue?"

"Mama, we are on the top of the last hill. We are overlooking Oregon City." Louisa's face wrinkled in surprise. She jutted her head forward as if to see what was ahead, but her vision was not up to her desire.

"Is it beautiful, Jessie?" she asked. "What's ahead? Is it beautiful?"

"It is lovely, Mama, the land is," she answered. "All greens around, with the river a blue line dividing the forests. The town, Oregon City, is small, though," and she let the words trail off. Cynthia, her large eyes looking forward, pressed her mother close and said, "The trees are tall and greener than ever I saw before. After crossing such treeless places, like the prairie, the trees here form a frame for what is ahead." She paused.

Her mother, encouraged, said "and . . . ," eager to know more, to have her daughter see for her.

"Mama, ahead is the river. The one we have been so many months heading for, the Willamette. It is broad and sweeps across the land as if making a statement. That must be the blue you could see in the distance. It is wide, with falls all the way across, and what looks from here like a spit of land and a . . ."

"Can you see the Methodist mission?" Louisa asked.

"No. But the falls on the river go clear across, a strong white line of froth kicking up as the water spills over the rocks. They look dangerous; I think it is what the travelers we met on the road warned us about. Across the river the land goes on and on. There are forests, miles of trees, possibly all the way to the Pacific Ocean." The girl straightened a bit, pulling at her mother's arm, held close at her side. "We have come across." And then with great excitement

Cynthia said in exaggerated words, "We made it, Mother," and she waved to her father to come join them. "Out there," she said loudly, pointing west, "out there, Father, is our land."

He joined them and took his wife's arm, freeing his daughter. The three looked westward, Cynthia with excitement about the future, her father with relief that they had made the journey, had crossed the continent, conquering the space between then and now, between there and here. They both watched as down Louisa Girtman's face tears flowed from exhaustion and a sense of deliverance. They had brought her across, both of them, holding her upright and guiding her every step of the way. They knew her heart felt gratitude and relief.

"It's all right, Louisa," said Levi Girtman gently as she wept into his shoulder. "We only have a short way to go now, to the mission. They will have a house ready for us and a schoolroom, because they need teachers for the children." Louisa nodded, a silent yes.

"Just a short way, now. And no more mountains to climb, but only a river to cross." The family sighed in relief.

Mrs. Perry to W. T. Perry

"William," she said breathlessly, "see what's ahead? Oregon City! It's . . . it's a batch of small houses, and a store, I would guess. But there are trees here aplenty all around. And water power, too. I don't see a sawmill up there, do you?"

He looked out at the collection of buildings ahead.

She replied for him. "There looks like one grand house, two floors and planed wood."

"Dr. McLoughlin's, I suppose," he said. "The Hudson Bay Company probably brought in the lumber on a ship."

"But the rest of the buildings are shaggy-looking places," Mrs. Perry interjected with excitement. "Oregon City needs a sawmill in order to go ahead, and that's what you can do. People are gonna come here, just as we have done, and they won't be satisfied with shabby houses. They are going to want to go ahead, have what they had before and then some. W. T., some of these people we have been traveling with are going on to other places, and many have already left, like all those young men, the Germans, and those Frenchmen who already went on to that place called Champoeg where they all speak French. Even those two young Indians who traveled with us are gone: rushing home, they are. There are only a few of us now, but others will follow year after year, now that we have proved it is possible. When they come to Oregon City next year and the years after, they can build their houses and stores with lumber bought from W. T. Perry Company."

"I don't know what Sister will do; she and Elbridge will decide that. We have come home, you and me, and little Susannah." Smiling at him, she added more quietly, "and there will be more. More little Perrys."

The Tompkins Women

MARTHA: This is Oregon City? This?

JANE: It isn't much.

MARTHA: There's nothing here, nothing ready.

JANE: But we made it across.

MARTHA: Yes. Yes, we did. Looking at this only makes me wonder why.

JANE: Well, . . . Father . . .

MARTHA: I know, Jane. I know. It probably suits you, but I can't wait to leave. To go home.

CAROLINE: I don't know what your Father would have said. I can't speak for him. But he wanted to come; he wanted to bring the news, to help create culture, to build up a place so that Oregon will prosper. I think he would have thought that this is just the place that needs a newspaper. It is a place to start.

Mother Bennett

As they walked into Oregon City, The Giantess seemed to shrink. The woman known on the trip as bossy, who commanded her family as a colonel with a small detachment, went up to her man Vardemon and took his arm. Her hair shone in the waning light, but it was also tangled and in need of washing and brushing, but it was unlikely that she still had a brush. They had lost much of what they had brought on the journey.

She looked at the rough buildings beyond them and shook her head sadly.

"This ain't it, Vardy," she said.

He nodded in agreement. "We'll go on."

"Yes," she said, sounding rather meek. Then with a toss of her hair she said, "We always wanted to go to California, where the girl can find a husband and the boys will be useful." He nodded his head.

"We might have to," he started, as if this couple were used to holding conversations, which had not been much evident to anyone who had been on the trail with them. But it was as if this start of a civilization, this pretend or almost city, this small rough town with no facilities, no real buildings, and seemingly no hope, had tamed her, brought her to a halt.

She finished his sentence with a sudden change of topic: "We gotta name the girl."

He let out a slow "yeah," adding, "It's about time we did. She can't be the Bennett girl forever."

Vardemon Jr., standing nearby, said a bit maliciously, "We could call her the Columbia, as she lost my best shirt in the river back there." He was roundly ignored.

Vardy offered another possible name. "Oregon? It's where we are," he said mildly.

"No," said Mary Bennett firmly, as if her muscles had just remembered that her whole family had gotten through. "We are going on to California, Vardy. Can't name her Oregon. She'd be a laughingstock down there. 'There goes Miss Oregon in California.'"

"Could be Georgia, where we came from," said Vardemon Jr.

"That's dumb," said someone.

"Then what?" he asked.

There was a long pause.

Vardemon Bennett said quietly, "She is the Belle of the Pacific. That's what I tell her. Belle is a good name."

But Mother Bennett, now fully recovered, said forcefully, "Pacific. Pacifica, we should call her that. We haven't see'd it yet, but we will and it ain't so bad being named for peacefulness."

"Might not always be that way," said Vardy. "She might not always be peaceful."

"No," Mary sighed. "But she's a peaceful child and we can hope. We done all right, getting across and getting us here, and now we gotta make plans to get us out of here and down the coast. California is the place for us because this ain't," she said, pointing to the poor building that served as a store and post office.

"Pacifica," she bellowed out, as if the air had filled her sails once again. No one looked up or answered. Seeing her daughter across the way, she yelled out again, "Pacifica," and pointed her finger indicating "you."

The girl dumb-pointed at herself as if to say, "Who, me?"

"I called you, didn't I?" yelled her mother, again in charge, again with a goal, a duty to drive her family.

"Pacifica, you pack up what we can save. Within a day or so, we're gonna get on along. We'll get to California, where there will be sun and space and lots of people dancing."

She looked at Vardy.

"We might dance," she said. "We just might dance."

He looked startled, but before he could say anything she bellowed out again, "We'll all get used to it."

MRS. SHADDEN

Did you hear? Did you hear what happened? It's just awful, plain awful! I can hardly believe, but Shadden just heard from the Crawford boy and he told me. A week, ten days ago, when Dr. White got to Oregon City, he made arrangements to go down the Willamette River to the Methodist mission and Nathaniel Crocker decided to go with him. You knew him, didn't you, Mrs. Tompkins? From back in your old home?

Anyway, they hired a boat, and some woman, I don't know who, but probably a missionary lady, was also to make the trip. They all got in the canoe and the boatman took them across the river to a landing spot near the top of the falls where there is a small beach, where the path leads back down the river.

Dr. White got out of that boat first, just at the top of the falls. Well, he leaned way forward to keep from stepping his shoe into the water, and doing so he pushed his other foot back.

And without any warning, he sent the boat straight into the current and it went over. It went right into the swirling white water, hit a rock, and flew over the falls, faster than you could say lickety-split. And, and, can you believe? That woman, and Nathaniel Crocker, and the boatman went shooting out over the falls, dropped down to the rocks below, and they all drowned. All drowned! Now, did you ever hear something as awful as that? Ever?

*

October 3: I can take off these boots at last!
—Martha Tompkins

TOMPKINS FAMILY OBSERVATION

All these months we have been heading for Oregon City. We had expectations of what it would be, with people on the streets who would welcome us. We thought it would be something like our village at home, being called a city and all, with shops and churches and a public building. And we only come from a village.

Oregon City now stands in front of us, a giant disappointment. It was started earlier this year, and there are a few wooden stores, an inn, a dirt road, and little else. We seem to have come so far to end up with something so lacking.

Mother expected a store like Mr. Benjamin's, where there would be fabric for dresses and molasses for baking and tin pots and pans, so that we might set up a kitchen. Perhaps a church or school. Martha is acting as if she knew all along that it was a hoax. Jane whistled and Wooley barked. Ned simply looked about.

Everything here for sale came from the sea—from San Francisco or the islands or from even farther away. It is a great disappointment.

We are not discouraged, but the city doesn't encourage us, either. Mother commented that the word *city* is given the site of a bishopric, and there is certainly no bishop here. A real city is a place of education and culture and commerce. There is little evidence of any of that, either. Perhaps a newspaper can make it so, she said.

Then Mother, looking down at her worn boots, smiled and said, "We will start here. When Oregon becomes a territory, we will move the press to the territorial capital. We will provide the news."

Oregon City

Looking down the rocky pathway that served as a street, past several homes, a blacksmith shop, and the boat landing, Caroline turned to Jane: "Sing, Jane," more a command than a question.

Jane looked perplexed. "I don't know what is . . . what to sing."

Caroline said enthusiastically, "Remember Cousin Smith's song . . . the one he wrote when he was at Andover Academy and taught us when he came to visit?"

Jane hesitated and then began, her clear voice rising up as she sang, "My country 'tis of thee." But she stopped abruptly. "This isn't our country, Mother."

"Sing," said Caroline. "It will be. We will make it ours." And as Jane's voice flung out the words, people began to appear on the empty street: someone came from behind the blacksmith shop, two emerged from the store, and one woman came down the street pulling a toddler. Behind them, members of the company, those few left, those still walking together, paused. Everyone stood still to listen,

"My country 'tis of thee," sang Jane, who then stopped.

Caroline rather firmly said, "Keep on going, Jane. We need a song now."

Jane continued, "Sweet land of liberty, Of thee I sing." People around shook their heads and smiled, nodding to the music. "Land where my fathers died! Land of the pilgrims' pride! From every mountainside, Let freedom ring!"

"A first," called out one man. Some clapped; a woman in the street wept.

Jane looked about, then stopped. "I don't know any more, Mother."

"We will all learn it, dear," and the people in the street, as if set back into motion, and those standing alongside began to move again. The people who had come with them, who had made a company, broke it apart; those who were starting out, these newcomers, all looked forward, westward.

There had been, thought Caroline, friendships made. Some were unexpected but felt true. But with the scattering of the emigrants, she wondered if she would see any of these women again. They were about to go—to other parts of Oregon, to California, and Martha, back to New York. Would she and her family and the printing press remain in Oregon City? The future seemed unclear, but the family was together—at least for a time, and they would go forward.

Caroline reached into the pocket of her apron and drew out a book. She walked over and placed it in Louisa Girtman's hand, gently pressing her fingers around the cover. "I could not bear to see *Gulliver* tossed away when we lightened our packs. It is yours."

Louisa gripped Caroline's hand and said, "Gulliver had an eagle fly him over the mountains to his destination . . ."

And Caroline continued, "and Ulysses had the gods blowing him home to Ithaca, even if it was the long way round."

Ellen piped up, "We have come from Ithaca and have done it on our own two feet! We have come all the way across without gods or eagles. And good for us!"

"On our own two legs," said Jane firmly.

Louisa pulled Cynthia close and said sweetly, "On our own four legs. You brought me forward, every step of the way."

"But we are here," murmured her daughter in her ear. "We are here and ready to start again."

At that, Elijah White came bursting from one of the sheds, a book in his hand. "I am here to take a census of Oregon to send to Washington DC, to show who is here, who is newly arrived, and who will stand for this land."

Duly counted in the census, they moved on, singly and in small family groups, forward into a new beginning.

Debts Owed

If anyone should thank her publisher, editor, designer, and, most important, her copyeditor, it is I. Everyone at the University of Nebraska Press made me welcome, starting with Matt Bokovoy, who sent the manuscript of *Lamentations* to Clark Whitehorn, editor of Bison Books; to the enthusiastic anonymous reader; and to Maureen Bemko, who copyedited the manuscript, untangling names and dates and doing so with great understanding of what I hoped to accomplish as she cleaned up behind me. I could not be more grateful. The editorial process has been nothing but educational, helpful, and so appreciated.

I was steered to Bison Books by novelist Lamar Herrin, who taught in the Cornell University English Department; by James Calder of the University of Oklahoma Press with whom I have corresponded for many years; and by Bethany Rose Mowry at the University Press of Kansas.

Before the manuscript ever got to the press, I was fortunate to have the attention and advice of my son Daniel and his wife, Bamidele, called Dele, who pointed me in a direction I had not considered and even offered to read the manuscript again. Their faith in *Lamentations* was crucial. My younger son Douglas and his wife, Johanna Maria, called Henny, cheered me on.

But also important to me was the enthusiastic reaction to the book by John Hopper, poet, known to all his admirers as Jack, who encouraged me to keep working at it, and to John Reps, ninety-eight and three-quarters years old, who emailed me shortly before his death and instructed, "Get this thing published."

My appreciation also to Bonnie Beuttner, who understood what I hoped to do right from the beginning and kept me at it, sharing my interest in the Overland Trail. I have been fortunate to have Susan Currie and Ann Mazer, who offered encouragement, and to Ann Martin, Bonita Voiland, Martha Hsu, and Nina Miller, who read variations of the manuscript. I also talked with Ashley Pierce about the birthing scene and watched *Call the Midwife*, the details of which I did not put on the page.

This book would have been impossible without scores of librarians and archivists who curated papers and made collections of materials available. The Huntington Library gave me a study in 1993–94 wherein I researched the history of the 1842 and later crossings of the country. Librarians at the H. H. Bancroft Library, the National Archives, Yale University, the Oregon Historical Society in Portland, and Cornell University found materials for me as I followed the strange and twisted life of Dr. Elijah White.

The record book kept by Medorem Crawford is the only surviving contemporaneous document from the 1842 crossing. Elijah White spoke of the crossing, probably from notes he had taken, in dictating his experiences. Those memories became *Ten Years in Oregon: Travels and Adventures of Doctor E. White and Lady, West of the Rocky Mountains with incidents of two sea voyages via Sandwich Islands around Cape Horn; containing also, a brief History of the Missions and Settlements of the Country-Origin of the Provisional Government—Number and Customs of the Indians—Incidents Witnessed while traversing and residing in the Territory—Description of the Soil, Production and Climate*, compiled by "Miss A. J. Allen" and printed in 1848 in Ithaca, New York. This book is usually cited as *Ten Years in Oregon* and contains a few pages about the 1842 crossing.

There are several memoirs of the 1842 journey written well after that date, some published by the Oregon Pioneers Association. Medorem Crawford wrote one. He also commented harshly on Lansford Hastings's pamphlet *The Emigrants Guide to Oregon and California*, published in 1845. Other memoirs of the 1842 trip include the "Reminiscences of F. X. Matthieu," originally dictated to H. L. Lyman in 1886 and published in the *Quarterly of the Oregon Historical Society* in March 1900. An interview with another member of the 1842 company, A. L. Lovejoy, appeared in the *Oregon Historical Quarterly* in 1930.

The historical literature about the Overland Trail and about Oregon's early days is extensive. For anyone interested in Elijah White during his first stay in Oregon, I recommend Robert J. Loewenberg's book *Equality on the Oregon Frontier: Jason Lee and the Methodist Mission, 1834–43* (1976). There is also Don Berry's novel about Elbridge Trask, titled *Trask: The Coast of Oregon, 1848* (1960), about his later years.

Stephenie Flora has compiled material about the 1842 crossing in "The Emigration to the Oregon Country in 1842," available online at oregonpioneers .com. She has reprinted Medorem Crawford's account and provides in "Emigrants to Oregon in 1842" a list of everyone who set out on the trip. She also has genealogical accounts of many of these travelers. Her work is very helpful, and when the spelling of a name was in doubt, I generally followed her version.

Available from the National Archives in Washington DC is the census that Dr. White took of residents of Oregon in 1842, just after his arrival. White's time in Oregon is discussed in many of the histories of Oregon, including Hubert Howe Bancroft's *History of Oregon*, published in 1886, and Samuel A. Clarke's *Pioneer Days of Oregon History*, from 1905. William Gray, whom the emigrants met on the road near the Whitman Mission, also wrote about Dr. White in his history of Oregon, as did many others, mostly expressing some distaste. The H. H. Bancroft Library at the University of California, Berkeley, has a collection of materials about and by Elijah White.

Reverend Samuel Parker's book *Journal of an Exploring Tour beyond the Rocky Mountains*, published in Ithaca in 1838, is crucial to this story, but of course Reverend Parker was not on the 1842 trip west. The map used here is the one that was tipped into Parker's book and most probably taken along by those crossing the country in 1842. There were few other detailed maps available. There is also a very useful essay by Kenneth R. Coleman, "White Man's Territory: The Exclusionary Intent behind the 1850 Donation Land Act," about the distribution of land in Oregon, available at the website of Oregon Humanities, https://www.oregonhumanities.org/rll/magazine/owe -spring-2018/white-mans-territory-kenneth-r-coleman/.